OUR DESTINY IS BLOOD

OUR

DESTINY

IS BLOOD

CLARE DALY

Published in paperback and e-book in 2017 by Clare Daly

Copyright © Clare Daly, 2017

First Edition

This novel is entirely a work of fiction. Any resemblance to real persons, living or dead is purely coincidental.

A CIP catalogue record for this title is available from the British Library

Paperback ISBN 978-1-9998362-0-7
E-book ISBN 978-1-9998362-1-4

Cover image by Janon Kas/Shutterstock.com
Book design by Design For Writers

www.claredalyauthor.com

For my mother

I

Far Eastern Siberia, 1827

CALEB TAMERSK WAS GOING to die. He had long accepted that fact. He'd even got quite comfortable with the notion, living precariously close to it as he did. Throughout his life he had taunted death, sent countless men into its open arms knowing that when it came for him, he would go out strong and fighting. He never thought when the moment arrived that it would be like this. This was beyond his worst imaginings and he wondered whether he was still asleep in his cell and this was some sort of macabre dream. The shackles cut deep into his torn wrists, the pain shooting up his arms. This was no dream. He was no longer within the walls of Castle Valla prison, he was outside them and that was the worst place he could be.

He'd been dragged out into the snow, forced to his knees as the guards chained him to a metal ring set in the ice. As the last of the daylight faded from the sky, they hurried back inside. He could just see the entrance behind him, the portcullis shrieking as it was lowered to the ground, the castle and all inside secure. He had never panicked in his life but it grew inside him – the uncertainty of what was to come. His teeth chattered against the cold and he cursed that the snow was deep enough to cover his knees but not enough to hide in, away from what was coming.

He pulled again on his chains in desperation, trying to shift the ring itself. It was unlike any metal he had ever seen – heavy as iron, but shiny like a mirror, his own reflection a distorted swirl as he tried to free himself. But there was no escape. His only hope was to freeze to death before it came, but the guards had seen to that too – the overcoat heavy on his shoulders. The sacrifice was no good if the offering was already dead. He must be alive.

As darkness fell, a loud crack echoed in the mountains beyond, and an avalanche descended as if to escape the one who thundered through. A blast of air flung his coat open and he braced himself as the icy air found the skin beneath his prison uniform.

'Please,' he shouted. 'Help me.'

He looked back to the castle. A lone figure stood on the battlements – the governor and orchestrator of his fate, a man known as Rako. He would not help him. He had signed his death warrant with Rako some time ago. Since his arrival last winter, he had aided four prisoners with suicide for no other reason than proof that he could – that he could push and prod and poke until his subject saw no other way. He even gave them the tools – a wooden spoon whittled to a sharp point hidden in their gruel or spare clothing in which to make a noose. Through thick walls and strong iron, he manipulated the weak-minded, his whispers echoing along the dark corridors and chambers at night. So delighted was he with his success, he was unaware of his growing infamy among the other prisoners, who for their own safety had reported him to Rako. Cowards. He would gladly have killed them all.

An image of his mother came to mind. He had not thought of her in decades for she was long dead but there she was smiling at him and he remembered how her lip curled so. Everything he had learned about manipulation came from her until the pupil saw the manipulation first-hand and would have a mistress no longer. He'd wiped that smile away when he'd killed her and here she was now forcing her way into his mind as he was about to die.

Do you wait for me, Lenka?

She had never permitted him to call her Mama, even as a child, and perhaps that's why it was easier for him to think of her as a stranger with a strange love he had no longer needed. She smiled again in his mind, the sweet turning sour this time.

He's coming for you.

Stop it.

You're going to bleed.

Stop!

The ground began to tremble, as if her presence had signalled the gates of hell to open and they shook the earth as they did so.

He's coming.

He blessed himself, trying to remember a prayer from long ago, but the words came only with practice and he did not know them well enough. If a creature such as this existed in the world then any God would have long forsaken it. The snow around him began to shift as it unleashed the smell of hidden decay, the kind that lives underground as it rots and becomes one with the soil. While acquainted with the scent of death, this was new to him, a deeper, more sinister offering. Perhaps it was the climb of the dead he had cajoled, come to claim their revenge. He looked across the ice. Something was coming, at great speed – a swirl of shadows, splitting and merging, until one long dark shadow came to rest upon him. He cowered in fear, squeezing his eyes shut. Something cold and wet touched his cheek and he jumped. Was that a tongue? But when he opened his eyes, all he could see were the folds of a giant cloak as it enveloped him, tearing his chains with ease.

'Please, I beg you.'

A husky laugh filled the fabric around him and in his mind that laugh became his mother's, rising in pitch as the laughter grew more hysterical and he was taken into the skies.

2

County Kildare, Ireland, 1847

'YOUR MOTHER SAID IF you got to eighteen, it had spared you.'

He coughed, the phlegm caught in his throat, before he swallowed it back down. The room was dark save for a single candle, the flame casting light up the walls of the cottage like a demon as the draught pushed it this way and that.

'You need to rest. No more talk now.'

He lifted his head. Beads of sweat ran back into his greying hair.

'It's important,' he said. 'She was so worried for you. Always so afraid.'

Evelyn wrung out the cloth in the bowl and brought it to his forehead but he flung it away. The fever was making him delirious. For the past hour, he'd been mumbling, so low at first that she doubted it, but when she lit the candle he was lying there, his eyes darting from one corner to the other. In his hand, he worked her mother's rosary beads, prayers lost on his lips. Since her death almost ten years ago, they had never left his pocket. While he had embraced the church during his grief, Evelyn had silently chosen to challenge it.

As a child, she sat diligently by her father's side at mass but as she knelt in prayer she sought to ask God the questions she felt he must answer.

They weighed heavy on her. Even her brother Michael took her stoic silence in church as devotion rather than rebellion. She needed answers and the one-way conversation was not satisfying her desire for them. She went to confession, not to confess her sins but to have somewhere private to talk to Father Mercer, who did his best to explain things to her. 'God works in mysterious ways,' he'd said, a look of concern on his face. 'You must have faith.' As her teenage years went by, her inquisitive mind delved further and she deemed that in being unanswered, the biggest question she was asking had been answered after all. However, she was fond of her talks with Father Mercer and in trying to bring her back to her faith, he had enlisted her help with various tasks about the parish that she was happy to assist with. If she didn't have her belief in God, she respected that he had his and she saw first-hand the comfort that his beliefs brought him and others who needed help. As famine tracked across the county, they needed it more than ever.

A drop of water fell on her cheek from the ceiling. The rain was coming through. They couldn't afford to fix it – at least not properly. Michael had patched the roof with brambles, but the rain found its way through its twisted branches. They had sold their workhorse three months ago, fetching a poor price because of its age, but a bad harvest meant difficult decisions needed to be made. As the money ran out, she knew that her father was going hungry so that they did not and when she did see him eat, he ate little, preferring to offer them most of his share. It was making him ill and he had grown weaker by the day. How long could he go on like that? She hated herself for even thinking it but he was bedridden, racked by fever, his body so thin.

It would be dawn soon. Where was Michael? He'd left after midnight, saying only that he would bring back something to eat. She wondered as she listened to her father cough if he would even be able to eat it. She brought the cloth again to him, pleased this time that its reception was met with relief, his eyes closing.

'You're a great girl, Evelyn. Just like your mother.'

'Dad, rest now. Michael will be back soon.'

'It's not the same for the boys.'

'I know.'

She didn't. She hadn't a clue what he was talking about but perhaps if she could get him to rest, he'd have come around a bit by the time her brother got back. If she could just keep that fever at bay, maybe he might stand a chance. He looked her in the eye.

'Your mother had lots of sisters. Half of them like her. All dead, she said.'

He never spoke of her mother's family. The only things he'd shared were his memories of her, of their time spent together, but never her life beyond him, before they met. She didn't even know exactly where she was from. She had a vague memory of sitting on her mother's lap – her telling a story about her childhood in the west, how the ocean tore the rocks to shreds in a storm and how she'd almost been blown off a cliff, and her mimicking, with flailing arms and whistling lips, the ferociousness of it all. It had made her laugh – a contagious giggle that went back and forth between them. Her father had once said she grew up on a strawberry farm with the sunshine in her hair but perhaps it was his own romantic notion. Maybe he wasn't sure either. And then she'd died. How would they ever know now? She had no family that she knew of, at least not until her father mentioned them. If he went too, then who would know their history? Not only would she lose him but also another piece of her mother, stories gone with both of them.

'What do you mean, half of them like her?'

His eyes had closed. Had he gone to sleep at last? He forced them to open again, his eyelids heavy, barely up to the task. Evelyn took his hand, listening to the rasp of his breath as he exhaled.

'Your mother...she was...extraordinary.'

He coughed again, a quick fit expelled impatiently as it disturbed his words.

'She thought you would have it. But you don't. You are eighteen soon and the worry will be gone.'

'I don't understand.'

'I know you think I've always stopped you doing things,

keeping you here to look after me and your brother, but I had to be sure.'

She waited.

'In case they came for you. There are things out there. Things that can see people who are different. I'm so glad you're not different.'

He coughed again. This time, a small line of blood coated his bottom lip.

'Your mother spent her childhood running from them. And then she came here, settled in with me and who would look for her here, she thought. And she didn't even use her gift. She said all she ever wanted was to be normal and how it would be a curse if you had it too. She didn't want that for you.'

Not different. What did he mean? She'd never fitted in. Every day she felt it and though it was hard to put her finger on it, she felt it inside – that if everyone had the same basic building blocks, she was missing some or they'd been built in a different order. Of course, she was different. A memory stumbled into her mind – hurtful and unannounced as the ones accompanied by grief always were. In the light August rain, she stood in the graveyard, her hand in her father's as they buried her. She'd only seen the figure in silhouette, the sun breaking through the clouds to shine right in her eyes at the precise moment he had turned to look at her. And he was looking. She could feel it. When the sun disappeared, so did he, walking away among the tombstones. When she'd asked her father who the man was, he said he didn't know but his grip tightened on her hand. In a way, he'd spent the last decade holding it, keeping her close.

She'd not thought of that in a long time. It had been smothered by loss, that aching hole in her left by her mother's passing. Had he been one of *them*? Had he been the one to find her?

'Tell me how she really died,' she asked, fighting the quiver in her voice.

Her father's expression changed. His eyes squinted as if the memory was too painful to resurrect. After a time, he spoke.

'One came for her. I didn't see it but I know it's true. Days before, she said she could feel it close. It watched her. She knew the feeling well. It wasn't the first time. And then one day she was gone. Her heart, the doctor said, for what else would cut a young woman down so quickly and silently? A sudden attack and I went along with it because I knew. It had made her heart stop beating. Had she more time, she might have fled but she was tired of running and she wouldn't leave us anyway, not you and Michael.'

'Does Michael know?'

'I never told anyone. Like her I was afraid. I told Michael only to watch out for you. Drove it into him all those years that you would be his responsibility if anything happened to me, at least until you were a grown woman. You can tell him if you like. It doesn't matter now.'

'You can tell him yourself when he gets back.'

Her father gave her a resigned look.

'You said she was extraordinary...how?'

He coughed again. A trickle of blood ran from the corner of his mouth and he closed his eyes. They were wet with tears.

'Please,' she said.

He caught her hand and brought it to rest on his forearm. On the scar tissue that distorted his skin, as it stretched, pulled and twisted from his wrist to his elbow. A scar he'd always had – ever since she could remember.

'She wasn't always able to control it,' he said.

* * *

A MILE FROM HOME, Michael's knees hit the road hard. Sharp stones skinned the palms of his hands, and his body seemed to lock, his legs telling him that they would not be leant on again, his body agreeing not to do the leaning. He rolled over on his back, grasped his sore hands, and looked at the gathering clouds. He needed to get home but his body was spent. He checked the package – a half loaf carefully tied to his ankle beneath his trouser leg – a cargo more precious than any diamond, richer than any amount of gold.

He knew that if he wanted his body to get him home, he was going to have to take a bite – just enough to fool his legs into working again. He cursed himself for using so much energy to get it in the first place. The queue had been orderly to begin with but when the relief cart ran out, things descended into chaos. Punches were thrown. Elbows flew into ribs. Hair was pulled by the handful. Desperate people did desperate things and like everyone around him, he had others who relied on his success. He had travelled miles to join the early morning queue and though he had come away with more than most, his right hand ached from the blows he had struck at those who tried to stop him. He didn't get far running along the road before his lungs were on fire. From there, he'd hidden the bread and it had been one slow foot in front of the other, in the hope that no-one stopped him. The fact that his body had given up on him was a harsh lesson indeed.

He crawled onto the side of the road and unwrapped the bread. The crust was hard. It was probably three or four days old but even still the smell of it made his mouth water. With eager fingers, he tore off a piece and ate it. The hunger reawakened in him like a beast and he fought the urge to just devour the whole lot and be damned. He wrapped it up, away from temptation, and rested his head back, waiting for the bread to fuel the fire inside him once again.

A man can do anything with a fire in his belly. A warming mutton stew, a bowl of steaming hot porridge, bread so hot from the griddle it would burn your hands but you don't care. You have to break off a corner, lash some butter on it and watch it melt as it touches your lips. Ah the warmth! And a potato – in that stew, seduced in that gorgeous gravy, its flesh scrubbed up – its pale inside deliciously breaking under the pressure of your fork. His insides ached at the memory of a good meal and he scolded himself for allowing it in. He was usually quite good at burying unhelpful notions. Like the one of leaving Ireland to make his fortune.

Most of his friends had taken the leap, long before the famine came – off to Liverpool, Boston or New York, the younger sons off to conquer the world, leaving the older ones to take care of the crops. Jack O'Keefe – he was in the West Indies they said, sailing on ships filled with sugar cane, while his eight brothers saw to everything back home. He imagined Jack soaking up the sunshine, his arms around an island girl with cocoa skin and flowers in her hair, oblivious to the devastation at home. Unlike Jack, Michael had no brothers nor a brood of sisters to rally the cause. There was just himself and Evelyn, two years younger than him, both forever tethered to their home and their father since their mother had died. Duty bypassed dreams as their father descended into grief and ill-health and both children realised that Cularne was where they would stay, until death saw fit to take them elsewhere.

A fly buzzed close to his ear. He swished it away but it was persistent. Can you smell the bread, fly, is that it? He hit out at it, his hand connecting with its wings as it flew away. The buzz faded but a distant hum remained and he looked beyond the roadside to a ditch further up. He willed his legs to stand and they obeyed. More flies hovered in the air, the hum louder as he moved closer. Death, he thought and the wind blew its scent to him.

Over the grassy bank, a thick swarm of flies were having their feast. A woman lay dead, her head rested to one side, her hair alive with the movement of insects. Her face was a horror of sunken flesh, one cheekbone free of its skin thanks to the night's predators. She wasn't alone. Her hand reached towards the child that clung to her. The little girl, no more than three, did not have the pallor of death and for a second he thought she might be alive. But the flies were having their fun with her too and one appeared from her nose to stake its claim to that part of its gracious host. On her face, old tears had dried in streaks and her lips were stained green from the clump of grass in her hand – the last resort of a starving child.

Michael staggered back to the roadside, feeling the bile rising in his throat, and prayed that he wouldn't throw up. If he did, he feared he would not make it back at all and what use would his journey have been then? He gripped his knees and took as deep a breath as he could. The dead were nothing new to him, not anymore. He had seen people he knew, strangers he didn't, who had lost the fight and he'd learned to use that to propel himself forward, to keep fighting for he was lucky enough to be alive to do it. Defiant, he made for home as the clouds won out and the rain began to fall.

3

EVELYN HAD WANTED TO ask more questions but her father was weary from all his talk. He had fallen asleep holding her hand, the rosemary beads snaked around his fingers. Was it true? Either way, he was convinced of it and his arm, well there was no doubt that he believed her mother had done it. Eventually she too must have closed her eyes for she when she opened them, the candle had burned out. Around the door a beam of daylight shone – just enough to make out the shape of her father lying there. But something was missing. There was no sound of laboured breath from his lips, no rattle of it in his chest. She listened to his heart, but it was silent – an empty cage bereft of its fluttering bird. He was gone.

The grief, that had nestled inside her these past weeks, began to grow. With it also came relief – not only for him, that he would suffer no more – but for herself. She was glad she would no longer have to witness it – even at the cost of her father's life. What kind of child would secretly welcome death for their parent? And why was it that emotion that would rise now above all others?

She crept to the door. The frame was rotten, the rusted hinges barely holding on. Without it, the wind that scoured through the valley would howl through them like a banshee and so she moved it gently, just far enough to bathe him in a narrow rectangle of light.

'Evelyn?'

She turned to see Michael coming up the path. His tattered jacket was soaked through. Water dripped from the strands of hair falling on his cheek and she could see the makings of a bruise over his left eye. Always the fighter, but she loved him for it and she thought of her father's words. He had always looked out for her. Whether it was childish squabbles in the village or when a suitor came calling, he was out front, ready to protect and defend her, whether she welcomed it or not. It was she who wanted to protect him now, to shelter him from the truth. He was carrying a package, offering it to her, his eyes full of hope until they met hers.

'I'm so sorry,' she said.

He hurried past her, looked at the pale, still figure of his father lying there and flung the package against the wall.

'There!' he cried. 'Eat!'

He would blame himself of course. There was no-one harder on Michael than himself. He turned to her and she thought she saw softness in his eyes, but no. The last of his energies went into a swift kick to the door. It collapsed outwards, hinges with it and he cursed.

'I should have got here sooner.'

'Don't.'

'I stopped. I shouldn't have.'

'It wouldn't have helped,' she said.

He looked back inside.

'This isn't your fault, Michael.'

'I should have been here...at the end.'

'You were out there trying to help.'

'And what good was it?'

She grabbed his arm.

'We will live a little longer.'

He pulled away.

'I'm not sure I want to.'

'Don't you dare give up, do you hear me?'

If he did, then all their fight would have been for nothing. She would not lose him too. Her eyes searched for the package he had thrown away. The bread had come lose and she dusted it off, tearing it in two. When he refused it, she forced it into his palm.

'Do you think I want to eat – right at this moment? Do you think he'd want us now to throw it away?' she said.

'He'd kick me from here to kingdom come.'

She nodded. 'So, we eat.'

Neither of them spoke as they did. She closed her eyes and forced herself to think of her father as he had been, before all of this. She would hear his unmistakable whistle as he returned from the fields each day. As a child, she would run out to meet him. He would take her hands and swing her around and she would laugh as the wind caught her hair and her feet would leave the ground for the twirling. She burned the whistle's melody into her mind as she looked at the fields, knowing she would never hear it again.

'What are we going to do?' she asked.

Michael took her hand in his. 'We're going to bury our father.'

'And after that?'

'We'll tend to the lazy beds as always and hope for a crop next season.'

Next season. There would be no next season for them. Usually the potatoes would see them through the winter but with blight there had been nothing to harvest and there was simply nothing to eat.

'There's talk of evictions,' she said. 'We'll have to go and see him.'

'Lord Stockett? Have you lost your mind?'

'We have to do something.'

"We'll be dead before he hears our plea.'

Later that morning, they buried their father in a shallow grave beyond the house. Though their limbs ached it was not something they would entrust to a stranger. The dead were too many for the graveyards anyway and here was perfect, just where the land started to rise into the hill beyond. Right at the twirling place.

4

THE GREAT HALL OF Castle Valla was a massive cave around which the prison's many cells, landings and nooks spread like weeds, with no form or design. The interior was built into the rock face, the castle's outer walls like an elaborate tumour on its side. Some of the cells ran back into the mountain, no more than carved out tombs within its dark crevices. Here, Rako kept the most dispirited ones. Men to whom even the society of Castle Valla was too much, for they had pulled their hair out in clumps, banging their heads off the jagged walls, that only solitude befit their existence. The mountain was their solace. They would converse with it like a sinner to his priest, draw on the walls their pictures and symbols, their words of redemption, handed down in their confessional.

Rako often thought of these men as his pen idled down the list of prisoner numbers. He did not take the selection for sacrifice lightly and so Caleb Tamersk or prisoner 6479 as he preferred, had been given due consideration among a prison full of dangerous men. There were a few who begged with pleading hands to be delivered to the creature – that the mountain demanded it. He wished it for some of them too – skin and bone, their beards allowed to grow only so long that they could not strangle themselves. These lost men. Where it up to him, he would release them all to the creature but the instructions were very clear and only men of a strong mind and body were required.

The stone walls began to close in and he breathed deeply, willing the room and his mind to settle. From the Great Hall, he could hear the familiar notes of violent song, angry roars tearing through the walls, the brutal tones of fists meeting flesh, all played to the background chorus of guards who had momentarily lost control. Every few months when the castle became an unbearable thief of their liberty, the inmates would revolt and a wave of violence would crash through its walls – until every man was engaged in it, compelled to fight.

Rako rolled up the list and made his way down the tower steps, stopping at a small balcony overlooking the chaos below.

'Enough!' he barked at them, his voice echoing off the damp walls.

In his right hand, he held up the paper scroll. He didn't need to say anything else. Trouble immediately abated, the tension evaporating as quickly as it had begun. The prisoners began to fix the overturned tables and benches, shoulder to shoulder with the man they had pummelled only moments ago. He surveyed the growing calm, all eyes cast to the floor for fear of meeting his gaze.

'Order is restored,' said an officer beside him.

Rako nodded. It never failed.

'Sir, one of the tower inmates has asked to speak with you, prisoner 6820.'

Rako sighed. 'Very well. Bring him to my office.'

The prisoner in question had arrived at Castle Valla just six months ago and Rako knew his number immediately for he memorised all those who piqued his interest, either as dangerous liabilities he needed to keep a close watch on, or those whom he couldn't quite figure out. From the moment he'd laid eyes on Vladimir Dermatov, he knew all was not as it seemed. He had looked up at the castle walls as if he were its Lord returning from war, marvelling at it without the slightest hint of intimidation, and Rako didn't like it. He'd also arrived with his brother in tow and though he had come across members of the same family interred before, there was something about these two that made him feel uneasy, and so he had earmarked their numbers for further scrutiny and a close eye. The fact that they had arrived with enough money in their pockets to ensure them a comfortable stay also made him wary, though bribes were always welcome. The castle made high demands on its staff and any added incentives were a bonus to them and the families they supported back home. He himself needed very little, just a comfortable bed and a soft pillow on which to lay his head. Castle Valla was his home. He had no need of anything or anyone else.

He listened to the slow progress of chains up the staircase. When the prisoner finally shuffled into the room, Rako was met with a cool glare.

'Are these really necessary?' the man said, shaking the chain on his shackles.

'You *are* a prisoner here.'

He pointed to the chair in front of Rako's desk.

'May I at least sit?'

'Be my guest.'

The prisoner lumbered to the seat and sat down with a sigh. He was tall and lean and though his beard was long, it suited him. Rako could smell soap, the same kind he used.

'You can leave us,' Rako said to the guard.

As soon as the door closed, the man spoke.

'I have been very generous, have I not? You and your officers are well taken care of?'

'Indeed, we are. Is there something you want? Some new clothes perhaps?'

Vladimir's shirt was blood-stained from the fresh bout of violence and he wondered if he were a willing participant or simply in the wrong place at the wrong time. It didn't seem to be his blood anyway. He pondered Rako's question, scratching his beard.

'There are some things I need. Nothing very important but I expect I'll have a few weeks to use them. Some new books perhaps?'

'You got books the other week.'

'And I've read them. But that's not why I'm here, Commander Rako.'

He leaned in conspiratorially.

'I want to go next,' he said.

'Next?'

'The next offering – to the creature.'

His brown eyes lit up as if to savour the look on Rako's face, waiting for his reaction, but Rako was calm.

'I thought that's why you *do* pay us. So, you won't be sacrificed,' Rako said.

'I paid you to show you I have the means and I will pay you handsomely for this opportunity. It will be sent after we are gone to him.'

'We?'

'My brother and I,' he said. 'I will go first, then he will follow.'

'And your brother, he is on board with this plan? He doesn't strike me as one who would choose such a gruesome death?'

'Death is only the beginning. I have watched all those who have gone before us these months and I am now ready. He will be too when the time comes.'

Rako had heard enough.

'Go back to your cell. This place…' he said, casting his eyes around the room, 'draws out the strange in some men and it swamps you now and clouds your judgement.'

'My judgement is sound. I know what he is and he's not the only one,' he said. 'Do you think I would come to this place of my own free will and take my brother if I did not believe it?'

'You came here for this?' Rako thought of the prisoners in the tombs, madness running down their bloodied faces versus the composed man opposite him.

'He has something to offer that transcends life. Don't you see Rako? He offers immortality. Didn't you ever think about it? What he was doing?'

'All of the men he's taken are dead.'

'Have you seen it?'

'He is not one to be questioned,' Rako said. 'And neither am I.'

'I can tell you there are others out there and they find their own prey. They don't ask for it. Why would he not simply sweep in here and take anyone he chooses, on any given night? This ritual is highly unusual. They are hunters, not collectors. You are providing him with an army handpicked by you and you don't even realise it.'

The balance of power in the room had shifted to the prisoner in front of him and he didn't like it. He paused, giving due thought to what he was about to tell him.

'I've seen him kill only once. When he first came down the mountain, to Castle Valla. I was twenty years old, a young officer, newly arrived. I hated it at first. You can see why. It's not the most hospitable of places and after a while, all the snow and ice makes you feel detached from humanity. But I made the best of it. I obeyed my commander, did what I was told, learned to handle myself and I was content. One night, as I patrolled the battlements, I met my commander taking in the night air.'

Rako was lost now in his memories as Vladimir listened.

'He often checked on us to make sure we were covering our posts and he must have been in a good mood for he offered me a cigarette. I took it gladly, the light from it a tiny orange glow in the night. Perhaps that's what attracted him to us but I suspect he knew what he was after. The temperature around us dropped. The stones changed from grey to white, glistening before our eyes. Our cigarettes froze. And the smell. Wherever it had come from, it was not a place either of us would ever wish to know. We hurried along the battlements when our path suddenly disappeared into shadow. Something was lurking there. It moved and we saw it was a man, walking towards us. He was covered in dirt, clumps of earth clinging to his body. It was hard to make out his face for the shadow never lifted from it, but I knew this was no ordinary man. It was a monster and he growled at us, a sound from deep inside him. We drew our swords but still he advanced. And when my commander faced him head on, he simply walked right into the blade, pushing it into his own flesh, blood spilling on the stones. He was pulling my commander to him, only the hilt of the sword between them. He grabbed his shoulders as light fell on his open mouth and a display of sharp jagged teeth. He bit him, clamped them to his neck and drank, until there was nothing left.'

'What did you do?' Vladimir asked.

'I froze. His form seemed to grow as if the drink had for-tified him. He discarded my commander and pulled out the sword, his wounds healing. His hands, reached for me, his palms white and unmarked by the blade. And he spoke to me. He told me that he would need more of it but not from just any man. Strong men. That when the moon was bright I was to leave one for him in a place he would make known. He would take their blood as he had my commander's.'

'Why not just kill you all?'

'Because then he would have no supply. As long as the prison functioned and new inmates came he could continue to get the best of them.'

'Chosen by you.'

'Only me. He said that I was commander now. I followed his orders to the letter. This has been going on a long time. It will continue no doubt after I'm gone, when he will choose my successor. I do not ask any questions of him. Frankly I don't want to know what he does with them but your theories, they are fantastical.'

'You think it impossible, after what you've just said?'

'I don't think at all. It's better that way.'

'Let me go to him.'

'So, you can join this *army*?'

'I must.'

'You will die. Just like my commander. Strong men mean strong blood, to make *him* stronger. Keep him alive. Your theory is wrong.'

'Then let me prove it…and come back.'

'No-one has ever come back and they never will. Now I have indulged you enough Vladimir and while I appreciate your enthusiasm I'm afraid there is no evidence of it.'

'Please you must.'

'He gave me a power that night to decide men's fate. I'm almost tempted to put you out there just to prove you wrong but I already have my next man chosen and I will not be dictated to. Also, your delusions make you unsuitable for the role.'

'Commander Rako…'

'I have heard enough. You will not talk of the creature again to me or anyone or I will put you so far below these walls that you will never see daylight again and no amount of money will help you.'

'You'll change your mind,' Vladimir said.

'Such confidence. We shall see.'

He called for the guards. The door opened immediately and Vladimir stood. He didn't say any more and Rako could tell from the glint of defiance in his eyes, that for him it was not the last of the matter.

He hadn't talked about the creature in over three decades. He'd told his story often when it had happened, to convince the other guards, and showed them the body to make them understand. But as the years went by, he told it less and less until he never spoke of it. The sacrifice was the way of Castle Valla now and new guards didn't need to hear it. They just had to believe it – and they did when they heard the screams for the first time. He was the only one with first-hand knowledge of it. How dare another, and a prisoner at that, think they should know more? He looked to his list, full of possible candidates and thought of all the prisoners that he'd given to the creature over the decades. An army? Chosen by him?

***

SINCE HE AND HIS brother had arrived in Castle Valla, Sasha had witnessed the screams of six sacrifices. Each time he strained his eyes at their window, no more than a long slit in the rock, trying to see what was going on. He found it hard to sleep and would sit there most nights in contemplation of the mysterious creature outside. That evening, he sat, an open book in his hands, his mind unable to read as he looked out into the darkness.

'Come away from there,' Vladimir said.

His brother sat at a small table also reading, the flame of the candlelight flickering in the draughty cell.

'What if one of us is chosen next?'

'Don't be ridiculous Alexander,' he said. 'I've told you, it's a trick to keep the inmates in line.'

His brother always called him Alexander and he hated it. Every time he said it, he felt as if their father were in the room. He even looked like him when he said it, that same look of disdain he had when he was angry. He didn't know where his brother had been that afternoon, but when he'd returned he did not look happy and had immediately gone to his shelf for a book to lose himself in. When he was like that, he was best left to his solitude. To his books.

Their mother had always joked that Vladimir had been born with a book in his hand, for he was always reading some text or other – a scholar of the world. He spoke English, though he had never encountered anyone to speak it with, and always seemed to have the answer to any problem. Even here in Castle Valla, Vladimir seemed to have it all worked out. His new-found wealth had afforded them certain privileges, notably elevation to a second story room high above the dungeon which was overrun with rats. They had also been allowed share a cell.

'I thought I could handle this but I can't stand it.'

'Calm down,' Vladimir said. 'You're letting this place get to you.'

'What do you think it is…out there, this creature?'

'Come now brother.'

Sasha looked to the window.

'They say he is a demon collecting the souls of the damned.'

'Well, he's in the right place then. You mustn't listen to them. They are stories to create fear. It's what this place is about. This creature is no doubt an overgrown mountain cat or a bear who stays in this area because it is fed by the lunatics who run this asylum. And it is an amusement for the guards to take our money for protection.'

Sasha felt comforted by this, his shoulders relaxing. He left the window, his thumb in the page of his book, and sat on his bed, a far cry from the straw bedding given to those below them.

'How long do we have to stay here?'

Vladimir sighed. 'Long enough to get what we came for. You know the plan. You just do as I say. Why do you question me?'

Sasha had never doubted his brother but he was beginning to wonder if he'd been honest with him about their scheme. He had promised him riches beyond their wildest dreams with a tale of a mystery benefactor who would fund their mission to the notorious Castle Valla to find an ancient artefact. Vladimir said it would take time to find given the size of the prison and having been six months already, Sasha was beginning to feel that his brother was not being straight with him or perhaps had been given false information and they were trapped there now. Every day he mapped another part of it, handing over his drawings to Vladimir who folded them into a book on his shelf for later consultation. He said there were clues to be followed and that he alone could work out the correct path. Sasha was a patient man but this was getting ridiculous. What was his brother waiting on so calmly and who was his strange benefactor? Whoever it was, they had gone to a lot of trouble to get them in there, arranging their entry on false papers, with a fake sentence handed down by a judge in Omsk.

He supposed it hadn't been wise to agree to this in the first place, but drunk on blackberry wine it had seemed like the grandest scheme and no one possessed the power of persuasion like his brother. From the time he'd been old enough to walk, he'd been following him from one adventure to the next. Their father, Abram, was an alcoholic with little time for his family, only peering out occasionally through the haze to tell them all how much he hated them with their judging eyes, mocking his failures as they clung to their mother. By the time he was three, his father counted Sasha among those failures and it was Vladimir, just approaching his teens, who stepped in to guide his brother on the best path around him. Their mother tried her best to shelter him from it though it had worn her down, her voice tender in his ear. *Be quiet my Sasha, don't cry.* Vladimir eventually became the man of the house and when she died from influenza in the winter of 1818, they left their father, lost to drunken sleep in his chair, with no goodbyes.

Sasha wondered if perhaps his brother's ego had finally succumbed to a challenge way beyond his skills and they would never be free of Castle Valla.

'Don't lose faith in me brother,' said Vladimir is if reading his mind. 'It may take a little longer but the rewards at the end of this will be…well…life changing.'

Sasha doubled up his flat pillow under his head and closed his eyes, the latest screams of the sacrifice still ringing in his ears.

5

EVELYN STOOD IN THE treeline, halted by the sight of Melmoth Hall, sprawled like a granite beast on the gravel in front of her. She had measured up the chances of getting Lord Stockett to listen to her, against those of dying without a roof over their heads and so she'd set out cross country, determined that the day couldn't possibly end any worse than it had begun. She hadn't lied to Michael exactly. She *was* going to go to call on Father Mercer and tell him what had happened but not until she had made a stop here, and abandoned any sense of self-respect she had. She wondered how hard he'd worked for such a home, if at all. How could one family lay claim to a house with, she guessed, fifty rooms at least? How could Stockett in all conscience throw people, who had nothing to begin with, further into decline by taking their homes and their livelihoods?

She was getting angry and it felt good. It had been building slowly since her father had become ill. Perhaps some of Michael's fiery nature was rubbing off on her at last. Their father always said he got it from his mother while Evelyn's even temperament came from him. For all his smarts, Michael tended to react with his quick tongue and clenched fists before his brain had had a chance to catch up, so it was best that he wasn't here or they would end up in more trouble with Lord Stockett than ever. When she'd left he was taking the barrow up the hill to the lazy beds and even though he was exhausted, she expected the thought of staying still with time to ponder events was not one he welcomed.

She had taken rest when needed, eating berries from brambles along the forest path. She had no idea if they were edible and so she let her palate decide for surely something so sweet and tasty could not do any harm. Those with a foul bitterness were not to be trusted and so would be spat out. Even the good ones made her stomach ache and she put her last handful away, fearful that she might throw up on Lord Stockett's doorstep. She had only ever seen him through the window of his carriage as he passed through town, his upper body like the bust of a statue, his beady eyes overlooking a long nose – his expression always one of haughty disdain. Perhaps today would be different. She took a deep breath, pulled her shawl tightly around her shoulders, and rang the bell.

***

INSIDE, LORD JAMES WILLIAM Stockett already had a visitor. He had called his 'middleman' Jim Corcoran to him for an update in the wake of the blight. He was not someone he would have hired himself but just as he had inherited Melmoth

Hall and its lands, so too had he inherited his Uncle's middleman, and he knew that it was due to Corcoran's force of determination that all rents were paid on time. He didn't have to like the man, he'd realised, he just had to let him do the job he was good at. But he was a little rough for Stockett's liking, one foot in the gentleman class and the other with the farming peasantry, for he too was a tenant, on a large stretch of land with a decent farmhouse and stables.

Both men were of similar age, in their forties, but there they parted ways for Corcoran had neither the manners or the grooming of a gentleman. He wore his hair short, the grey hairs like those of a wire brush standing on end, and his face was ruddy from the outdoors and bloated by the alcohol he was so fond of. Stockett could smell it when he walked in and wondered how the man ever got to do any work but he seemed to function well and if he was suffering the ill effects of last night's drinking he certainly didn't show it.

'So, tell me Corcoran, what's the situation?' he said, offering him one of the armchairs by the fire.

The man sat before answering him, his hands out to the flames.

'Cold out there,' he said, rubbing his palms. 'Perhaps a nip of whiskey?'

Stockett almost refused then thought if rumours were true and circumstances were indeed to get tougher, he would need the man's help. He handed him a small measure from a decanter on the table. Corcoran smiled.

'I'll tell it to you sir,' he said taking a sip. 'It's bad. The worst I've ever seen. Every field, every potato. Four of them dead this week and I mean families…every last one. Empty stomachs bring sickness. They won't last.'

'What's to be done?'

'Well sir, even now, they crowd my door, begging for mercy. Their hope is to live free on your land until it passes.'

Free. That was not a word Lord Stockett was fond of. He sat down at his desk, his tenant ledger open in front of him.

'Then the time has come to protect my assets. Evict those who can no longer pay. Let them try to survive under their own steam. I will not see my lands turned into a mass grave for starving peasants. What good is that land to me then? If I let them stay they will eventually turn on me with their desperate hunger and violent ways and Melmoth would lie in ruins. Let them try their luck elsewhere.'

His clipped English accent was a product of good stock and public-school education, but even he was aware that when it came to conversing with the Irish, he leaned into it more to make the sounds more nasal, bringing an authoritative gap between him and his tenants. Corcoran's hatred of the English was not lost on him. He'd caught him once in the reflection of a window sneering at him but he had the foresight to not let it get in the way of business. He lived in Ireland now, held lands there, and it was a pleasant country not unlike his own. Until now.

He would need Corcoran. Especially if it was as bad as he said. In truth, he was afraid. Things were changing. His wife Jessica had left Ireland a month before, upon hearing news of riots in the south west. Try as he had to dissuade her, she had left for their London residence with their two children. Now he wished he'd gone with them. Corcoran was married too, he was sure. Certainly, when he'd first arrived in Cularne, he'd seen him with his wife in town, she scurrying a few paces behind him. Since then rumours abound that she had left him and gone to England. Wise perhaps to get the distance of water. He would not have been pleased.

A loud knock came on the study door. The butler announced that a Miss Evelyn Mooney wished to see him on behalf of her father Patrick Mooney. Recognising the surname from his ledgers, he threw a look at Corcoran.

'Do you want me to deal with it?' 'Corcoran said, standing up.

'No,' he sighed. 'Take a seat.'

***

EVELYN HAD INSISTED THE butler request her meeting, her face determined as she stood in the doorway. When he tried to shut the door on her foot, she threatened to scream the house down and so he relented, allowing her into the hallway to wait, her tiny form lost in a sea of white marble. Standing there alone she glanced at the mirror hanging on the wall and understood his reluctance to let her in. Her blue eyes, once bright, lay heavy in their sockets, dark circles creeping down her cheeks. To him she must seem a ragged wisp of a girl, her long dark hair matted and pushed behind her ears. Her gauntness wasn't helped by the clothes that had once fit perfectly and now hung shapeless on her thin frame.

She shuffled from one foot to the other as pins and needles battled in her feet, from the exertion of the walk, she assumed. Rather than lessen, they grew in intensity until her hands too began to tingle. She rubbed them together and was alarmed at their warmth. Her knees felt weak and she grabbed the cool surface of the side table to steady herself, forcing long breaths of air into her lungs as a wave of nausea struck her insides. She cursed the berries, begging them to stay put. She imagined them spilling out – a purple stain on the pristine white floor. Not the impression she wanted to make. When the butler returned, she forced herself upright to follow him down a long corridor to two large ornate doors.

He knocked once and showed her into a room – a man's room – dark panels of wood lining the walls, closing in on her. Behind a large table sat Lord Stockett, his head bent into a ledger. She stood in front of him, waiting for him to meet her gaze. When he did finally, he cast a look behind her and she turned her head to see Corcoran seated in an armchair. Her heart sank as did any chance of appealing to Stockett's good graces.

'Pardon my Lord, but I needed to speak with you urgently,' she said. She could feel her legs begin to tremble and she willed them to hold strong a little longer. 'Our crop has blight, all ten acres gone. I beg you to allow us another harvest before our rent.'

'You'll be dead by then,' said Corcoran, unable to resist, his deep voice resonating in the panelled room.

'I'm afraid Mr Corcoran is a little put out that you didn't bring this conversation to him. He is after all my middleman,' Stockett said. 'Why do you come to my home?'

'I meant no offence but I didn't know what else to do. My father has died.'

She fought to keep the tremor from her voice.

'I have come because this is no ordinary crop failure. We're starving and we need help. My brother and I will surely die.'

'So, Mr. Corcoran is correct then. Either way I won't get my rent.'

He stood up and approached her, looking down his nose.

'I am sorry for your loss my dear. It is the way of life and we must all face it but business is business and these are harsh times for us all. Therefore, if you cannot pay rent, you leave me no choice but to evict you.'

'Sir, you can't. We have nowhere to go and winter is coming.'

He raised a hand to silence her, disinterested in her pleas.

'You have one week to pay or the bailiffs will come. Mr. Corcoran will monitor the standing and visit you in a week's time. Now leave my house....' He paused, wrinkling his nose. 'You pollute the air with your stench.'

He smiled to himself, pleased with his childish insult. Evelyn had heard enough. She took a sudden step towards him.

'How many are dead because of your greed? If I die because of you, I'm coming back here to take you to hell myself.'

Stockett gasped.

'Why I've never…'

She heard no more of his response. Corcoran grabbed her, pulling her backwards out of the room. The force from his boot sent her sliding across the floor into the hallway.

'Get her out of here,' he said to the butler.

'And don't think about burying your father on that land,' he said to her as he walked away. 'They can throw him on the heap at the workhouse with the rest of them. You'll join him soon enough.'

Evelyn knew better than to talk back to him. Her side ached from the force of his boot but it was a small price to pay for not allowing that pompous, cruel man have the last word. She picked herself up off the floor. She would not have the butler's hands on her too. Though he didn't seem to relish the thought either, for he simply opened the front door as wide as he could, as if the world outside might extract her itself. She straightened her shawl. A young maid was dusting the hall table, trying to ignore the commotion, her attention set wisely on her work. She rubbed a dark stain in the wood and as Evelyn passed her, she saw it was scorched black, the shape not unlike a handprint – small and delicate. Just like her.

6

She didn't slow her pace until she reached the woods again. She had scurried away, rubbing the palm of her right hand with her thumb. It was no warmer than any other part of her, though she was warm all over. She had lost her temper – not exactly how she had foreseen their meeting would go. Of course, she had expected it to be difficult, but naively she had hoped to get through to the man with a heartfelt, honest and yes, desperate plea for help. He was human after all – wasn't he?

The deeper into the trees she went, the cooler the air, the smell of damp leaves and moss heady after the rain. The truth was that, no matter how well intentioned, she had made things even worse. How could she tell Michael, after he had already warned against it? And what news to bring him today, of all days. But she was at a loss as to a solution. Maybe he'd think of one – when he'd calmed down. Like burning Melmoth Hall to the ground. Destroy his home before he could theirs. And Stockett, trapped, his frock coat alight as he banged on the window for mercy. She paused. This flight of fancy was not unusual for her, but one so dark? Her father called that 'unholy thought' and she reckoned that perhaps in dark times, people were forced to think like that − to dream darker.

Her attention turned to the sound of horse's hooves behind her. Someone approached at great speed. There was no mistaking the rider as Corcoran's hulking frame came into view. He spotted her, pulling on the reins. His face was a menacing snarl, his eyes demented and she knew that her greatest mistake was not upsetting Stockett, but putting herself in the path of his middleman. She'd gone over his head and worse still she'd done it right in front of him. Had Lord Stockett reprimanded him after she'd gone? Most likely and he wasn't happy about it. A beating was coming, of that she was sure.

She ducked off the path into the trees. She would never outrun him − he was strong and healthy − so she searched desperately for a place to hide. She dropped down into a patch of dense undergrowth, and peeked out through the leaves. On the path, his horse stood alone. To her right, she heard the crunch of twigs underfoot. Then silence.

'You can't hide from me.' His voice boomed among the trees.

She didn't dare move. The ground crackled again, louder this time. He was getting closer. A bead of sweat ran down the side of her face, her body a sudden furnace of intense heat. Closer. She could see his coat, just a few feet away. Could he see her? Not yet, but he soon would. Damn it! She burst out from the bushes, running as fast as she could. Within seconds his hands were on her, dragging her down to the sodden leaves, her feet slipping as she tried to escape him. But he was quick. He was on top of her before she had a chance to move, his face so close she could smell the alcohol on his breath.

'Told you I'd find you.'

She struggled underneath his weight.

'My brother will come,' she said.

'Your brother has no idea you're here, or you wouldn't have come alone.'

He chuckled, savouring his position and she hated that she'd given him reassurance of it. No-one would come and he knew it. He leaned back, delivering a powerful blow across her face with the back of his hand. Pain, as the vision in her left eye swam into a blur. As it righted again, she saw a change in his expression. In it was violence, but also desire and she realised that there were worse things than a beating. Much worse.

She screamed as loud as she could. Was there anyone out there to hear it? Please let there be. Someone to intervene and put a stop to it. She screamed again and this time he clasped his hands tightly around her neck, her cries stifled as she gasped for air. But there was uncertainty in his eyes. Either his hands were ice cold or her feverish warmth was more pronounced than she thought, but he had noticed it too. Her insides heaved as it spread through her body, the intensity growing the tighter his grip became. The tingle in her limbs she'd felt in Melmoth Hall returned. Was she ill? Or was it true and she hadn't been spared her mother's gift after all?

She fought against him, her hand grabbing his neck as he had hers. She was weak, her grip having no impact but she held on as the heat surged. It rippled through her arm, up to her wrist and into her fingers until it reached the tips, where it shimmered through her skin onto his, growing hotter by the second. Disbelief and panic married in Corcoran's eyes. He let go of her, forcing her hand away and pinning it to the ground. He was staring at it, his eyes wide. There nestled in her palm, was a golden flame. It danced hypnotically, majestic in the darkness of the wood. And then it disappeared. She clenched her hand but it was gone, the magic lost.

Corcoran's hands went back to her throat, not to subdue her but to end it, for he leaned his body forward, adding his weight to the task. White clouds drifted across her sight. She was dizzy – disoriented – unable to breathe. She would soon lose consciousness – that or the sheer force would break her neck. Whichever came first. Her hand grasped the air before finding the sleeve of his coat. The tingle returned to her fingers and she felt the tiny flame ignite once more. Corcoran held fast, determined to finish what he started. The threads in the fabric began to singe, the flame getting to work, growing until it reached its fiery tip to lick his face. He had no choice but to draw back and tear the burning coat from his shoulders. This was it – her only chance. Air struggled to reach her lungs but all she could think of was escape. She only got four or five paces before something heavy struck her on the back of her head and everything plunged into darkness.

***

The world is red. I can taste it.
It fills every part of me.
The world is blood.
And in it I drown.

Evelyn's eyes opened suddenly. She was no longer in the woods and her mind struggled to connect with her strange new surroundings. Everything seemed slower here and it was only as a lock of her hair drifted in front of her face that her mind caught up. She was in water. Far below the surface. And she couldn't move. It filled her mouth and she expelled it in a trail of bubbles into the murkiness around her. Pain raged in her head, thanks to Corcoran, and she knew then where she was. Still in the woods but far below the trees. On the riverbed. He had wrapped her in sackcloth and tied her hands and feet. She wriggled, fighting against what she knew to be inevitable. She couldn't hold her breath forever.

When it did invade, the water was a mix of silt and the taste of her own blood trailing from her head. It found her stomach, her lungs. She had lost. Death was approaching as surely as if it had opened a door to greet her and she was drifting into its embrace. In its midst, she heard a voice whisper in her ear – the tone urgent.

He said only one word.

Fight!

She felt it strike her like a blow, her whole body reacting as her eyes shot open again. An image came into her mind of that flame in her hand. Her flame. She imagined it spreading all over her body, her heart a pulsating orb of fire as it strengthened her. The heat inside her rose again. This time, it erupted from her in a ball of white light. Her bindings and clothing disintegrated, the heat so powerful as to change them to particles that shot out like exploding stars around her. She was free. Her feet brushed the stones on the riverbed and she sprung off them, rising quickly to the surface. When she reached the bank, she coughed up water until there was no more and she lay on her back in the grass, her arms outstretched, air at last in her lungs.

It was nightfall. A bright moon shone in the sky and her thoughts turned to Corcoran. Was he still here? Was he lurking somewhere in case she re-surfaced? How long had she been out for? He probably thought he had done enough. He'd certainly tried.

She looked to the old stone bridge that lay above her. He must have thrown her in from there. Long ago, people used to fish there, her own father included, until Lord Stockett took over Melmoth and outlawed it. The first wisps of mist began to descend on it. And only there, for when she looked around, the night was clear. It cascaded through the air, to slowly unveil the figure of a man. He was finely dressed, his jacket neatly buttoned over a white shirt and neat grey cravat, his dark hair slicked back off his face. He was smiling at her, his brown eyes warm. It was *his* voice she'd heard. She had no doubt. He bowed his head to her before the mist covered him and when it curled away on the air, the bridge was empty, the night once again clear.

Who was he, this stranger? Or maybe he wasn't a stranger. She thought of the man she'd seen in the graveyard that day with her father. But she was just a child and she hadn't seen his face. Was it him? Was she in danger? But he'd saved her – urged her to use her power when it mattered most. If he'd wanted to destroy her, he could simply have left her to drown. She felt the first chill of goose bumps on her skin as she returned to normal. But then she would never be normal again. She *was* different. She *was* extraordinary and she would see him again.

7

FAR AWAY, THE SAME man opened his eyes to the city skyline, a panorama of rooftops and chimney stacks all the way to the Hudson River. Exhaling, his misty breath clouded the air, a souvenir of his projection to the girl. Manhattan's nocturnal soundtrack returned. The sound of horses' hooves in the warren below, human sounds of laughter and cries for help intertwined, the barking of loose dogs that roamed the streets, the distant bells as ships made their way across the bay. And music, far off in the distance from the Five Points. Music for revelry and celebration. *Prepare yourself city! Soon you will have a new daughter.*

She'd seen him – a feat indeed! He stretched his arms out like a bird flexing its wings before flight. He liked to come up on the roof alone at night to survey his city, to watch it pulsate below. Nothing happened here that he did not know about. If it involved an act of darkness, he knew of it and who was responsible. He controlled the subterranean tide of this great city, the one that sat silently heaving with the human world beneath heaven and above hell, a darkness within the mortal world where creatures roamed and evil seethed. Without his control, it would spill over into theirs and there would be chaos. He kept order and if he did not allow your entry to this great island you went away with your pointy tail between your legs. Object and you might find yourself visiting hell a little quicker than you thought.

She was coming to him at an interesting time. He removed his jacket and loosened his tie. He did hate such restrictive clothing but he wanted to make a good impression should his suspicions of the girl prove true, and he was glad now that they had at last made a connection. She would recoil if she were to see his true self, the one he kept hidden, buried deep. Anyone would.

8

RAKO AWOKE TO THE shrill sound of a bell ringing. He heard it
clearly as if the ringer were close to his ear and then it stopped.
He listened for a moment. Nothing. The castle was quiet,
the sun only beginning to rise in the sky. He often dreamt in
sounds as much as images and knowing there was no bell to
be found within its walls, he knew his mind was already sig-
nalling a busy day. There would be a sacrifice tonight and a
prisoner to prepare. Dragomir Letski, prisoner 5382. Trouble.
No other inmate could match his strength and size and as
men do, in challenging others, he had left a wake of beaten
men in his path, some who died instantly, others weeks later
from their injuries. The creature was welcome to him, for
with him here, the list of good candidates was getting thin.

He sat up and rubbed his face. His fingers touched something wet on his forehead and he drew them back. In the
half-light, they looked black but he knew blood in any light.
He pushed off his blanket and went to the small mirror on the
wall. Streaks of it smeared his face, tiny droplets dry on his
nose. His bed was the same, covered in drops of blood. His

heart leapt. *He* had been here. In this room. He shuddered and peered into the darkened corners to see if his eyes would meet the monster's gaze, but the sun was rising and he knew that with any luck the creature would have returned to its lair, for he had never encountered him in daylight.

A fresh drop of blood landed on his shoulder and he looked up. It was coming from the ceiling. He lit a candle and climbed up on the bed, his arm extended as far as he could reach. There, in the shadows, written in blood with a childlike abandon to form and size, were a row of numbers.

Rako looked closer. It was a prisoner number. It had to be. They could have no other meaning. Hurriedly he washed his face and pulled his uniform on, his fingers fumbling over the buttons on his shirt. The creature had never asked for anyone before. He left it to Rako and Rako had already chosen. In his office, he thumped down the heavy book of records and though he suspected he knew its owner already, he ran his finger down the list of inmates. When he found it, he sat back in his chair to ponder it. The creature had chosen this man? Why?

***

THE GREAT HALL WAS its usual state of organised chaos as prisoners queued for their morning gruel. Rako stood on the balcony watching them, when he spotted the Dermatov brothers standing in line. When they reached the large cauldron, they each received a ladleful from its smaller cousin behind, the steam from its heat leaving a trail after them as they found a seat. Most of the prisoners were used to some getting preferential treatment. You got what you paid for and if you had no money than cold gruel was the best you could hope for.

He watched as Vladimir walked towards Dragomir Letski's table, a no-go for any man not in his circle. What was he doing? The mountain of a man sat with his back to him, eating his own gruel – grey and running off his spoon. He could have demanded a hot breakfast from the guards, but why bother when he could simply take it from another? He would surely take the Dermatovs'.

Vladimir sat at the empty bench beside his, where he proceeded to eat his breakfast, loudly savouring each spoonful. When Letski looked at him, he winked. His brother Sasha had stopped in the middle of the room, unsure whether to follow him, when his brother shouted to him.

'Alexander, here.'

With unsure steps, he followed him and sat down.

Letski was already on his feet, filling the space around him as he stood up, his own men giving him room to manoeuvre.

'It's good, huh?' Vladimir said to him, his mouth full. 'Nice and creamy today.'

Does he want to die? No-one goaded Letski. It didn't take much to get most of the men going. They were hungry most of the time and hunger is great fuel for an argument.

'Did you want some? Vladimir asked, holding out his bowl to him, before tipping its contents out onto the floor.

For a big man, Letski was fast. A fist the size of a boulder came at his head but Vladimir was quick too. He dropped the bowl as he swerved to avoid him, sinking a punch into the man's lower back. Letski faltered as Vladimir grabbed onto him, one foot on the bench as he climbed up the man, using all his weight to knock his balance until he crashed to the ground. Letski clasped his hands around the smaller man's skull but Vladimir took a blade from his pocket and drove it upwards into Letski's jaw. His grip released as his head fell back, blood pooling on the flagstones.

The room fell into silence. Somewhere in the kitchens, pots clanged. All eyes were on Vladimir. The guards rushed in, forcing him to the ground, but he didn't fight back. He lay there grinning as they shackled him. His brother was staring at the dead man and back to Vladimir, dumbfounded. He was a man of constant surprise it seemed, even to his own family. Slowly the prisoners returned to their seats, Letski's gang silently eating their gruel, eyes cast deep into their bowls.

***

'YOU CAN'T KILL THE inmates,' Rako said as Vladimir was led to the same chair in his office. The bloodied knife lay casually on the desk between them.

'You allow me to carry protection. Did you think I wouldn't need it?'

'For protection. Not ambush…and Letski of all people.'

Vladimir wiped his bloody hands on his trousers.

'You'd chosen him to go out there. The man was a thug. Not worthy of the honour.'

'How do you know that?'

When the list wasn't with him, it was locked in a drawer in his office.

'Letski was a bit obvious don't you think? I told you I wouldn't give up. With Letski dead, now you can send me.'

The man had hidden resources, he had to admit. A shame. He might have been a good candidate after all.

'You murdered Letski for nothing,' he said. 'You were right, for years, it's been up to me. Who I saw fit and I had put Letski to the top of the list. But your intervention will have no effect. *He's* making the decisions now.'

He let his words sink in, for a moment even pitying the man before him. All that he had done, only for his great adventure to misfire.

'He has decided who he wants next and it's not you.'

Rako ran his finger down the page, checking the number again, though he'd already done it dozens of times. There was no error.

'He wants your brother.'

The words hung in silence as Rako waited patiently for his reaction. When he spoke, Vladimir's voice was no more than a whisper.

'There must be some mistake.'

'Tonight.'

'Why would he want him? How does he even know about him?'

'It is not for us to reason,' Rako said.

'He can't have him before me. I won't allow it.'

'I will. Make no mistake who is in charge here. Me over you and the creature over all of us. It's my job only to give him what he wants, not what he doesn't.'

'But he doesn't know what I know.'

'Then I suggest you tell him.'

'He won't understand.'

Rako sighed. 'They never do.'

***

SASHA WAS PACING BACK and forth in their cell when Vladimir returned. Though he waited for news, he was surprised to see him. He expected him to be deep in one of Rako's solitary chambers, as punishment for murdering Letski. He'd never seen his brother move like that – didn't know he could and he wondered what other talents he kept hidden. There was no warning from him, no citation of the day's plan for blood-shed and so he couldn't work out why he would even do such a thing. Had he cracked at last? Gone mad? He shuffled in, sitting down so that the guards could remove his shackles. All while he stared at Letski's dried blood on his hands. When the guards left, he rose to the basin of water and sunk his hands to the bottom.

'What did Rako say?' Sasha asked.

He could tell his brother was in no humour for conversation but he knew losing himself in a book was not going to do the trick this time. He was ashen faced.

'Nothing' his brother said.

He moved his hands slowly in the water.

'He's not going to punish you?'

He gripped the side of the basin, his knuckles white. He didn't speak for a moment as if deciding the best way to tell it. Eventually he turned to him, looking him in the eye for the first time since he'd returned.

'He's separating us,' he said. 'Rako will take you to your new quarters tonight.'

'And where will you be?

'Here…for now.'

Something switched in his demeanour as if he'd been trying to work out a problem and had at last fallen on the best solution. His expression brightened.

'I did Rako a favour getting rid of Letski. We talked and I suppose, in an effort to see the back of us, he granted us our expedition. You are just going first, my own delayed start a punishment of sorts. He said there were ways other than murder to get his attention but once I had it and agreed to share some of our fortune, he conceded.'

'So, we'll be free soon?'

'Yes…you first and then me. It's very important you know that. I will follow you.'

Sasha couldn't believe it. At last! He pulled his brother in for a hug.

'I should never have doubted you,' he said. 'I'll admit it, I was beginning to think we'd made a huge mistake but it's come good, just like you said it would.'

The door of life's possibilities was open again. Re-joining it in all its wonder, was a pleasure he thought lost to them. Vladimir handed him the book of maps he had collected which he accepted with eager hands, putting it securely into a satchel that had lain empty since their arrival. Now he would take it out of there.

'Rako will tell you where to go,' Vladimir said watching his every move. 'Get you set.'

Sasha suspected his brother was a little jealous but now was not the time to rub salt in the wound. If Vladimir hadn't killed Letski, he would not have this chance. He owed him everything.

The wait seemed endless but when the door finally opened that evening, Sasha jumped up, keen to get started. Rako, who was accompanied by four guards, looked puzzled by his high spirits. It was only when he saw the shackles that Sasha knew something wasn't right.

'Has your brother explained it to you?' Rako asked.

Vladimir shifted uncomfortably in his chair.

'Yes, I'm ready.'

'You won't need that,' Rako said, looking to the satchel, then to Vladimir. 'You didn't tell him, did you?'

Slowly Sasha put it down on his bed and looked to his brother.

'Vladimir?'

He didn't look up.

'Just take him Rako,' he said.

The guards stepped in, one of them with a heavy coat draped over his arm and Sasha knew then that there was no expedition. He backed away to the tiny window, the icy air circling in – a reminder of the fate that awaited him. Outside. Alone. With what, he couldn't be sure. But he wouldn't be coming back.

'No!' he shouted. 'Vladimir? You can't let them take me.'

He kicked and twisted his body but he couldn't fight them. The shackles bit into his skin as the guards dragged him to the door, his hand gripping the door jamb in one last plea for help. Vladimir did nothing. He just sat there with his eyes to the floor.

'You lied to me.'

One of the guards struck his fingers to pry them loose. As they took him away, he heard the faint words of his brother delivered to the empty room.

'I'm sorry Alexander.'

9

MICHAEL HAD WORKED TIRELESSLY all afternoon and as night began to fall, he threw his spade in the barrow to head for home. At the end of the furrowed rows, a heap of blackened potato plants lay ripped from the ground. There were too many for him to clear them all. Not today. Not on his own. Voices carried from the fields beyond and in the distance three figures toiled as he did, shouting across to one another. He looked around, imagining his father, calling out to him as he always did. *You alright, son?* And Michael from the time he could hold a shovel, would wave his hand in the air and smile back at him. As their father had grown weaker, it was Michael who looked out for him. He worked close beside him to spare him the hard graft. Not that it had done any good. His father was dead. Buried on the land he'd worked so hard on all his life.

The thought made his chest heave. Grief would have its say no matter how hard he tried to push it away. Angry tears fell as it swept over him, for grief and rage were born together from death, each screaming for attention. His body folded, the seat of his trousers meeting the ground, his head collapsing into his hands. He dug his heels into the ground, pushing the soil back and forth. Stones ran into the hole in his boot and in the disturbed earth, he saw something. An object, half buried. He dug it out with his fingers. It was a piece of whittled wood – a dog, small but carved with great skill. A child's toy perhaps lost or discarded but not one he recognised. Their father was good at many things but the detail in this carving was beyond even his handiwork. It looked like a wolfhound but with more muscle, built like a beast, it's shaggy coat expertly rendered, its head large with a vicious open mouth, baring its teeth. Perhaps not a child's after all. He put it in his pocket to show Evelyn – the only prize from his toil that day, when he saw the plume of grey smoke rising in the sky.

He ran as fast as he could but by the time he reached the cottage, thick smoke billowed out the empty door frame, the roof ablaze. Neighbours ran with pails of water but it was too late. Where was Evelyn? He looked for her among the faces. Maybe she was still with Father Mercer. A man came towards him, an empty bucket in his hand. It was Foyle, a local farmer, who sometimes collected rent on Corcoran's behalf.

'I'm sorry son, but it was too far gone,' he said, Michael only barely listening. 'We couldn't get to her on time.'

Her?

'She was inside. I heard her scream as the place went up.'

He reached for Michael's shoulder but he was already gone, in a sprint towards the blaze. Yellow and orange flames raged and with a loud crack, the ceiling beams – no longer able to hold – collapsed sending a shower of sparks into the room below. Still he rushed forward. If Evelyn was in there, he had to try. And if he failed? Then death was better than being without her. He felt someone grab him, then many hands, as they dragged him back. A safe distance, they said. Nothing you can do now. They sat with him in the grass, all of them watching.

As the last embers burned, he refused offers of shelter for the night, some with more swearing than was necessary. How could this happen? Most of the neighbours had left after he'd shot down their attempts to explain it. Chimney fire? He kept it swept. An ember from the fire falling on the straw? Evelyn was careful. She'd never let anything near the fire. In the end, he lost patience, especially when the ones who remained, did so holding hands – a *Hail Mary* on their lips for his father and sister.

'What good are your prayers?' he said. 'There's no God here anymore to hear them.'

If there had been, he would have spared her. The blight was strangling their community and his sister was out there doing her best to peel its fingers back one by one. He was done with prayer. There was nothing left to pray for. In his eyes, the glow of the embers became a copper haze. The last of the faithful left, and he moved closer. He had to be sure. There, beneath the blackened beams she lay.

They should have let him run in there. Losing both his father and Evelyn in the one breath, was too much to bear.

He could hear her voice in his head, calling to him. Did she scream for him as she died? Over and over, he heard it. Was she to torment him? Haunt him? The very thought of it. He pushed his hands against his ears. He would go mad from it. Around him, the wind picked up blowing ash out onto the road. He watched it as it drifted, the rise and fall hypnotic and there in the middle of it all stood his sister, her face in sorrow as she looked at their home.

She was strangely dressed. A man's overcoat, her hair damp over the lapels, her legs and feet bare. He stood transfixed by this apparition. But she was no ghost come to haunt him, for when she put her arms around him, she collapsed into him, her embrace so tight his ribs ached. She was real. Breathing hard against his shoulder. She didn't speak and he didn't know where to begin.

'You were inside.'

He knew the futility of it for she was here in his arms.

'He said you were and then I saw you…'

'Who said?'

She was looking at him strangely.

'Foyle. He said you were in there and then it all fell down.'

'Was Corcoran with him?'

'No, why? You think he had something to do with this?'

'I know he did.'

She went to the house and peered inside.

'I suppose a body isn't hard to come by. They can't bury them quick enough,' she said.

'I don't understand. Why would he do this?'

'I went to see Lord Stockett. I'm sorry. I know and… you were right it was the worst thing I could have done.'

His attention turned to her appearance as she said it. Christ, what had happened?

'Whose coat is that? Did he hurt you?'

'No, but he wouldn't listen to me, he said he was going to evict us. And Corcoran was there too. When I left he followed me into the woods…'

No matter what she would say next, Michael had already decided his course of action. She told him of the attack – how he'd caught her and fought with her. How he'd hit her with something and then tried to dispose of her. Get rid of his problem and cover his tracks. She was keeping something back – he could tell. Was she trying to spare him the most awful of truths? She only wore his coat. Nothing else. He could see a secret in her eyes and he was terrified as to what it might be. Either way, he'd decided. He was going to kill him. He would find a safe place to hide her until this was over. He told her as much before she disappeared around the back of the house, returning with the sharp prongs of a muck rake, curved like a claw in her hand.

'Corcoran's mine,' she said.

10

EVELYN PULLED THE COAT tightly around her, the irony of finding it thrown in the gorse not lost on her. It was heavy and warm and it overlapped to double up on her, such was their difference in size. She felt the burnt threads and marvelled again at the gift that had saved her. She would have doubted her sanity where she not wearing the proof of it. She hadn't fully understood its magnitude when her father had told her. How could she? It was fantastical that a person could create fire from nothing. But now that she'd felt its power for herself, it was incredible. If only she could talk to her mother. How could anyone else possibly understand it? Would her brother? On the way home, she'd debated whether to tell him. She was going to but that was before she'd found their home destroyed and him possessed of an urge for violence. Losing their father had struck Michael hard. Perhaps it was enough for one day and besides, Corcoran needed to be dealt with first.

***

THE FARMHOUSE WAS IN complete darkness to the front. By now, she hoped he'd have retired to bed, for murder must surely be an exhausting practice. Michael went first as they rounded the corner to the back yard. There was a soft glow from the kitchen window. Candlelight. He was still up. She ducked below the windowsill, peeking above an empty flower box that hadn't seen a flower in a very long time. Inside, Corcoran and Foyle sat at a large table, a bottle of whiskey, almost empty between them.

Michael tightened his grip on the drill spud in his hand, its long, concave blade more used to sowing crops than vengeance. It was all he could find but it was sharp and more than adequate. The presence of Foyle certainly didn't deter him. It seemed to enliven him and he motioned that he was going to check the back door. She stood still and listened, the men's drunken voices carrying through the thin glass. She peeked again.

'That's the drink talking boss,' said Foyle shaking his head.

'You didn't see her. Huge fuckin' flames shooting from her hand at me.'

Corcoran picked up the bottle for another swig. Nothing but a trickle on his tongue.

'Jesus, you drank the lot.'

'Did not,' Foyle said, his elbow slipping off the table.

Corcoran rose and took another bottle from the cupboard. He opened it and threw the cork across the room, swallowing a mouthful. Foyle's eyes were closing.

'A toast,' he said. 'To the witch. May she burn in hell.'

He swung the bottle upwards as whiskey splashed in the air, taking another gulp before he sat down. A long hunting knife lay on the table and Corcoran picked it up, running his fingers along the blade.

'Wish I'd had this with me today, I tell ya.'

His hands were trembling. It could have been the drink but she'd gotten to him, she knew it. Is that what he'd told himself – that she was a witch? They needed to get in there but Michael was nowhere to be seen. Then, something moved in the shadows opposite Foyle who had fallen asleep. From behind Corcoran's back, Michael raised his blade high. What was he doing? Corcoran must have caught a reflection in the knife, for he turned just as the blade came down. It struck the back of his shoulder, half of it disappearing as Corcoran let out a roar.

He jumped up, his knife swiping through the air as Michael leapt back, his own weapon still embedded in the man's shoulder. Evelyn ran for the back door. She heard Foyle's raised voice, first to protest the noise disturbing his nap, and then to shout at their intruder. She hesitated. She needed the fire. Could she summon it? She didn't know how it had come to her before. She flexed her fingers, willing it to come but it was no use. The feeling wasn't there. From inside, the sound of glass breaking. She was going to have to get in there regardless, before they both got killed. She moved into the room. Foyle had broken the empty bottle and he held it by the neck, pointing a long shard at Michael. Corcoran had fallen to his knees, his arm extended as he tried to remove the blade from his back, his own weapon still in his hand.

All three men saw her and paused. Michael's face flashed with worry. Foyle cried out with fright while Corcoran's look of shock disappeared in seconds as he readied himself to take her on. He left the blade in his shoulder and stood. Now, she had at least evened the fight. Foyle hurled himself at Michael, both men falling to the floor, the shard dodging precariously between them.

Evelyn swung the rake as Corcoran came at her. She grinned. The heat began to grow, spreading rapidly from her hand into each prong, until the iron turned amber in her grasp. She swung it out to block him and it cut clean through his knife, the handle still in his hand. He would not best her this time. He took a step back, fear in his eyes as he looked at her weapon, the tips white hot. He opened his mouth to say something. Would he surrender? Try to reason with her? Beg her forgiveness? It was too late for that. Her mind had already made that leap, decided it the moment she swam out of that river. Was her gift responsible too for these thoughts? Was it affecting her mind as well as her body? She wanted to tear him apart, watch him burn, then continue to Melmoth Hall and do the same to Lord Stockett. Whatever this power was – it was dark and capable of making its host do violent things. Is that why her mother didn't use it? But think what she was capable of. The power it brought.

The terror it could reign. She had been so thankful of it in the river – it had saved her life – but now it frightened her. Or was it the terrifying thrill of being able to stand up to Corcoran when it counted? Had she not found it, would he have left her alive – battered and broken – only to do it again? It wasn't in her nature to be violent, yet here it was, when she needed it. She should be thankful. She was still breathing because of it.

The heat spiked in her veins and she ran at him, twisting her body to bring the rake up, slashing him across the chest. He stumbled back into the table. She had scorched deep tracks into his skin, tearing his shirt and he lay panting, the wound in his back adding to his misery. She was conscious they were not alone but her brother and Foyle were fighting too hard to notice. She wanted a slow death for him, but death itself would have to be enough. She raised the rake again but didn't strike him. Instead, she rested it on his chest, leaning over him to curl her hand around the blade in his shoulder. Instantly, his body began to shake as the heat flowed through it. She concentrated, increasing the intensity, controlling it. He tried to speak but his mouth made no sound, opening and closing in a futile attempt to cry out. She imagined the heat running through his body. His eyes throbbed in their sockets. His tongue swelled. Would his heart do the same? Still she held on, her face close to his. A sheen of perspiration glistened on his face. She didn't let go until he was dead, his final breath an agonising groan.

Among the splinters of broken glass, Michael wrestled with Foyle. He'd been cut – a deep gash across his jawline – before he had forced it from Foyle's hands, smashing it. Now Michael was on top of him, punching him in the face. Foyle had passed out and as Michael continued to hit him, Evelyn caught him by the arm.

'That's enough,' she said. 'It's done.'

'He's still alive.'

'We came for Corcoran.'

Michael looked at his dead body and back to Foyle.

'We can't let him live,' he said his fist raised. 'He'll tell.'

'Tell them what – that a dead girl killed his friend or that he staged her death to cover up a murder when she was alive all along? C'mon, we need to go. The sun is coming up. We've done enough.'

'But…'

'I won't take a man from his family. He has children. They'll starve without him. Check his pockets and look for any food we can take with us.'

Michael did as he was told. She opened the pantry door and looked in amazement at its contents. The long narrow room was packed floor to ceiling with food. Bags of flour. Jars of preserves. Sugar. Oats. Tea. Bread. Cured meats. Even a few rabbits hanging on hooks from the ceiling. He was of course allowed to hunt on Melmoth land. She took a small sack and filled it like a pirate taking their share of buried treasure.

'Jaysus.'

Michael stood at the door, his mouth open. Evelyn threw the sack to him to fill. She went back to the kitchen and searched through the drawers in an old dresser. Corcoran was not tidy. The drawers were a mess of odds and ends. At the very back of one she found a small sewing box, wooden with painted flowers, a feminine possession lost in a heap of manly disorder. A keepsake of his wife's perhaps? She stuffed it into her pocket and ran upstairs. She was still wearing Corcoran's coat and hoping she was right and that he had no mind for the clearing of old belongings, she looked in every room for signs of feminine occupation. At the end of the landing in the smallest room, a few trunks lay gathering dust. They surrounded a child's cot – just an empty wooden frame without bedding, never slept in. It looked handmade. Had he made it himself? In the first trunk, she found the bedding, carefully folded away. In the second, women's clothes. They smelled musty but Corcoran's wife had a petite frame and she chose a high-necked dress that would cover her bruising, some underclothes and a pair of boots which were a little big. No matter. She pulled the laces tight and charged back down the stairs.

Michael had relieved Foyle of two silver coins in his pocket, payment no doubt for his part in all this and she pocketed what money she found on Corcoran. It wasn't much and he probably had more hidden away but unfortunately, they didn't have the luxury of time to find it.

'Take what we can carry and let's move,' she said taking a sack from him with a thankful smile.

Foyle let out a low moan and as he passed him, Michael gave him a kick, silencing him again. He eyed Corcoran's body on the table, his shirt covered in blood, his skin gleaming with sweat.

'I don't know how you did it,' he said.

'The rake was sharp and he was in such shock – I got a good strike at him. I guess I was lucky. Besides you injured him to begin with. You gave me the advantage.'

She ushered him outside. Further scrutiny of Corcoran's body would only bring more questions. All the same, he was staring at her in disbelief. Maybe he thought she wasn't capable of it. A day ago, she wouldn't have thought so herself. They ran for the stables. Corcoran's horse was still saddled and Michael climbed up, pulling her up behind him. Foyle was awake again. He was howling – the sound of someone demented by drink and the horror that now dawned. As they galloped away, Evelyn watched the house grow smaller, the faint sound of male laughter echoing in her mind.

II

Twing – Shook.

Twing – Shook.

IN THE PIT, THE two men kept a steady pace, their shovels biting into the earth. Muck flicked up on their faces and spattered their clothes. One of them, the younger, stopped for a moment to adjust the cloth over his mouth.

'Don't lose the rhythm, Charlie,' said the other man. 'We need to get this done before the sun comes up and every child in town is here staring at us.'

He hadn't yet noticed her and Michael. They had slowed to a trot as they approached the workhouse, hoping to cut across the lands of the nearby Castletown estate. A shrine to poverty and disease, the workhouse seemed to kill more people than it helped.

'I think it's big enough,' Charlie said.

'God help us, it will never be big enough,' he said. He slammed his shovel down hard into the soil, picking up a full load and throwing it out to the surface, careful not to disturb the fifteen souls waiting at the trench's opening. Fathers, mothers, sons and daughters lay in wait for their burial. The older man patted the younger on the back.

'Nearly done.'

Michael kept his eyes on the road but Evelyn was transfixed. She'd never seen so many people, like that, together. She caught the older man's eye and he cocked his head sideways to tell her to keep moving.

'I wonder what Foyle will say about us,' Michael said, as they made their way into Castletown. 'Maybe he won't remember anything at all when he sobers up.'

'That's the best we can hope for. Other than that, it's just the mad ramblings of a drunkard. That cut doesn't look good.'

'Yeah, he got me good alright.'

'I'd better fix it up, before it gets infected. Stop over there.'

He drew the horse into a small clearing in the trees. Signs of an old campfire lay strewn about, the rocks and grey ash a reminder that they weren't the first to cross these lands uninvited, and they wouldn't be the last. The migration of people on the roads, was growing to such numbers as to lead more through the less travelled forests, where they may have a hope of catching a squirrel or stumbling upon a bird's nest. A roast pigeon was a fine feast indeed. They dismounted and she took out the little sewing box, her hands trembling as she tried to thread the needle.

'You okay?' he said. 'You've been through a lot.'

'And you haven't?'

'Yeah well, you know, you're a …'

'If you say girl, I'm going to hit you.'

'I was going to say – you're not cold hearted like me.'

'Are you sure?'

'It'll never happen Ev,' he sighed. 'No matter what happened with Corcoran, you're one of the good ones.'

Was she? He had such belief in her. Even still after she brought this down on them. Would a good person burn another to death? She knelt beside him and surveyed the damage to his face. The cut was severe. A crooked line ran from below his left ear across his jaw. It had stopped bleeding but congealed blood oozed from the open wound. Wiping it as best she could, she drew the needle in. A tiny wave of heat sterilised it, and she was grateful for its help even though it seemed to come of its own accord. Carefully she worked stitch after stitch, to pull the cut closed. When she finished the eighth one, she tied it with a knot that she bit with her teeth.

'There – you won't be pretty – but then you never were.'

'Funny.'

'Makes you look rugged.'

He smiled, his cheek stinging and settled for serious again, his fingers lightly touching the stitches.

'We should eat.'

They devoured the salty ham and half the bread washed down with a flask of milk. Remorse for how they'd come by such a feast, would have to wait. If she would ever feel it at all. She wasn't the good person he thought her to be. A truth he'd hopefully never discover. She should never have brought him into this. She should have gone straight for Corcoran, before returning home. Then he would be safely out of it. But what would she have done after? Go back home like nothing had happened? And besides she was no mastermind when it came to covering up murder and how would she explain how she had overpowered him? No. She would always have had to leave. To have her brother with her and not think her dead, was a favour to both of them. Perhaps their destinies lay elsewhere, beyond Cularne, after all.

As they rode on through the trees, Castletown House blinked into view. Larger than Melmoth Hall, its main house was set back from the wings by curved sweeping colonnades. Such beauty and grandeur. A glimpse of a dream she would never realise – for grand houses and wealth don't befall a murderous peasant girl with a gift for fire. She was suddenly conscious of her hands around Michael's waist. What if she burned him by accident – the fire uncontrollable? The smell of smoke still clung to his shirt, a reminder of what they'd lost and she drew closed her fists, resting her head on his shoulder as they left Castletown behind.

They followed the River Liffey that ran through its lands until they reached a pretty stretch deep in the valley. She'd heard her father talk of it before, calling it the Strawberry Beds. They would take them into Dublin, Michael said, and so they joined the road, already busy with wagons and carts. While the time for strawberries had passed, the riverbank was full of industry, shepherding people and trade along its waters. Alongside them, trailed a pilgrim-age of the starving and downtrodden. Withered by famine, they moved slowly, seeming to drag themselves along, their gait heavy and laboured. What belongings they had were tied to their backs, their clothes no more than rags, torn asunder by hardship and life on the road. Mud caked their bare feet; dried in splashes on their legs. Their dirty hair, matted and polluted from sleeping outdoors, gave them the appearance of lunacy, as if a local asylum had emptied its wards onto the streets, but it was their complexion that shocked Evelyn the most. Famine had struck a cruel hand in Cularne, but wherever these people had come from, it had all but laid them to rest. Their skin, stretched over the bones of their faces, was grey and almost translucent as if the dead walked among them. They were beaten down, heads hanging low.

As they journeyed downhill into the tiny village of Chapel-izod, the situation worsened. In other circumstances, you would think it a market day, for the narrow streets were thronged but these people sought survival not commerce. A boy, no more than five or six, held his mother's hand, watching them from the roadside. His black hair hung low over one eye, the other rimmed in dirt, starkly green and staring. He had no expression to his face, no downturn to his mouth, just pursed lips and an emptiness – a lifeless thing. As they passed Evelyn looked back at the boy, his head turning to follow them.

'We have to give them something,' she said to Michael who was already handing her the bread from the bag. As she took it, he grabbed her elbow.

'We can't stop,' he said.

She nodded, breaking the bread into chunks. She gestured to the little boy to come to her. His speed shocked her as he darted through the people, his little hands outstretched as others saw her charity and came to them. She gave some down to his desperate hands and to the others now raised in the hope of a tiny morsel.

'I've never seen anything like this. What has this famine done to us?' she said.

'Broken us,' he said. 'And there's no one stepping in to fix it.'

***

As THEY REACHED THE outskirts of the capital, a patch of blue peeped out behind the dark clouds, as if a secret, brighter world lay beyond. The city itself was divided north and south by the river. Under its many bridges, the Liffey flowed, brown smeared with green, the tide high against the stone walls. Gulls screeched as they circled above. On the quayside, the sound of clopping hooves and clattering carriages filled the air, as Evelyn and Michael marvelled at the city around them. Bewigged barristers and officers of the court scurried under the giant Corinthian columns of The Four Courts, upon which sat a green copper dome, a giant judicial eye presiding over the city. On the opposite bank, at the top of a sweeping green slope stood Christchurch Cathedral, a chorus of bells ringing from its gothic belfry.

If the island of Ireland was shrivelling beneath a blanket of death, Dublin was the only place left it seemed, where the pumping heart of humanity still survived. People thronged the pavements, men in long overcoats and tall hats, their shoes finely polished, buckles gleaming. Women with large hats atop a bundle of coiffed hair and tailored dress coats, glided by. Even the street urchins and peasants looked nourished if hardened by the city's streets. Following the river, Michael pulled the horse to a stop at Carlisle Bridge. From here the road widened to their left, revealing the expansive thorough-fare of Sackville Street. It was double the width if not more of all the roads around it, on each side a uniform line of five storey buildings, their elegance only interrupted by the majesty of the General Post Office, it's imposing portico jutting out into the street. Opposite, Nelson's Pillar stood victoriously in the centre, the horse-drawn traffic weaving around its foundations.

'How much money do we have?' Michael said. 'I took two crowns from Foyle.'

She dug into her pocket. 'I've got a guinea and three shillings.'

He took the guinea from her, putting it with his for safe-keeping. A large black carriage, its roof laden with luggage, thundered by them in a hurry and Evelyn watched it plough on down the quayside, to the waiting ships. Where were its occupants headed? Her eyes followed it until it disappeared among so many others – a mass exodus towards the sea. A gull cried out overhead and her attention was taken to the sky, as it circled back to the water and down to the towering masts. She lost sight of it and she yearned suddenly to have their freedom of flight, to venture anywhere, unhindered. Michael was talking to her, but she wasn't listening. She couldn't take her eyes off those ships. They called to her and the city faded around them.

'We'd need to sell the horse,' he said. He was smiling. 'If that's what you want?'

It was. It was all she wanted. To feel the wooden deck under her feet, to taste the salty air as they sailed out into the ocean. It pulled on her very soul. There were no other options now.

'This city will make paupers of us by nightfall anyway,' he said.

She drew her gaze away, her eyes meeting his. They were filled with excitement – his own yearning for adventure.

'Well, then we sail,' she said, '...for America.'

It came to her only the moment her lips said it. Yes, America. It had to be.

'The land of opportunity,' he said. Isn't that what they call it? Well then, America it is.'

12

MICHAEL DISMOUNTED IN THE hope of finding the nearest market. The sooner they could get the fare, the quicker their new lives could begin. But he wasn't getting very far. Though the pavement on Sackville Street was crowded, no-one would stop to hear his request, their eyes flickering to the blood on his shirt, and the cut to his cheek. Evelyn looked at the passing faces, wishing for her mysterious stranger among them – standing there as he had on the bridge – tall and silent, his eyes on her. Was he here? Watching her? The more people passed by Michael, the more frustrated he became. The cut did make him look rugged but also dangerous, especially with the intensity in which he asked for their help, like theirs lives depended on it. She supposed they did. She slid down to help him as they made their way up the street.

Half way, under the portico of the post office, a crowd had gathered, a mix of morning patrons awaiting the opening of the doors, and those who saw the stationary crowd as a captive audience to their protest. They held placards high above their thin arms, strong in their will if not in health.

SENTENCED
TO
DEATH

DON'T
STARVE
US!

The words adorned them in large ugly letters, and Evelyn resisted the urge to join them as they raised their voices. A man lay in a doorway close by, a sign around his neck that read **LEFT TO DIE** and she couldn't be sure if he was still living, until he let out a cough. It wouldn't be long. She didn't know what was more horrifying, the fact that the man lay there or that he was being ignored by everyone who passed him. One woman, her gloved hands holding tightly to her purse as she waited for the post office to open, shouted at them.

'Don't bring your disease here. God inflicted the blight and you must pray for his mercy. Constable!' she cried. 'Constable, here....', pointing now to the fallen man. 'Can't you move these people on?'

A young policeman, no more than twenty puffed out his chest.

'Yes Madam?'

'Take these wretched people away!' she said.

'Have you no heart Missus?' someone shouted. It was a woman's voice, loud and shrill, her inner-city accent used to being heard on the busy streets. An old woman, her face corrugated with wrinkles and framed by a black bonnet, poked a finger at the woman. From her tiny frame again came that big voice.

'You should be ashamed of yourself. Jaysus, would you not help them, God love them.'

She fished into the pocket of her long overcoat and produced a ha'penny, which she gave to the youngest of the protesters.

'I don't have much, love, but you need it more than me,' she said. The young man took it gratefully as the constable looked on.

'Come on, May, get that cart out of here.'

'Ah hold your horses, copper. I'm going' she said scowling at him.

She moved back to her cart, a sea of colourful flowers peeking out beneath the cloth and pushed it out into the street in front of Evelyn.

'Sorry love,' she said. 'Have to move on or the copper will have me in irons,' she chuckled.

'Do you know where we'd find a market or horse trader?' Michael asked.

The old woman eyed him suspiciously.

'What happened to your face?' she said.

'I met the wrong side of a bottle,' he said truthfully and the woman smiled.

'Jaysus he gotcha good, didn't he? Wouldn't like to see the other fella. Don't let the constable see you like that or

87

he'll have you before a magistrate before you can say bloody murder.'

She beckoned for them to follow her as she wove her cart left into the adjoining street.

'Something tells me you're in a hurry,' she winked. 'You'd be wanting one of Bricker Murphy's boys. They'll take it no question. Give you a few bob for it. Where you headed?'

'America,' he said.

'You and your girl, get yourselves to the Gresham Hotel back up there on the right. A coach goes from outside to the docks and it'll take you where you want to go. Find you the right ship. It's a shame to see so many of you leaving,' she said. 'It's disgusting what's happened to this country.'

She spotted a scruffy-looking boy in a worn peak cap and gestured to him. The boy was barely in his teens yet he carried himself with authority – his shoulders back, chin high, his face serious with the business at hand. He leaned into her as she whispered something in his ear. He looked up at Michael and then to the horse and cocked his head for them to follow him.

'Good luck to you both,' the woman said and she pushed the cart onwards, singing to herself.

The boy smiled at Evelyn – a practised smile – the corners of his mouth rising but that sobriety still lingering in his eyes. What choice did they have but to follow him? They needed that money. To their right, a laneway ran back from the cobbled street. Half way down, the boy put two fingers in his mouth and whistled. Behind them, three more boys appeared, one slightly older than the other two, wearing a battered old top hat, sitting on a bird's nest of unkempt hair and a coat that was older than all of them put together.

'You want rid of your horse?' he said.

'How much?' said Michael.

The boy laughed. 'We won't be paying you today. We'll just be taking. Lads…'

One of them sank a punch into Michael's ribs, before snatching the reins of the horse. Evelyn caught his arm. She would not be the victim again. She would fight them if she had to. Burn them all. No-one was taking that horse. A high-pitched whistle sounded behind them, accompanied by the heavy footfall of two burly constables. The gang scarpered, the young boy reefing his coat away just as she felt the heat intensify. He flung himself onto the horse's back and kicked his heels into it, saluting Evelyn as he galloped away. The others had either run or shimmied up the drainpipes to the low roofs behind. Quick and efficient with practice.

Michael pulled her arm, making a run for it, the two constables in pursuit. Victims, they may be, but the horse wasn't theirs to sell, and as for the wellbeing of its owner – well, it was best to avoid that conversation altogether. They had no choice but to flee.

Michael was finding it hard to catch his breath as he ran. He'd been winded and the running wasn't helping. He stumbled and she thought he might fall but he swerved to his right, into an open doorway. A darkened hallway, with boxes stacked high either side, led to a bright room beyond and a startled shop girl, who jumped back in fright. *Flanagan's – First Choice for Gentleman.* The words were printed on a sign over the counter with a portrait of a tailor, presumably Mr. Flanagan. The real man stood below as if he'd only just sat for the artist, right down to the pomade in his hair and the tape measure around his neck that he held looped with one hand. He stood behind the counter of silk neckerchiefs and cufflinks, stunned by their invasion. He was slight of frame and had no desire it seemed, to intervene.

'Lock the door,' a constable cried out behind them. But the tailor froze. One of his customers, an elderly gentleman, in an attempt to find the quickest remedy, held the shop door open. As he passed, Michael took a hat from a nearby stand and Flanagan found his voice.

'Thieves! Thieves!'

But they were gone, back into the bustle of Sackville Street again, the pavement thronged, the road a sea of moving carriages. They ran between the horses, Michael taking her hand as he eyed a coach loading trunks outside the Gresham Hotel.

'You do the talking.' he said, planting the hat firmly on his head and pulling down the brim.

Evelyn paid the driver and soon they were safely inside, as the coach rumbled along. Outside the post office, half a dozen constables had gathered. One of them, his uniform decorated with medals, held one of the boys by the scruff of the neck. She sank back into the seat, away from the window. Above them, Horatio Nelson towered atop his granite pillar – a captain at the helm of a sinking ship.

13

THE SIGHT OF THE river was a welcome relief. Even the smell of sewage into the cabin, would not deter the gladness of its waters as they rode over the cobblestones to the docks. Sitting opposite them were a couple in their twenties, their young son asleep on his mother's lap. The father stared at Michael, assessing the danger of the dishevelled man opposite, his grip tightening around his wife's shoulder. Evelyn was worried. How were they going to board a ship if they couldn't afford the passage? Stowing away would be tricky, especially for two of them and it was a long journey to remain invisible from crew and paying passengers. They wouldn't survive it. Perhaps they could get as far as Liverpool? Her dream of America was fading before her eyes. Michael's thoughts had also turned to their finances. He dug his hand into his pocket to count their coins. When it came up empty, he patted them all in desperation. Their money was gone.

'He must have taken it when he punched me,' he said in a low voice.

'And it didn't even take until nightfall.'

'I'm sorry.'

'It's not your fault. We didn't have far to fall anyway. We were paupers to begin with.'

The coach jolted as it came to a stop. A sign, painted emerald green across the front of a large warehouse said 'Fortfield's Shipping'. There was an office to one side, while the rest concerned itself with the storage of goods for distribution or export. The driver began to unload the passengers' luggage, seeing the uncertainty on their faces.

'If you're stuck, just ask Maggie. You can't miss her. She'll set you right.'

The room inside was very official. Two men and a woman sat behind a counter topped with iron bars. So, this was the pit into which the Irish economy had fallen, the poor simply tipped upside down, their pockets emptied and sent abroad. A queue wound back from each agent, and so they joined what must be Maggie's line and waited. Above their heads on a large chalk board was the next departure:

3 O'CLOCK – THE ELEANORA –
LIVERPOOL, ENGLAND/NEW YORK, AMERICA – £4

She desperately wanted to be on it. Whatever they proposed, she would take it. She was going to New York – even if she had to swim there. The young woman ahead of them turned to leave, her hand gripping a piece of paper tightly to her chest, as if a sudden wind might erupt and blow it out of her grasp. They stepped forward and Evelyn felt the woman's eyes judging them already. She must see thousands like them – nothing left anymore to hold them in Ireland – and she sent them out to conquer a new world or let it be their ruination. She did not feel the burden of it, she was sure for her manner was so brisk, you could cut yourself on the edges of her.

'Destination?'

'New York,' they answered in unison.

She raised an eyebrow.

'And I presume you don't have the fare?'

'We've nothing,' Evelyn said.

'Well then, these are the terms of travel. Take it or leave it. If you wish to sail, you sign a contract of indentured servitude – meaning on arrival at port, the Captain will pass on your contract to those looking for workers. You will work for a period of five years for your employer after which you'll be free to go about your business.'

Satisfied that they hadn't run away at the notion, she took out two pieces of paper and began writing.

'You first,' she said to Michael. 'Name? Age?'

'Michael O'Neill. Twenty.'

'Read and write?'

'Yes.'

'Skills?'

'I'm a farmer,' he said.

'No good for this. Anything else?'

'I'm good with my hands, carpentry, that sort of thing.'

She scribbled something down before stopping midway to look at his face.

'Are you a drunk?'

'No. Chance would be a fine thing.'

She cracked a smirk. 'New York will eat you alive if you are.'

'I'm a hard worker. Just fallen on bad times.'

'I can see that,' she said.

Her eyebrows rose again and Evelyn wondered how many times a day they did that. They must ache at the close of business. She threw them now towards her.

'Are you Mrs O'Neill?'

'No, he's my brother.'

'Right, well. There's no guarantees you'll get to stay together over there. You take your chances like everyone else.'

'Yes ma'am.'

'Name and age?'

'Evelyn, seventeen. I can cook and sew.'

'A maid,' she said as she wrote. 'Good.'

'Read and write?'

'Yes.'

Her mother had instilled the importance of it from a very early age.

'Okay...sign here.'

She handed the sheets of paper to them and they each signed their names.

'Now take it to Captain Pearse on the Eleanora. He'll give you the once over and if he thinks you fit for the contract, he'll sign it for you. He wants to be paid in New York mind, so you'll have to show some enterprise with him. Go on now, take yourselves off.'

'Mr O'Neill?' Evelyn said as they stepped back out on the river.

'Yeah, do you like it? New start – in case anyone comes looking for us.'

'Well, I'm dead,' she said. 'Or so everyone thinks.'

'Well, then it's the freshest start anyone ever had, isn't it?'

There was something delicious about the notion – a chance to reinvent herself. Be someone else, someplace else. They crossed the grey cobblestones to George's Dock and looked for the Eleanora. There were ships all along the quay wall. Most were large cargo ships, bringing in coal, sugar and other luxuries destined for this and other ports. The Eleanora drifted shabbily among them. Its paint was peeling on the portside and where there had once been a clean red stripe of paint, it had been flayed away by the salty air, revealing the timber underneath. They joined a queue of people making their way slowly over the gangway. Two boys were talking in front of them.

'I heard they can get three hundred on board, pack us to the rafters,' said the older boy of about fourteen, jumping up and down to get a better look.

'Three hundred! She'd sink, Tom. She's not going to sink, is she Tom?'

The smaller boy's lips were trembling and he looked on the verge of tears.

'Don't be silly, these things are as strong as an ox. We'll be grand. You stick with me, Bill. I'll look after you.'

'I can't swim,' said the boy, a tear escaping to roll down his cheek.

'Well I can, so we'll be grand,' Tom said.

He noticed Michael and Evelyn behind him and put both hands on the boy's shoulders.

'It'll be brilliant, you'll see.'

As they reached the gangway they caught their first glimpse of Captain Pearse. He was smartly dressed, the buttons gleaming on his navy double-breasted coat, his grey ponytail neatly tied under his bicorne hat. He was examining someone's ticket with great interest, turning it over in his hands. Had it been a coin, he would surely have bitten it between his teeth.

'Very good,' he said ushering the people on board.

'You're travelling alone?' he asked the two boys, taking their tickets.

'Yes, Sir' said Tom. 'We're joining our father in New York. He sent us the tickets. Ma is too sick to go but she'll follow when she's better.'

'Very well. Below deck now with you boys. We sail in an hour.'

He waved an impatient hand for Michael and Evelyn to come forward, taking their papers. 'Servitude?'

'Yes, Sir', Michael said.

'Do you understand the contract? Five years?'

'Yes, Sir.'

'Have Doctor Elliott look at that face when you board. And I can tell you, I won't have any trouble, do you hear?'

'There'll be no trouble from us, Captain,' Michael said.

'Good. I'd hate to have to throw you to the sharks.'

He leaned on a wooden crate beside him and signed both contracts, handing them back to them.

'Miss O'Neill.' He nodded towards Evelyn.

'Thank you, Captain,' she said and they crossed the gangway. There were over a hundred people on board already. Many had taken a look below at their lodgings and come straight back up, keen to take in the civilised air again before they had to succumb to their dwellings. Some clung to the sides, shouting farewells to loved ones on the docks. Michael and Evelyn held onto the ceiling ropes as they made their way down the narrow stairs.

'How are you supposed to do this at sea?' Michael said.

'Maybe we're not,' she replied. 'Maybe we're to stay where we are.'

A peculiar smell was coming up the stairs, stronger and more pungent with every step. It emanated from the main hold – a mix of urine, sweat and vomit. An old mop and bucket stuck out of a nearby doorway but Evelyn doubted any amount of mopping could make it go away.

'Christ,' Michael said, putting his sleeve to his mouth.

The room extended the length of the ship. On each side, built into the hull were two dozen large wooden bunks, big enough to take four adults lying down end to end, though they were already overpacked and creaking with the extra weight. Running down the centre was a long dining table with benches either side. Two lanterns lit the entire room, which meant that most of it was in shadow. They could just make out the notice that hung on the wall.

STRICTLY FORBIDDEN:

1. Smoking
2. Naked flames and candles
3. Swearing
4. Fighting
5. Gambling
6. Spitting
7. Alcoholic Beverages

By order of Captain John Pearse

'Rules me out so,' Michael said. Evelyn gave him a playful jab in the ribs. He groaned in pain.

'Sorry, I forgot,' she said. 'Let's find the ship's doctor and get him to have a look at you.'

She eyed the list again as they passed and shuddered at the thought of a fire below deck; a flaming ship with hundreds of burning souls, clawing their way up the narrow staircase. She flexed her fingers. Would she be able to control her gift in such a confined space? Was she a hazard to them all?

By the time they fought their way back up the stairs, there was barely an inch to move. With the last of the luggage on board, Captain Pearse signalled to the first mate to begin preparations for sailing. Crewmen stood on the pin rails either side, holding onto the rigging and shouting at the top of their voices. All passengers were to move below deck. Evelyn felt Michael's hand pull her towards the rail. A tall man of about thirty stood there talking to a number of passengers. There was no mistaking the ship's doctor. He wore a long black fitted overcoat, black trousers and a white shirt with a pale blue cravat tied neatly at his neck. He had brown curly hair with long sideburns that he grew along his jawline almost meeting his large mouth, which grimaced as he examined a man who stood with his mouth open, tongue extended. On his nose, were a delicately balanced pair of wire rimmed spectacles that he adjusted upwards every few seconds as he spoke. Michael and Evelyn waited patiently despite the cries of the crew to go below deck. The doctor at last turned to them.

'I'm afraid you must go down to the hold,' he said.

'Please doctor,' she said. 'My brother was attacked as we travelled and I did what I could to sew his wound but I fear for infection. Could you take a quick look? Please?'

'*You* sewed it?' he asked. He turned himself to get a better view of Michael's face.

'Ah, it's nasty but not too deep and the bleeding has stopped. You did a good job my dear, very good. You must keep it covered now to prevent infection. I'll give you some dressing.

Just for a few days and then the sea air will do it good. I'll remove those stitches then. I recommend you allow a beard to grow, Sir, as you'll not be able to shave for some time until it heals.'

He took up a worn leather bag at his feet. Inside it, were all sorts of medical provisions, tiny jars strapped into leather encasements. He opened one and tapped a little of the powder into a vial, handing it to Michael with the dressings.

'It's willow bark. Take it with some cold boiled water. It will stop the inflammation and help with any pain.'

Michael thanked him. The doctor smiled at Evelyn, and then said, 'You are lucky to have such good help, Sir. This young lady is good to have in a dangerous situation. Are you hurt yourself?' he asked.

'Oh no. I'm fine.'

'You take care and if you need me on the journey don't hesitate to come to me. I'll be very busy, you'll see, but I try to make time for everyone. Now I suggest you go downstairs before Mr. Harper there, throws you overboard.'

The second mate, Ronald Harper was scowling at them. The deck was almost cleared and they were among the last above, save for the crew, which Evelyn counted at nine – ten if she included the doctor. Below deck there were others too, a handful or so. They'd passed the cook on the stairs, his apron already grubby and a sailmaker who carried reams of extra fabric should they be needed on the crossing. As the gangplank was taken aboard, two of the men climbed up the main mast to secure and check the middle and main sails. The ship creaked and popped under the weight of its cargo.

They joined the queue as people filed into the hold. Already the place was suffocating. Every bunk was full to capacity and the long benches were all occupied, with some sitting on the table. They found a spot beside the door and sat down on the sawdust, their backs propped against the wall. The first mate, a man called McGregor, strode into the room and stood at the top of the long table.

'Ladies and Gentlemen, if you please!' he shouted.

His deep voice, with its heavy Scottish accent, boomed around the crowded room. Silence fell as they all turned their attention to him. He leaned forward on the table, his huge hands spread like plates before him. He looked like he'd been fighting with the sea all his life. His skin was red from the elements and Evelyn guessed, a fondness for alcohol. That was the battle perhaps. The drink and the sea.

'Listen carefully. It concerns your welfare aboard this ship. I draw your attention to the rules of passage. Breaking those rules will not be tolerated and will have repercussions. All passengers will stay below deck in bad weather. On fine days, you will be permitted in small numbers to take air on the deck and cook your food on a deck stove. Here is a list of rations,' he said pointing to a notice on a centre pillar above the table. 'These will be distributed to those travelling to America. We expect to reach the port of Liverpool at seven o'clock this evening depending on sailing conditions. Have your trunks ready to be unloaded. Those going on to New York we will set sail at six tomorrow morning. There is no need to disembark. Any ailing passengers may seek the advice of the ship's Doctor Elliott, and be sure you do if you have a fever, for all our sakes. God speed!'

He left the room and there was an immediate chatter of conversation, deafening in the confined space. Passengers crowded around the rations list.

WEEKLY PROVISIONS:

21 quarts water

$2 \frac{1}{2}$ lbs Bread or Biscuit

1 lbs Flour

5lbs Oatmeal

2oz Tea

$\frac{1}{2}$ lb sugar

$\frac{1}{2}$ lb molasses

Michael got up to look but Evelyn didn't care what was on the list. They would have food. That was good enough. For now, they were on a ship bound for America, something she wouldn't have thought possible, only days before. How quickly everything had changed. She had lost her father, her home. Corcoran had made her suffer and she…well, she had brought a wrath to bear on him, that she never could have imagined. They lunged forward as the ship pulled away from the quay wall. A loud cheer erupted and she let herself rest finally, comforted by the notion that the worst was behind them.

14

SOMEONE WAS SHOUTING – loudly above their heads. She stretched her aching body, stiff from slumber and listened. McGregor was bellowing orders at the crew. Michael stirred beside her. Neither of them had been disturbed by the crossing but from the looks of things, others weren't so lucky. Many had been sick and while most had availed of the buckets provided, the young did not possess the same self-control. There was vomit on their clothes, on the floor, their bunks. A crewman shouted into the hold: 'Clarence Dock, Liverpool.'

Departing passengers gathered their things as people scrambled for their lodgings. Michael threw himself into a low bunk beside Tom and Bill and another young man, who introduced himself as Lawrence Sherlock. Lawrence was from Portlaoise he told them, and with starvation a sure outcome, his father had given him the last of his money to make a new life, in the hope that he could send back some of his good fortune. All three were pale and gaunt and it had not taken long for Tom's enthusiasm for the voyage to falter. Their clothes and straw mattress bore the proof of it.

The Eleanora came to a stop with a whoosh of the anchor into the deep water. Almost half of the ship's passengers were leaving and once they had all alighted, the business of rations began. The cook, his apron even filthier than before, doled them out, warning them that they would not receive more for another week, and to use their judgement and common sense in the matter. He was a serious man, and she expected that rationing at sea was a serious business. Should circumstances make the journey longer than planned, it was his job to make sure they wouldn't run short. They were among the first group allowed on deck to cook and as Evelyn reached the top of the stairs, the air was sweeter and fresher than any she had ever breathed. Liverpool by comparison to Dublin, was a huge port with ships as far as the eye could see, and a lively swarm of dock workers.

'Why don't they let us off the ship?' she asked McGregor as he passed.

'The Captain has learned it's best for onward passengers not to venture on land here, Miss. There are men who would have your belongings in a moment for a lie of good lodgings told, and you run the risk of getting the fever more out there in those slums, than you do here. Believe me, you are safer here', he said. As if to second his response, there was a loud caw from above as a crow flew in, circling the sails before landing on the mast above them.

Despite having a bunk that night, she found it hard to sleep. She couldn't relax her mind, and when at last she did, it was plagued by snatches of unformed dreams that wouldn't let her rest. She woke weary. Maybe the ocean's waves suited her better. She ignored the noise of the cabin and turned over, thinking she would try again when she realised Michael wasn't there. She looked about. There he was, pushing against the throng of people trying to get by him, as they made for the stairs.

'What's going on?'

'C'mon, you have to see this,' he said.

She could hear it from the bottom of the stairs – the shrieking. But it was not human. It was a squawking chorus, that drowned out the sounds of passengers, as they clamoured over each other to investigate. When at last she could see it for herself, she gasped. On every piece of rigging that could accommodate them, hundreds of black crows sat looking down on them, cawing loudly. All of a sudden, their racket ceased. In place of their town hall chatter, lay an eerie silence, each bird perfectly still. And then one loud squawk from the highest placed of them, shattered their display, as one by one they flew away, each one following the path of the other until a single black line cut through the sky. Beside her, one of the crew blessed himself.

'Never seen anything like that in all my years,' he said. 'On no other ship did they land, but ours. It's a bad omen.'

'Come now, Spike, don't be alarming the passengers with your superstitions,' said Captain Pearse. 'We have two hundred people to board. Let's get on with it, shall we?'

Michael gave Evelyn a shrug but she knew the crewman was right. They had chosen this ship for a reason. Had they assembled like that for her? Michael put his arm around her as people began to disperse.

'I bet you've forgotten,' he said.

'Forgotten what?'

'Yep, I thought as much.' He leaned in and kissed her cheek. 'Happy Birthday Ev. He would be very proud of you today.'

She was eighteen, the day her father would have rejoiced upon. If only he knew all that had happened. Although she wasn't sure he'd approve.

'I didn't have time to pick you up something – too busy on the run from the law,' he said, 'but I did find this in the lazy beds yesterday.'

He handed her a small, beautifully carved animal – a dog – the detail and craftsmanship exquisite.

'It's a bit on the scary side,' he said, pointing to its snarling mouth, 'but then everything is a bit scary at the moment.'

'I love it,' she said.

And she did. There was something elegantly grotesque about it. She held it tightly in her hand, watching as the last of the birds disappeared from the sky.

As the Eleanora prepared to pull up its anchor, the last of the new travellers settled on board. The crowd at port was heaving with heartfelt goodbyes. Women selling lemons in large baskets from the dock, threw them aboard on receipt of a ha'penny, a godsend for the sea sickness ahead. A large steamer towed them out of the docks and into the mouth of the River Mersey. Soon they left Liverpool behind and sailed northwards, moving up the English coastline before turning north west at Scotland, sailing over the crown of Ireland.

With the ship again at full capacity, the hold was packed and Evelyn was thankful for the bunk space, restful sleep returning to her. Not all had the pleasure – and those suffering lack of sleep were travellers that would slowly become encased in their own wooden prison, their minds unable to find any peace among the toppling waves. It was not until they were beyond the coasts of Europe that they felt the isolation truly set in. The ship which seemed a leviathan at port, was dwarfed by the watery universe, no more than a bobbing cork in a vast oceanic world. It was as though nature had cast its watchful eye over them and flew hurdle after hurdle, testing them with all its might. They fought hurricane winds that swung the ship from side to side, the sea a huge swell trying to envelope them.

In the third week, the rains came and for five days straight, sheets of water fell from the skies. Though cooking was done under a makeshift canopy, people retreated to the hold for fear of influenza from a soaking in the icy air. Eleven days from New York the waters began to freeze as they sailed northwards. At midnight, the sea froze around them – a hard layer of salty ice. The air grew colder and the ice deepened halting the ship's passage. The crew were quick to respond hoisting themselves down onto it, their hammers and axes hard at work at the bow. If they didn't try to break it, they might be stuck for weeks and rations would run out, not to mention the freezing conditions that would put them all at risk. So, the ship kept momentum, slowly moving forward, one swing of a pickaxe at a time. Michael volunteered up on deck to help and Evelyn watched him tie his rope carefully around his waist before climbing over the portside.

A mist had swept in and though she could hear their axes she could no longer see them at work. Exasperated voices drifted on the air as they pounded the ice to no avail. She swung her leg up on the rail, pulling herself over the side of the ship. The mist was thick and she dropped down, the ice solid beneath her feet. Kneeling, she put both hands out in front of her and concentrated their heat into the frozen sea.

Clever, she heard a voice say in her ear.

The heat sent cracks running into the ice and she pushed her palms out further still, to channel it to the front of the ship. The ice started to melt slowly at first and then she heard the crew's shouts that their efforts were working. The ice was breaking. She looked around wishing for him. The sound of his voice had awakened her desire to see him again and there he stood, out to sea, across the icy mass. He wore the same suit, this time accompanied by a grey top hat which he removed to greet her. His expression was warm as before but there was something else in it too. Pride perhaps. Yes, he was proud of her.

Voices floated across the mist, as the men began to ascend the ropes and he disappeared, the mist clearing as the icy ground began to rock beneath her. She quickly took one of the lagging ropes and climbed it. She was standing on deck as Michael climbed back up over the side.

'Go below Evelyn. You'll catch your death up here. The ice is thinning, I think the worst is behind us.'

The energy she'd ignited still ran through her and she rubbed her hands on her skirts to banish it before going below. That night she was unable to sleep, thinking of him. She should have spoken to him. Walked out on the ice to meet him. A proper introduction. Next time. She would speak to him next time.

15

AFTER FORTY-EIGHT NIGHTS AT sea, The Eleanora dropped anchor in New York Harbour. Its passage through The Narrows had been slow, as they crept silently by the sleeping monsters of Long Island on its starboard, and Staten Island, portside. A swirl of light from Robbin's Reef lighthouse rippled across the bay, and a few miles ahead, a sprinkle of tiny gas lights grew to a glow, as the island of Manhattan revealed itself. Everyone crammed together on deck for their first sight of a new world, their first breath of American air. It almost tasted different, as if it had been magically altered and hope had a taste, a sweet smoky flavour that made all who inhaled it salivate for the new possibilities life held.

'The land of second chances,' Michael said, his voice, for the first time in weeks spurred with that infectious optimism. Tom and Bill had squeezed through to the front, Tom clapping his hand on the side of the hull to congratulate their steed on her magnificent journey.

'If we pass quarantine, you'll have your feet on American soil by dawn,' Captain Pearse said to him, making his way to Doctor Elliot, who was for now the most important man on board. He'd lost weight, a man whose fabric had been stretched to its very seams, one man single-handedly battling the onset of fever and disease. Every voyager owed him a great debt, and he along with the Captain had been adamant not to let sickness take hold. Every morning the floors had been mopped and scrubbed. The sick were kept to one end of the ship and the doctor worked through many nights fighting illness with only the contents of his medical bag and his wits. The esteem with which he was held on board was second only to the Captain himself. His brow furrowed as he discussed their status with Pearse, who looked nonplussed by his concerns. Miraculously, they had not lost a single soul on their voyage and the Captain rested a hand on the doctor's shoulder, confident that they would pass quarantine on that principle alone. They ushered what passengers they could below deck, as the officers boarded them for inspection.

By first light, they sanctioned the Eleanora safe for docking, after much reassurance from Doctor Elliot that the relatively small number who were ill, had not infected anyone else. He agreed that the sick should be transferred to the quarantine station at Tompkinsville on Staten Island, for care and observation. Among them, Lawrence Sherlock, for whom the journey across the Atlantic had been as tumultuous as the waves, plagued first by sea sickness and then dysentery. He was a good humoured young man. Many's the night he'd kept the whole bunk awake with stories of his antics on the farm, joking that he still had to grow his sea legs, and that by the time he'd get to New York, he'd be rightly pickled from all the lemons he'd eaten. He'd kept his humour as best he could, but when his condition worsened and he'd been moved to the sick bay, that spark began to fade in his eyes.

He'd often talked about this moment, when he would lay eyes on America for the first time, and now it was tainted. He was almost too weak to open them but he did, just for a second, to catch the sunrise as they lowered him into the quarantine vessel, and then he was moving backwards, away from Manhattan and his dream. What if Staten Island was the only piece of America he would ever see and he'd crossed an ocean for nothing? What if they all had, for none of them knew what lay ahead? The one thing Evelyn was certain of as she looked at the city, was that *he* was there, waiting. He had brought her here, as sure as if he'd tied a length of ribbon around her waist and pulled her slowly to him. This was his city, his island. She couldn't explain it, but she knew it was true.

If she was scared, she might have considered telling her brother, but she wasn't. And how would she begin – with a secret told from their father's death bed, that he never wanted to share with him? Would be feel betrayed, insignificant to a man that he idolised and who was not there to explain himself? And when he'd got over that, what of her gift? Would he refuse to believe her, angry with her for listening to the feverish ramblings of a dying man? Then, she'd show him and she would see the true measure of him. At first, he might be afraid. A natural response. Then maybe delighted – not only for her – but for himself and he would have ideas for what she could do with such a talent, and he would continue to stand over her as he always had. Maybe even in the way of her and this man. What if he was jealous, resentful? And what would her stranger make of him, of his intrusion into whatever it was that was going on between them? No, it was better for now to keep Michael in the dark, about everything.

McGregor's gruff voice startled her.

'Have your papers ready,' he said. 'You'll need them for the port officers.' He looked at Michael. 'And they are strict mind, so don't think about dodging them and making a run for it. They'll have you back with us and our timber out of here, or worse in one of their prisons. You'll wish for servitude after that.'

'Anything is better than what we left,' Michael said.

'You'd think so, but be careful. This city is not for the faint hearted and it's sure not like home.'

It was home now. Good or bad. Come what may.

'Don't worry,' Michael said. 'I'll look after you.'

'I can look after myself,' she snapped, regretting the words the moment they left her lips. Her hands began to tingle. 'I'm just nervous, here…' she said, giving him the contracts, 'you mind these. I'm afraid I'll lose them.' Or set them alight.

She picked up her skirts as she made her way down the gangway. There was something about leaving the ship that made her feel like she was leaving a part of herself behind.

Shedding her skin like a snake, the old one left, never to be worn again. She'd left Ireland a girl, fleeing a country torn apart by starvation and had arrived in New York, a young woman, ready to embrace a new life, and new abilities. The indentured servitude meant nothing to her. She had no wish to start life in America as a fugitive, looking over her shoulder and *he* knew where to find her anyway. So, they would do as they had pledged. Keep within the law, at least for now.

They watched as their contracts passed through a series of hands. First the port official at the end of the gangway, then to another who escorted them to an office. From his hands, they went to a clerk where they were stamped and recorded before passing to another, who would assign them to their new employer; their fate passed around on pieces of paper, as if they were nothing. Many foreign ships had docked that morning and the room began to fill with more immigrants all vying for the positions available that day. The far wall of the office was lined with agents and employers keen to get the best, able bodied and fittest workers.

Evelyn felt eyes scrutinising them. She was glad at least that Michael's scar was now concealed under a growth of beard. They looked like any other hopefuls in the room. Her eyes combed the prospective employers. One of them, a man in his fifties was arguing with one of the clerks. Though both American, their accents varied drastically. The older man spoke with refined pronunciation, while the other had a twang and rhythm to his voice, that she tried her best to follow.

'Look, you know the situation here. No refunds and no returns. You gotta look after these people or they will die on you every time. Jeez some of you treat animals better.'

'Now, see here,' the older man said, poking a finger at the other's chest, 'Mr. Dermatov treats all his staff well and they didn't *die*, they absconded.... with most of his silver.'

'That's a matter for the police, Mr. Baker.'

'I see, well I have spoken to them and they better find them before the master does. There'll be hell to pay. But you need to find me workers not petty thieves.'

'I have you on my list here today,' said the clerk. 'I'll find you someone good.'

'I need two,' said Mr. Baker his eyes scanning the room as the man flicked through the sheets of paper in his hands.

'Alright let me see what we got.'

The older man caught Evelyn's eye, holding her gaze for a moment before he turned back to the clerk.

'Make sure they speak English,' he said.

Michael had been watching too and he pushed through the line of people, dragging her behind him.

'Sir, we will work hard for you. Me and my sister.'

Mr. Baker glanced at Michael and then back to the official. 'I don't want Irish. The last ones were Irish.'

'Please Sir, we are honest hard-working people. We just need a chance.'

The man looked slowly around the room and pointed to another couple. 'What about them?'

The clerk checked his list. 'They've come off the Zoektocht, a Dutch vessel. They don't speak...'

'Alright, alright,' he said impatiently. 'I don't have all morning. Show me their papers,' he said pointing to Michael and Evelyn. He took his time reading through the information, as if expecting to find some shocking revelation that would instantly dismiss them from contention. But there were none.

'Fine, I'll take them,' he said to the clerk, his mouth twisted into a pinch as he took out his pocketbook from his coat. He handed over a large bunch of notes to the official who didn't bother to count them. He knew better.

'Sign here,' he said holding out a copy of their servitude agreement to them. 'You are now in the employ of one Mr. Vladimir Dermatov.' He paused before saying wearily, 'Welcome to America...land of the free.'

Mr. Baker shot him a bemused look and ushered them outside to his waiting carriage.

'You have no luggage?' he said. 'You travel very light.'

'We lived very light,' Michael said.

'Well, you are now house servants of Mr. Dermatov, one of the wealthiest men in Manhattan. You will be treated well and in return you will treat your employer with respect. Mr. Dermatov doesn't tolerate fools or thieves. I hope you're neither.'

The streets around them smelled of old fish and sulphur and Mr. Baker took a neatly folded silk handkerchief from his pocket, flushed it open with one hand and carefully covered his nose and mouth. His gaze turned from the two young immigrants, to the world outside. Almost immediately a stench rose, like the innards of a hundred ships – the familiar smell of overcrowded living. The carriage rolled through the streets of tightly packed tenement buildings, some no more than wooden shacks leaning into the falling down bricks, like an infant clasping their father's leg. The voices of children carried on the air as they played, their Irish accents unmistakeable. Evelyn looked at the interior of the carriage, its dark leather upholstery, its cushioned head rests in the deepest plum velvet.

'I don't mean to sound ungrateful Sir, really I don't, but why would a man of Mr. Dermatov's wealth hire people like us? There must be thousands of good workers in this city.'

She could feel Michael's eyes boring into her. Mr. Baker smiled. Evelyn was sure it was a rare occurrence for it didn't sit naturally on his face.

'Mr. Dermatov came here just like you to make his fortune many years ago. He likes to give something back to the city and those hoping to change their path in life.'

Evelyn wasn't convinced. There was something about Mr. Baker that made her doubt every word he spoke.

'Well then, I'm sure we are the luckiest two immigrants in this great land,' Michael said, giving her a swift nudge of his elbow.

They didn't speak the rest of the journey. The carriage weaved out of the maze, poverty receding like the tide as dirty streets became tree lined avenues. They turned onto Washington Square with its pretty park before making their way up Fifth Avenue. Mr. Baker wasn't lying. If this was where Mr. Dermatov lived, he was in very wealthy company. Evelyn was in awe at the splendour of the mansions set back from the road. On their own they were magnificent, but to feature on the same street was exceptional, each trying to compete with the other in size and style, from Italian to French, Greek to Roman. It was only as they progressed northwards, that the last remnants of country life could be seen. Farmland stretched out before them, the buildings growing sparse and there perched on the corner of East 38th Street, stood their new home.

The driver pulled the horses to a stop. Mr. Baker got out, offering his hand to Evelyn. She took it, his grasp limp, that strange smile returning to his face.

'Ms. Rosev the housekeeper will see you settled in the servants' quarters. Make sure you do as she tells you. She's very particular. It's the way the master likes things done. Please her and you will him. He's away this week on business, so please do try and learn the ropes before he returns. It will ensure a smoother transition.'

Where Melmoth Hall's design was one of overindulged decadence, the Dermatov mansion was a picture of classical splendour. From its windows buried beneath the pavement to the three stories above it, it bore all the marks of wealth with a reserved eye for understated elegance. Whoever this Mr. Dermatov was, he had done well for an immigrant. Perhaps America would be their making too.

16

THE WEEK PASSED AS they settled into their new home. Ms. Rosev was a taskmaster. If she was pleased with their efforts she didn't show it, only telling them that she would be reporting to the master and if she wasn't happy, contract or no contract, they would both find themselves on the street. As Evelyn lay in her bed that morning, she could hear her heels clicking on the stairs above. She pulled the blanket up over her head. Please could she enjoy five more minutes in bed, before those heels stormed in with the day's commands?

She wriggled her feet against the warm sheets. The novelty of having a proper bed would never wear off. That first night when she'd been shown her basement room, she had just starred at it and when left alone, she kicked off her boots and snuggled under the blanket. Every bone in her body receded into the soft mattress and though the pillow was battered and old, when she lay her head down, it was heavenly. She'd allowed herself to float for a moment, lost in its luxury until the familiar pangs of guilt brought it to an end. Memories of all that was lost and that which had been sacrificed.

She pushed the blanket back, as the footsteps approached. Ms. Rosev didn't even knock. She barged on in, ready to roust the sleeping girl. She was not impressed to find her awake.

'Well don't just lie there, girl,' she said. 'Get up and be about your chores.'

'Yes, Madam,' she said sitting up.

'The master returns today. Everything must be in order.'

She seemed slightly more frazzled than usual. Perhaps she had caught the best of Ms. Rosev while the master was away. This morning, the bun in her silver hair was a little higher and tighter, not a strand out of place. She turned on her heel with a tut, and left her to dress.

Evelyn put her uniform on, a black long-sleeved tunic dress, over which she tied a white apron. She suspected it had been worn by the last parlour maid, (perhaps the one who had left with the silver), who was a considerably larger girl. When she'd first tried it on, Ms. Rosev had almost hyperventilated at the shambles of a maid that stood before her, hanging as it did off her body. Thankfully she'd been permitted to alter it and now it fit her perfectly. On her feet, she had new leather shoes, which made the endless trips up and down the four flights of stairs more bearable. Black stockings completed the ensemble and Evelyn too wore her hair tied neatly in a bun, crowned by a white headpiece.

The staff assembled as the cook, Mrs Osborne prepared breakfast. Michael was there, chomping into a piece of bread with a cup of hot tea. He poured her one as Ms. Rosev gathered herself to address them all. For a large house, they were a relatively small staff of five, six if you counted Mr. Baker, the master's steward. He operated outside of them, for he kept his own hours in accordance to the master's needs. Outside of him and Ms. Rosev, there was the butler Mr. Watson, under whom Michael worked as valet, and of course the amazing Mrs. Osborne who could turn any meal into a feast. All of them had worked a long time for Mr. Dermatov. Ms. Rosev had explained that though the house was very large, the master lived alone and rarely had visitors, so he preferred to keep his staff small and pay them well.

From the opposite side of the table, Michael winked at her and she knew he too was enjoying their new home. They both worked long hours, their limbs sore and hands raw, but they knew again the warmth of a good meal and they were already showing signs of better health. Ms. Rosev cleared her throat loudly, her face stern.

'Good morning,' she said, 'So with Mr. Dermatov returning, there are additional tasks to be set today…'

She went through a long list, mostly comprised of chores for Michael and Evelyn that involved preparation of the master's study and sleeping quarters. The study was locked when he was away and Ms. Rosev carried the key proudly on her apron string. She brought them to the heavy door and unlocked it, squinting at them as if she doubted their trust-worthiness. But a fire needed to be lit and settings laid out for lunch and so she allowed them to enter. She explained that he would eat breakfast and lunch there every day, sometimes dinner too.

'The master is a man with many interests,' she said as she swept back the heavy velvet curtains. 'When he is working he is not to be disturbed. Mr. Watson takes his meals to him and no other. You and your sister should be seen and not heard. Do you understand? You do not address him, unless he speaks to you.'

Evelyn couldn't help but be intrigued. As the study door opened, the air filled with the fragrant aroma of burnt incense, the sweet woody notes, still hanging in the air.

'You can empty that too,' she said pointing to a gilded censer on the mantelpiece. 'Remove the ashes and when the fire is lit, place a hot coal in the base. The master will burn fresh incense on his return. And be careful with it. It's very old.'

Evelyn admired its beautiful workmanship, but Michael's eye was drawn below the mantelpiece to the long sword and scabbard mounted above the hearth.

'Mr. Dermatov is a collector of antiques from around the world,' Ms. Rosev said. 'It's from Japan. That's very far away. Don't touch it.'

Unlike the censer, it didn't look too old or if it was, it had been carefully maintained. Its blade looked sharp and the golden dragon on its hilt gleamed in the morning sun. Michael's face was like that of a child on his birthday and Evelyn knew how badly he wanted to reach for it and swipe it gloriously through the air.

'Can I trust you two alone in the master's study?' Ms. Rosev asked.

'Yes Madam,' they said stepping back. She left the room, casting a backwards glance at them.

The room was a large rectangle, lined on two sides by bookcases, the shelves stacked from floor to ceiling. In the farthest corner, a spiral staircase disappeared into the room above – her Master's quarters she presumed, given the geography of the house. Along the wall behind the door, were rows of glass display cabinets. She couldn't help but take a quick look. There were old books, their yellowing pages of text opened for display, several religious relics and crucifixes, some plain and rusted by age, others ornate and bejewelled. The next case was devoted to weaponry. A bow and arrow lay beside daggers reposed on satin pillows, as if to rest them after a long bloody war.

As Michael set the fire, Mr. Watson's head came around the door. His eyes scanned the room looking for any sign of displacement. Did nobody in this house trust them?

'Hurry now,' he said gruffly. 'The master will be here soon.'

By midday, they stood in a row on the chequered floor of the hall, like pawns on a chess board, ready to welcome their king. Ms. Rosev straightened her apron looking down the line at Evelyn and Michael. She hissed at her, pointing to a stray hair hanging down and Evelyn quickly tucked it into her headpiece. Michael winked at her excitedly, as the carriage drew up outside. Ms. Rosev was almost knocked to the ground as the door flung open. In strode the master, with Mr. Baker following close behind.

He seemed like a giant to Evelyn. On his large frame hung an expensive woollen coat, its collar of black fur stretching across his shoulders and down his lapels. He wore it like the conquest of a hunting expedition and with his mop of unruly hair and speckled grey beard, he was not unlike an animal himself. His eyes ran down the line, narrowing on the two new additions and then he was gone, straight to his study, calling Ms. Rosev behind him with a wave of his hand. She scurried after him as Mr. Watson and Michael went to the carriage to take in the masters' luggage, carefully overseen by Mr. Baker.

'Careful with that. Its contents are most fragile,' he said.

Ms. Rosev appeared a short time later, the Master's coat hanging over her arms. She handed it to Evelyn, the soft fur brushing her face and she pitied the poor creature it had come from.

17

THE VAMPIRE STOOD IN the deserted alleyway, listening for signs of life. He could hear the rats as they devoured the night's garbage, their tiny nails scraping the ground, the grind of their jaws as they ate. He could even hear the rapid tempo of their beating hearts. To humans, they had no value, but to a vampire they were a tasty substitute to human blood, even if it was only a short burst in a case of emergency. He would certainly never go hungry in New York. It was raining and he let the cool drops run down his face as he contemplated the door in front of him. He hated to admit it, but for the first time in years, he was nervous. An image came to mind of the mirrored ring in the ice and he felt his throat tighten, his mouth dry. He placed his fingers on the door, as if touching it would give a sense of what was within, when a small metal slot flew back and a pair of green eyes appeared.

'I need to see him,' the vampire said.

The green eyes narrowed. 'See who?'

He didn't know his true name. He was a shadow man, they

all were – mystical figures, beholden of many different names. He spoke none for fear of being mistaken.

'I need to speak with him,' he said.

'The roof,' the green eyes growled, severing their exchange as the slot snapped shut.

The vampire looked up at the dilapidated building, with its broken windows and crumbling bricks. The city had many decadent dwellings, intimidating in their grandeur, but he chose this place – run down and insignificant. Perhaps that was the trick, to have his enemies underestimate him and the power he wielded.

Come, said a voice. This was his last chance. He could walk away, decide once and for all to let the past go, but it wasn't an option. He flew up to the rooftop, his feet landing softly. Strangely it was dry up there, the rain falling like a curtain around it on all sides, into the alleyways below.

'I was never fond of rain.'

A man stood with his back against the chimney stack, one foot on the bricks. He didn't know what he had expected. For one thing, he was just a man. He took human form – was that his choice or thrust upon him? He was younger than he'd imagined or maybe it was that look in his eyes, the energy he exuded. His dark hair was slicked back at the roots and underneath his morning coat, he was bare chested, his body pale and lithe. Black trousers hung low on his hips, the ends buried in heavy infantry boots. The kind that looked like they had just stumbled off the battlefield for they were caked in mud or was that blood? Yes, he could smell it as he moved closer.

The man was looking at him oddly, sizing him up, an agenda of his own and the vampire was glad he'd come, for he knew that to go against his wishes would have been very foolish indeed. He had heard the stories about what happened if you dined unannounced in his territory. You had to ask permission, put yourself in the very position he was in now. If you didn't, you would be struck down or so the stories went; passed on from one vampire to another, about the places where humans gathered in great numbers. London, Paris, New York, Constantinople, all the great cities, each protected by fallen angels – those who fell out of favour with their creator – sent to earth with no chance of redemption. Only a promise to fall further, if they didn't safeguard his greatest endeavour, humanity. Not from themselves, for what is in human nature cannot be altered, but from that which exists around it, seething in the wings. Only they could keep order – have those with the impulse to dominate on earth, annihilated.

'I like to come up here at night and behold my city,' he said.

'It's impressive. I've never seen such a place as this.'

'She is the greatest city in the world, is she not?' he said with pride. 'You see there,' he pointed down into the catacomb of tiny streets, as the rainfall parted. 'Such poverty. They fight for survival, every minute they breathe. It's fraught with injustice, cruel and wicked how they behave to one another, but that is their kind – how they were made. There are many here to sustain your appetite – if I let you. But there is only one you want. I can see it in your eyes. Someone to whom you cannot bear to allow breathe any longer. Tell me.'

He could see his brother, sitting in their cell at Castle Valla, his words cutting him still – '*Just take him, Rako.*'

'Vladimir Dermatov,' he said.

'I see.' He pursed his lips, supressing a smile.

'You know my brother?'

He leaned towards him.

'I know all sinful men. So, what did he do to deserve your wrath?' he whispered.

'He fed me to the creature that made me what I am.'

'A beautiful vampire? Is that so bad? Your body, never to age another day, your hair like spun silk, your skin as smooth as the finest marble, the golden sheen in those chestnut eyes. And a complexion to which many in society would give their right arm – though I detect a little ruddiness in your cheeks, from a recent feed perhaps?'

The vampire shook his head. 'You mock me.'

'I do not. On the contrary, I only remind you of the advantages of being such a thing. I counter that it is not the vampire you've become, but the act of betrayal that you cannot forgive.'

'I've grown accustomed to it, I had no choice. He must know the pain he's caused me.'

'You feel foolish for letting him put you in its path.'

'I was a naïve young man. I'm not anymore.'

'Have you considered that your brother may have prepared for this eventuality?'

Sasha paused for a moment. He had not thought that after twenty years he may be expected.

'I think my brother has long forgotten me.'

'Don't be so sure. Go. Begin the merry dance. I watch with interest.'

Sasha bowed his head in thanks. He had gotten what he needed. Why, this man was fair, even just. He understood what needed to be done.

'Before you do though, there is one condition.' The convivial atmosphere changed as if a darkened cloud had drifted into the clearest of skies. 'I will need something from you in return.'

'I see all in this fine city, through its walls and every dark crevice. There is a girl in your brother's household, an immigrant servant, recently delivered to him. I want you to keep her safe as you orchestrate your little campaign and when it is done, you will turn her and bring her to me.'

'Turn her?'

'Yes...oh my, you've never turned anyone, have you?' the man said disappointed at the novice to whom he had assigned a most important task. 'Well, she will be your first. Think yourself lucky and privileged to do so.'

Sasha had never turned anyone and with good reason. He would never wish this existence on anyone. He had found a way to live with it, even found some joy in it occasionally, for one cannot survive such an immortal curse without partaking of the small joys it offers, but to turn someone else? His own transformation had not been quick. It had been long and tortuous and he decided long ago that he would never put another human through it. He'd been lucky enough to meet others of his kind that the thought had never occurred to him. He neither needed nor required a mate but now, he would have to bend his principles to have what he wanted. Refuse and he would get nothing.

'Are you up to the task?'

Sasha nodded.

'Believe me when I tell you, you will thank me for it. She's a wonder.' He slapped him on the back. 'How fortunate it is you came along.'

'Your wish is a small price for my vengeance,' Sasha said. Now, if he could only convince himself that was true. The thought of killing the girl made him uncomfortable, never mind the turning. He'd never even drank from one. It hadn't been a conscious decision but somehow every kill had become a ritual, a rehearsal for the moment he would kill Vladimir. He'd spent two decades thinking of nothing else. The man was clasping his hand in his, thrilled with their transaction.

'Please, you must call me Gabriel.'

His name — he had spoken it. At least the one he wanted Sasha to use. A bargain had been struck and it seemed he would be spending more time in New York than he had first thought.

'Do you travel alone, Sasha?' He knew his name. Of course, he did.

'I have a small group of companions, like myself.'

'Bring them tomorrow tonight,' he said. 'I give you permission to hunt, once it's in small numbers. I can't abide greed. Now, go, plot your course, until we meet again.'

Sasha stepped up on the ledge, the rain parting for him. He would need to stay focussed on his own game in hand. He would meet this girl soon enough.

18

THE MASTER WAS LIKE a ghost in his own home. Most days he moved only between his chambers and the study, the house quiet as if he'd never returned. That morning, her work done in the kitchen with Mrs Osborne, Evelyn went to the study door and knocked lightly. The master had gone out earlier with Mr. Baker but caution was always wise. Ms. Rosev had unlocked it so she could see to the dusting and so she entered, glad of another opportunity to breathe in the heady smell of incense.

It was even more delicious in the darkness, as if she were in some exotic outpost, and she smiled to herself as she pulled back the heavy curtains. Daylight streamed in, illuminating *the wall of wonder* as Michael had named it and rightly so. It was a marvel, with its ancient artefacts and yellowing scripts. How had Mr. Dermatov managed to come by them? She didn't dare open the glass, they weren't permitted to, but she could run her cloth over the spines of the books on the shelves. *The Divine Pymander, The Clavicle of Solomon, Dragon Rouge, The Fourth Book of Occult Philosophy.* Curious she lifted out the latter, opening it midway. The title on the page read *Heptameron: or Magical Elements*. Would she find mention of her power inside? Would they help her to understand how she and her mother came to have it? She began to read some of the text forgetting her place. Had she the luxury, she would have pulled up a chair and folded into it. So engrossed was she, that it was only when a shadow fell across the page, that she realised someone was standing behind her. She jumped, the book falling from her hands. The master caught it in one swift movement before it hit the rug.

'I'm so sorry.'

She blurted out the words but they sounded empty. An apology wouldn't be enough to erase her stupidity. These were his prized possessions. He carefully stroked the cover, examining it for any damage before placing it back carefully in its position on the shelf. He was standing so close, his breath in her ear but she didn't dare move away.

'Should I dismiss you?' he asked. 'This room is for my work, not to amuse my staff.'

'I meant no harm, Sir.'

Where the hell had he come from? Was she so engrossed that she didn't hear his footsteps on the staircase? He would want rid of her now and maybe Michael too. From his pocket, he pulled a pair of spectacles and he put them on looking at her face, examining her as a spider would a trapped fly. A wisp of her dark hair had come undone and his hand grasped it gently, sweeping it behind her ear.

'Where does your curiosity lie?'

'Sir?'

'You have an interest in magic?'

Behind his spectacles, his glare softened, his eyes warmed now by the conversation. Evelyn nodded.

'Where are you from?'

'Ireland, Sir.'

'Ah, a land of mysticism. Have you heard the banshee's howl?' he said. 'One day I hope to add an account to my memoirs.'

There was something attractive about his fervour, a childlike excitement at the prospect of witnessing such a thing, that made Evelyn see not her master, but a willing accomplice. Perhaps if she engaged him, he may forget her indiscretion.

'When I was a child and my mother died' she said, 'a storm raged like none I had ever heard. Me and my brother, clutched to my father all night, as the wind howled in and out of every crevice. I remember thinking the very wind was crying, like an animal writhing in a snare. It swirled around us taking most of the roof, as it tried to escape. It was as if her spirit were fighting with the next world because she didn't want to leave us. At the burial, my father told me that the banshee had fought for my mother, to let her stay but she had lost her battle and the spirits had taken her.'

She closed her eyes, and for a moment she was back home, the master beside her as the wind howled around them. He was staring at her, fascinated.

'Would you like to learn more?' he asked pointing to the bookshelves.

'Yes Sir, I would.'

'Well, then we should start again.' He bowed his head, extending his hand. 'Vladimir Dermatov.'

'Evelyn O'Neill,' she replied putting her hand in his. Her palm was warm but the master, if he felt it, didn't comment.

'We shall be friends then Evelyn' he said, his Russian accent changing the shape of her name on his lips. 'You will share stories from your homeland and I will tell you all about my collection. You may read any book here, once it does not leave this room.'

'Thank you, Sir.' For not dismissing her, for listening to her, for letting her explore the secrets hiding in those books.

'Come after lunch tomorrow and we'll begin with the ancient Egyptians. And no more of that Sir nonsense. Vladimir will do.'

She daren't smile, but she imagined Ms. Rosev keeling over if she ever heard her call the master by his first name. As if on cue, the shrill pitch of her voice rang through the hallway, as she called Evelyn to her.

'Sir,' she said, bowing her head as she left the room.

From then on, Evelyn brought his meals to him, much to the annoyance of both Mr. Watson and Ms. Rosev. But the master wanted it this way and so neither of them complained, except to each other. A few days later, when she came in at noon with his lunch, he was reading a letter, clutched tightly in his hands.

"This came this morning?' he asked, not looking up from the paper.

'Yes Sir, I brought it straight in.'

'Fetch Mr. Baker...now.'

Sunday November 30th, 1847

My dearest brother,

How long I have searched for you. With the rising of each new moon I wished for success in my quest to find you and at last I have. You have not made my task a simple one, but then what's one year or twenty when you have eternity like me. Perhaps when we meet you can regale me with tales of your travels and adventures and what led you to settle finally in this beautiful metropolis. I, in turn can relate my tale of survival beginning with the night you gave my life so readily to another.

Did you think me dead? Imagine my bones left to decay in the frozen forest? You must be intrigued. Maybe even a little fearful? Worry not brother. You have nothing to fear from me. Cannot two estranged brothers simply meet and make amends? I would very much like to see you. If I wanted my return to truly be a surprise, I would simply appear one night, when the last curtain has been drawn by Ms. Rosev and the house has shut its eyes until the dawn. But you see there are a great many ways in which I have changed, and such behaviour would be unbecoming the gentleman I now consider myself to be.

If you should be willing to meet and I truly hope you are, please send word by return. I eagerly await your reply and look forward to introducing my long-lost brother to the rest of my family.

Sasha

19

Michael was well up to the physical tasks assigned to him by Mr. Watson, but it was the mundanity that set his mind wandering, slowing his progress until a swift clatter across the head, set him back on course. Like his sister, he was curious about the master's study and he would imagine various scenarios in which he had come by his treasures. That afternoon, as he washed the front railings in preparation for a fresh coat of paint, he imagined his master as a younger man, running for his life through a sweaty jungle, a bloodied crucifix in his hands. In pursuit, an ancient Pygmy tribe, their poison darts whizzing past his ears. His daydream was interrupted by the solemn face of Mr. Baker coming out the front door towards him. He seemed flushed, his usual cool demeanour gone.

'Michael, come with me.'

He threw his cloth into the bucket as Baker walked past him to the carriage. Mr. Watson sat up top looking very displeased at Michael's unfinished chore.

'Well, come on.' Baker beckoned him into the waiting coach. 'The master has a job for you, boy, if you're up for it?'

'Yes Sir,' Michael said. A chance to do something new, out of the house was a very welcome change. He handed Michael a small envelope, its contents sealed with a 'D' in crimson wax.

'I want you to deliver this letter and report back to me. The address is not known to us, but there can be nothing reputable in that area, just brothels and gambling houses. You will bring the letter and you will await a reply, do you understand?' He paused, then added: 'Can you hold yourself in a fight?'

Michael started at the question, his adrenalin kicking in with giddy excitement at his mysterious, and seemingly dangerous task.

'Yes Sir, I can punch well above my weight,' he said.

'Good lad, you might need those skills this night. Good luck and speak to no other of this matter, but myself and the master.'

He climbed up top with Mr. Watson. He did not favour his mood, had he sat in the carriage. He'd been excluded from whatever it was that was going on, but he didn't seek to enquire further. He only glanced again at the address on the envelope and shook his head. He pulled the carriage to a stop at the south west corner of Canal Street and Broadway.

'I'll wait here,' he said. 'I'm not taking the master's carriage and horses in there. It'll be dark soon.'

Michael was expendable but not the master's horses, or was Watson scared? Could he hold himself if things got rough? Undoubtedly not. He was past the age of fisticuffs, if he'd ever had to engage in them at all. Head clattering, yes, punches, not so likely. Michael got out, his confidence shrinking with every footstep he took further into the slums. He felt the envelope in his pocket, hard and crisp and strode on, his head low, avoiding eye contact with vagrants that huddled around an open fire. He could be one of them, he knew that. Still could be. With any luck, he would return unscathed and please his master. He had no desire for himself and Evelyn to end up here.

As the last light of the afternoon disappeared behind the rooftops, he came to the address on Orange Street – a run-down tavern called The Shrieking Widow. The door gave a loud creak as it opened, the smell of stale liquor and tobacco pipes filling the air. Inside, a boisterous crowd chattered, their voices raised in high spirits helped by the flowing alcohol and the convivial atmosphere. A long bar ran down the left-hand side, bottles stacked high behind it like a fairground game. In one corner, a man played a fiddle while a trumpet played merrily in the back. Men sang songs around both, each instrument competing with the other. The fiddler was winning, with some locals dancing and Michael felt an unexpected pang for home.

Behind the bar, a woman shouted orders to a younger man, her apron strings barely tying behind her swollen physique. In her hand she held a cloth, though it looked like the counter had never known its touch. As Michael approached, she scolded her apprentice, for his slow pace.

'I'm looking for Mr. Alexander Dermatov,' Michael said tapping his pocket self-consciously.

The woman let out a cackling laugh.

'Who? We don't get them Russians in here boy – you're barking up the wrong tree here.'

She threw her head back and he could see her rotten teeth, the molars long gone – her mouth a black chasm of laughter.

'Now, are you having a drink?'

Michael took a step back and looked around. He took out the envelope, checking the street address. When he looked up from it, a tall man was standing beside him.

'You have something for Sasha?' came the deep American drawl.

'I have a letter for Alexander Dermatov,' Michael said, unsure as he looked up at the man, who stood a good three inches taller, wearing a wide rimmed cowboy hat.

'Yep – that's Sasha alright. Only his brother calls him Alexander,' he said.

'I have an urgent matter with him. A letter from my master.'

'Well, then I better take you to see him, *mo chara*.'

He grinned, his teeth perfectly aligned and unusually bright. It was an affecting smile and Michael felt himself smile back, the tension easing.

'How does a cowboy like you, know Gaelic?' he said, listening to the words as they came out and regretting his familiarity, even if he had just called him his friend.

'I get around.'

He clapped Michael on the back and motioned for him to follow. As he did, he took in the size of the man, his broad shoulders and strong build. He had only ever seen drawings of cowboys in the penny novels he came across with the other boys from home. This man looked like he had been flung out of the pages. He wore a buckskin jacket over a leather waistcoat with a plain shirt, a neckerchief tied at the collar. His trousers were cotton, missing the chaps, but on his feet, he wore leather boots with metal spurs that spun when he walked. On closer inspection, he would not have been surprised to see the badge of a lawman pinned to his lapel. His face though, did not have the weathered look of a man who spent his days outdoors. It was pale and angular, a neatly kept moustache giving him a debonair look, a wave of brown hair peeking out underneath his hat. It was his crowning glory and he walked with a confidence that Michael couldn't help but admire.

'You finished checking me out boy?' he said as he opened the back door, holding it as Michael stepped out into the alleyway, following him close behind. It was empty save for some cats hunting the nights offering of rats and rotten food.

'Hey now, where is he?' Michael said, as Baker's question of his fighting prowess came to mind.

'You ever see the devil, son?' he said. 'You one of them Irish Catholics? You know all about the devil, don't you?'

A plain wooden door stood opposite them and the cowboy knocked lightly. It had no handle, only a small slot that flew back and a pair of green eyes that greeted them. They disappeared almost as fast, as the door opened slowly and Michael saw that behind the wood, the door was reinforced with thick steel. Inside, a musical din rose from deep within. It was like no other music Michael had ever heard. There were strings he was sure, but he had never heard a fiddle sound like that before and the ground seemed to vibrate beneath his feet such was its power.

There was no sign of the owner of the green eyes behind the door, just a dark corridor beyond. He looked at the cowboy, awaiting a sign for him to enter.

'I thought we were coming to you, Sasha,' the cowboy said into the darkness as a man appeared out of the doorway.

'Change of plan,' he said, his Russian accent soft as if smoothed by a sculptor's touch. He was only a year or two older than Michael – mid-twenties at best. He wore an elegant wool suit, his blonde hair resting on the nape of his neck. His brown eyes were friendly, though Michael thought them very capable of swift change. The door closed silently behind him.

'You seek me?' he said.

'You are Alexander Dermatov?' Michael asked.

'The very one, but you must call me Sasha.'

He held out his hand to Michael and he shook it. It was warm but there was something odd about it, an unnatural feel.

'My companion here is Wade. What's your name?'

'Michael O'Neill.'

'Well Michael, has my brother not given you something for me?'

Michael produced the letter from his pocket and handed it to him surprised that this young man was his master's brother. He could so easily have been his son. Sasha turned his back on him and carefully tore the envelope open whipping the letter out.

Sir,

What trickery is this? My dear brother perished many years ago in my homeland and you seek to mock his very memory with such an aberration. You wish to meet as do I, to expose you for the liar and confidence man you are. You call yourself a gentleman yet you seek to cause me deep upset for my poor deceased kin. So, you shall come to my home you know so well. The next Friday night when the moon is full. Don't bother bringing your 'family'. Come alone.

V

Sasha re-read the letter and turned to Wade.

'My brother wishes to welcome me back,' he said. 'With open arms, as I suspected. Well, it would be a shame to refuse such a lovely invitation.'

He looked at the cowboy, a wide grin on his face.

'Tell my brother I graciously accept. We have a lot to talk about. Oh, and tell him I will bring three friends, and we expect dinner. It's the least he can do.'

With that he turned and went back inside, the door opening for him, no look out required. The cowboy followed him.

'Be seeing you, Michael,' he said with a tip of his hat.

Again, came the drift of distant music and Michael strained to see inside, his eyes following them down a staircase until they disappeared into the shadows. Out of nowhere, the owner of the green eyes appeared – a little old man, his grey hair long, his skin so wrinkled it swallowed his features, save for those emerald eyes that shone brightly as he pulled the heavy door shut with ease. Michael stood there bewildered. He heard a noise in the alleyway up ahead, a cat probably but spooked, he hurried along the laneway and out into the street, anxious to deliver the news back to Mr. Baker. When he reached the carriage, Watson seemed surprised to see him in one piece and he knew better then to discuss the evening's events with him. By the time they reached the house, Baker was already on the front steps pacing them like an expectant father, a look of genuine relief when he saw Michael return unscathed. He ushered him quickly into the study. Their master sat in his armchair beside the fire, straightening as Michael entered the room, his hands gripping the arms. Michael recounted his meeting, first with the cowboy and then Sasha in the alleyway. For some reason, perhaps unsure what to say of it, he didn't mention the door and its dark innards. He relayed Sasha's message. Both men exchanged a look between them that Michael couldn't read.

'Very well, you can leave us,' Baker said handing him a few coins for his trouble.

'Thank you, Sir,' Michael said as he headed to the door. He heard his Master's voice then softly ask: 'Did he look well?'

Michael turned to him. 'Very well. He's a fine gentleman like yourself, Sir.'

'And how old would you think him to be?'

It was an odd question but thinking about it he said: 'A little older than myself perhaps.'

A flicker of unease at his answer.

'Thank you, Michael. I may have need of you again.'

'Yes, Sir.'

Michael left the room, closing the door gently behind him. He lingered a moment listening to the men inside. Someone was pouring drinks.

'And so, it begins,' the master said.

'You're sure it's him?'

'He was always impertinent.'

'What happens now?'

'Now,' he sighed. 'Now, I go and see my very old friend and better the odds.'

'Perhaps you worry unnecessarily.'

'Perhaps but prepare the night as planned. We will soon have our answers.'

20

St. Patrick's Cathedral stood on the corner of Mott and Prince Streets, its arched windows reflecting the low winter sun. The air was cold and crisp and Vladimir swept a long scarf around his neck so that it wrapped his chin, partially covering his face. Not that anyone would recognise him here, but he felt it right to conceal himself. This was clandestine business after all, and would not be welcomed by those who preached from its pulpit. The cathedral was the first Catholic Church to be called such in the New York diocese – a beacon for European settlers who sought the sanctuary of its teachings, as they tried to settle in their new home. He wondered why his benefactor had chosen it. Perhaps it gave him comfort.

He slipped in through the heavy door. Services were done for the day, and there were only a handful of people sat outside the confessional, waiting for their turn to repent. He made his way to the alter and genuflected at the foot of the steps, looking back to the line of sinners, their heads bent low in prayer.

Behind the altar, to the left of the tabernacle, a narrow door led to the crypts. He went inside, quickly making his way down the curving stone steps. At the bottom, he loosened his scarf. A box of used candles lay in an alcove and he took one, lighting it from another on the wall. He peered into the pitch-black darkness ahead. He'd been in many tombs over the years but this place made his skin crawl, or was it that he was always on edge meeting him? Even though he had requested it, he still felt the urge to turn back, but Sasha's letter, buried deep in his pocket, pushed him onwards. This meeting was necessary, imperative if he was to survive. He moved along, bathed in a sphere of light, the path behind him lost to the black, when the flame went out. He cursed loudly in Russian. Something, an animal, brushed up against his leg. Was it a cat? If it was, it was bigger than any he'd encountered.

'Oh, for God's sake,' he muttered.

He didn't like the darkness or cats and he reeled, as it rubbed itself against his other leg. A small flame ignited in the darkness. Then another four, revealing a silver candelabra held by a white hand. It moved towards him, the light slowly illuminating a slender tattooed arm – a twisting branch of thorns that seemed to move as he did.

'I would have thought you were quite at home in the dark,' came the silky voice.

'Yes, my friend. I have a problem I need to talk to you about.'

Gabriel came into the light his skin glowing softly. By his side, was a lynx, its golden eyes gleaming. Its ears stood on end, tufts of hair at the tips making them appear longer. No wonder he had found him in the dark. He had probably heard every breath he took.

'There can be only one problem that you would have to discuss with me,' Gabriel said, laying the candles down on a nearby tomb.

Vladimir took the letter from his pocket and handed it to him. He turned it over delicately in his fingers, before unfolding the sheet of paper.

'I didn't think he'd be strong enough to survive, not without me to guide him,' he said as Gabriel read. 'But your prediction was right and now he's come for me. He's not aged a day since.'

'You've seen him?' Gabriel said looking up.

'No, but I have a good report of it. He has come for revenge. That's what I would do. He means to kill me. He thinks I lead him to his fate.'

'You did.'

Vladimir was about to say something and thought best of it.

'It would seem he has in fact fared quite well,' Gabriel said, handing him back the letter. 'Do not mistake the hands of time, ceasing for his mind. Immortality gives you a unique perspective on the world and how life must be lived. He is not the young man you knew.'

'He'll kill me, don't you think?'

'How come he hasn't done it yet?' Gabriel said. A flicker of light cast moving shadows across his face.

'Because he toys me with me for sport. He wants my mind to suffer. You must get one of your hunters to kill him.'

'I must not do anything. Know your place here Vladimir.'

'Please Gabriel, what if I can't destroy him? You have to help me. I would not have been in Castle Valla where it not for you.'

There, he'd said it. Twenty years of blame, blurted out in a second. Twenty years of lost possibilities.

'Tread carefully. It was you who failed your task. You could have played such an important role. But you brought your brother, someone to bask in your glory and he chose him over you. How disappointing.'

'It was destined to fail. The creature knew. He knew it and you let me walk in there thinking I would succeed. Like it was easy. That's why I took Alexander.'

'You could have returned to him afterwards.'

'He was my responsibility.'

The words hurt him to say aloud.

'You knew the risk. It was always a life or death mission. You said a chance of immortality was worth it. And how strange that you have never sought it again all these years. Never asked me about other ways to have it. You lost your nerve.'

'You weren't there.'

'Ah yes, but you were. You pleaded with Rako to let you watch, so that you would have at the very least, an account of him to report. And he let you, so you could see for yourself the fate that befalls those sacrificed. But let's remind ourselves, shall we?' He gripped Vladimir's shoulder.

Suddenly the candles faded, their light dimming as snow began to fall all around them. It was night, a full moon in the clear sky. They were standing on the battlements of Castle Valla and they were not alone. Rako stood to their right, looking out to the prisoner chained in the snow. Alexander.

'Stop this. There is nothing to be gained from it,' Vladimir said, his words unheard by the governor.

'Isn't there?' Gabriel said. 'We're just in time.'

A swirl of shadows flew across the ice and then the creature appeared beside his prey, his cloak billowing in the wind. They could hear his breathing, a deep growl from his chest as he bent down to touch Alexander's face, his long nails reaching into his hair. He lingered a moment.

'What's he waiting for?' Rako said.

He'd been on edge all evening, Vladimir remembered. The first victim chosen by the creature himself. Vladimir had done his best to bury the details, but they returned to him with the full force of terror in which they had been received the first time, and he steadied himself for what was to follow. Gabriel watched the proceedings, rapt.

The creature ran his hand over his brother's head, a master stroking his favourite pet before standing to allow the wind to once again catch his cloak. The fabric multiplied but instead of swaddling his prey, it passed over him like a wave, as he moved closer to the castle. Rako gasped. Vladimir took a step back but Gabriel was behind him, his hands on his shoulders.

'Let's see what happened, shall we?'

The creature rose on a dark cloud of fabric, until he was level with them on the castle wall. His hood was deep, his face hidden. From the folds of his cloak, his hand stretched towards Vladimir. It was a memory, the event long passed, yet he could feel his sharp fingernail as it prodded him, like a knife to his chest.

'You were sent to spy on me,' he said. His words were of a dead language but he understood every one.

'No,' Vladimir said. 'I wanted to join you.'

He spoke the words, just as he'd done before. The creature laughed.

'Your master would destroy me, given the chance,' he said.

He moved, the lower half of his face catching the light from the flaming torches on the battlements. Even though Vladimir knew what was coming, he felt the fear double – the memory of it from the first time and now re-living it anew. Maybe he could just shut his eyes this time, not have to see it. He tried but they wouldn't close, the memory taking precedence. He would have to look upon the creature's face once more.

His skin was the colour of old parchment, and just as thin. The blood moved in tiny rivulets under it, red and purple, a map of decay. His mouth was a wide slash like an open wound, the flesh around it mottled. Vladimir wanted to run but he couldn't move. The creature parted his lips, his mouth opening to reveal his blade like teeth. They were all sharp, every one of them designed for one thing only. Two larger canine teeth sank lower from the top ridge of his blackened gum, their edges jagged, a cutting machine designed for carnage.

The world slowed, the snow stopping mid-fall. There was no Gabriel, no Rako, or Castle Valla – just him and the monster. All notions for an immortal life disappeared, the memory reinforced, crisp and focussed. He can't hurt you. It's just a memory. But still he felt his legs go weak, his heart beating out of his chest, sweat weeping from his pores and his fear was real again.

'Spare me. I beg you.' He remembered the words so clearly.

'You are not worthy of my blood,' he said. 'Tell your master I will show no mercy when finally we meet.'

He receded back into the shadows, dropping from the battlements to swoop down over his brother's body. Only the chains remained as his cloak drew back across the ice, Alexander's cries lost within it. Slowly the scene disappeared, the candelabra coming back into focus, the crypt illuminated once more. Vladimir was shaking. He had buried that fear a long time ago and now it played again with his mind, making him search the shadows, should the creature be hiding among them.

'Do you know why I sent you?' Gabriel said. 'I saw your potential. If I wanted to send someone to their death, I could have chosen any number of people. But you – I thought you stood a chance. You were clever, cunning, your mind your greatest asset, and your resilience. You were perfect. And he would have seen it too. He would have gladly turned you. But it was a lone mission. You would have discussed it with no-one, but you had to concoct a fallacy to bait your brother into going with you and all your talk brought you both to his attention. And he saw your ruse. He took your brother to punish you. And then you begged for your life – a weakness, even he could not overlook. You should have begged him to take you too.'

'He would have killed me,' he said quietly, reflecting on his words for a moment. He'd never shared the details with Gabriel preferring him to think that the creature simply took his brother and never returned. It was better than the truth.

'I'm not proud of it,' he said. 'Rako banished me after that for upsetting his precious monster, sent me back to Omsk, never to return and I left my brother, never to be seen again.'

'Until now.' There was something in the way Gabriel said it. 'You must be curious to see his transformation. To see what you might have become?'

'I have a thousand questions, but if his aim is to kill me, then what is the use of asking? I need your assurance that you'll protect me.'

Gabriel was silent, his fingers curling through the flames. 'You have it.'

'He will bring others.'

'Then preparation is key on your part. Any son of Woltacht is a very powerful vampire make no mistake.'

He'd never named the creature before. *Volt-act.* He almost wished he hadn't. To give the thing a name made it all the more real.

'You have replied to his letter?'

'Yes, I thought it best. He will come, Friday evening.'

'Good. You know the preparations that need to be done. Tricky creatures, vampires, such varying weaknesses. Oh well, we shall see, won't we?'

'It's a relief to know that I have your help. Thank you.'

'Least I can do, given it's all my fault.' He wasn't smiling and Vladimir couldn't tell if he was mocking him. The dormant candle in his hand fizzed with light and he knew it was time to go.

'Thank you, Gabriel.'

'Mafdet will accompany you, should you lose your way.'

The lynx rose from Gabriel's feet and padded towards him. He dreaded the feel of its fur again in the dark and so he began in earnest. He had got what he came for, even if did require a visit to the past. He would have the upper hand on Alexander and he began to look forward to the adventure that awaited him.

21

IF EVELYN HAD ANY doubts as to how Ms. Rosev felt about her spending time under the tutorship of their master, she only had to look at her face. When she would find them sitting at his desk, books piled high, her eyes would narrow, her lips a hard, thin line across her face. The master never looked away from Evelyn or his text, seeing her interruption for the unwelcome distraction it was. Even as Ms. Rosev stood before them and requested more staff, given that Evelyn's time was being taken up with her 'studies', the master barely registered her.

'Do as you see fit for the household, Ms. Rosev,' he'd said.

But Evelyn knew she had no intention of hiring another girl, instead making her rise earlier and work later into the evening. It was worth it though. She loved every moment she spent in that room and the extra work was a small price to pay for something which gave her so much joy. The master was a great teacher, his own passion for learning contagious. It was an unusual arrangement but it was working, for everyone except Ms. Rosev.

And Michael was happy too. He had been elevated beyond his own position, running errands for Mr. Baker directly. Their master had a brother, Alexander, that he never mentioned, but then he never spoke of family or his homeland. No portraits hung of beloved family members, no mementoes that he spoke proudly of. Everything Vladimir loved was in that room and that was it. Now that preparations were being made for a reunion, she was excited for him, that he should find a connection again with his family. He had to be lonely, living here by himself all these years.

That evening, as she knelt in the hall, scrubbing the skirting boards on Ms. Rosev's orders, she heard the master's voice beckon her to the study. She dried her hands in her apron, his voice a pleasing sound to her – perhaps another opportunity to learn from his books.

'Evelyn, there you are,' he said, his expression brightening as she entered. 'As you know, there is a gathering of sorts planned this Friday. I should like you to attend as my guest. Ms. Rosev will give you a clothing allowance. Buy yourself a dress befitting the occasion.'

'I'm not sure I understand Sir.'

'Think of it as a study Evelyn, but this time our subjects are living, breathing ones.'

***

THE DAY BEFORE THE reunion, Evelyn hurried down Fifth Avenue as the winter's afternoon fell to night. The boxes were heavy in her arms. She held another on her shoulder, a hatbox on a pink ribbon. Inside was the most elegant headpiece, a mix of beads and peacock eye feathers, inset with a stunning blue opal that would sit beautifully in her dark hair. The master had given detailed instructions to Ms. Rosev on how he wanted her to look. Perhaps he doubted her own sense of finesse given her background, but he'd even gone so far as to have the housekeeper make an appointment at the boutique of Francisco Barossa, the most sought-after dressmaker in Manhattan. She had spent the afternoon there, as he altered a dress for her. He had pulled the corset so tight she fought to breathe, the lack of air making her swoon as she looked at her reflection. She barely recognised the young woman looking back at her but in there, was a woman she wanted to be. Strong, powerful, desirable.

Is that what Vladimir wanted? Was he interested in her romantically? The idea was absurd and then she remembered the glare from Ms. Rosev. She knew it. Knew the path the master was taking with her. Surely not. She was a million miles away when she collided with a man walking towards her. His broad shoulder hit hers, knocking her balance and sending the boxes up in the air. They fell to the pavement as the man grabbed her arm, steadying her, before she followed them to the ground.

'Are you okay?' he said releasing her.

'Yes. Sorry, I wasn't looking where I was going,' she said bending down to pick everything up.

'With all these boxes, it's a wonder you can see at all,' he said smiling. 'Please let me help you.'

He handed her the lid of the hatbox as people stepped around them on the path. His voice was accented but she couldn't tell from where. It was soft and smooth, each word hypnotic. *Handsome.* The word forced its way into her mind. She almost spoke it and she pursed her lips, should it escape without her consent. He was like a prince from some old fairy tale. His elegant Homburg hat, his fair hair long beneath it, touching the collar of his wool coat. His eyes had a welcome familiarity to them, something she couldn't quite place and when he smiled at her, she held her breath for fear of showing signs of affectation. He gathered up the boxes, letting her see to the undergarments that had strewn from one of them. Embarrassed she grabbed them, shoving them back inside.

'Please let me carry these for you. It's the least I can do,' he said.

'I haven't far to walk,' she hesitated, 'but yes, thank you… I would like that, I mean appreciate that.' She blushed and he smiled, his eyes meeting hers.

'My name is Sasha,' he said offering a gloved hand from under the boxes.

'Evelyn,' she said. She felt a charge when her hand touched his, an energy pass between them.

'You're not from here,' he said.

'No, but I live here now.'

'Is this city not a crossroads of the world?' he said as they walked on. 'It's like the earth were a sheet of paper with the corners drawn up, sending us sliding neatly into this one place. Do you like it?'

'Very much,' she said. 'I have more now than I've ever had.'

'And yet it makes you sad.'

'I lost a lot in Ireland. My father died before I left.'

'Oh, I'm so very sorry,' he said.

He seemed genuinely touched by her loss and she felt it stir her grief, giving it permission to surface. She quickly changed the subject.

'What brings you to New York?'

'That is a very complicated tale for another day,' he said. Something changed in his eyes. She caught it like a tremor rippling and then it was gone and he went back to his talk of the city. She didn't feel like a servant and she allowed herself the dream, for she was sure she'd wake up any minute on the floor, Francisco flapping around, having cut off her air supply with that corset. There was an ease that seemed to come as a surprise to both of them, and he kept looking at her in earnest, as if taking mental notes to remember every detail. She stopped just shy of the mansion, not wanting to be seen with a stranger.

'I can take it from here,' she said as he placed the boxes on a nearby stoop.

'Very well,' he said. 'It was lovely to meet you, Evelyn. I do hope we meet again soon.'

He extended his hand again and this time when she took it, he brought the back of her hand to his lips, grazing them softly on her skin. She felt her whole body bristle as he kissed her, the same sensation she felt when she summoned fire, that tingle, that warmth.

'Thank you for your help,' she whispered, her heart beating so loudly she was sure he could hear it. He turned reluctantly before walking away back down the street. She stood there for a moment not quite knowing what to do, when he looked back at her. He did not smile but there was a look on his face of contemplation and she knew that she would see him again.

22

THAT NIGHT, THE CLOUDS parted to reveal a crescent moon in the black sky. In the alleyway, the door swung open and a group of revellers stepped into the moonlight. The first was the cowboy, the fringe on his jacket swinging as he walked. Tucked neatly in underneath was a crisp white shirt, finished with a black string necktie. On his arm was a beautiful red-haired woman. He leaned in to kiss her on the cheek and she pushed him away with a playful shove, before grabbing his jacket and planting a passionate kiss on his open mouth.

Behind them, came a black man, well dressed in a tailored suit. He wore it well though his frame was thin, his long legs stretching out in front of him as he walked. His hair was shorn close to his head and there was an intensity in his dark brown eyes, despite the smile on his lips as he observed the lover's kiss in front of him. The last one to step out was Sasha. He buttoned his long black overcoat as the door closed behind them.

'You haven't told us the plan for tonight's festivities,' Wade said.

'Think of it as an aperitif for tomorrow,' he said. 'Gabriel thought we might like a game of poker. A diversion until I see my brother and the life he's built for himself.'

'So, you can take it?' the girl said, a grin across her ruby lips.

'Velle, your criminal mind never ceases to surprise me.'

'Oh, I'm way past criminal don't you think,' she laughed, reaching out to take his hand. 'We stick to the plan then?'

'You always did like a nice slice of retribution.'

'Oh yes,' she said licking her lips.

'The plan stays as is,' he said.

'And the girl?'

'We do as Gabriel has asked.'

'I think you made quite the impression on her,' Wade said.

'I like her,' Velle said, resting her head against Sasha's shoulder as they walked.

'Well, nice to know you're keeping an eye on me, mom and pop. I'll be more discreet next time.'

'Don't be defensive. We just wanted to see her for ourselves. Same as you,' Velle said. 'Will be nice to have another gal around.'

'I don't know what Gabriel has planned for her. He'll take her when it's done,' he said, his mind already struggling with the idea.

'Not if she chooses to stay.'

The three vampires looked at their companion. Lincoln was a man of few words but when he spoke, he never wasted a single one. He had never seen the need for floral language.

He had never needed it. His voice was smooth and deep, like molten rock buried deep beneath the earth's crust. Sasha loved the sound of it, its frequency all too rare.

'Indeed, she may decide her own fate,' he said, buoyed by the idea and that his friends wouldn't be troubled if she did. He tipped his hat to Lincoln, who raised his hand to tip an invisible one back.

He had been the last to join their family. It was at the State Fair in Syracuse in '41. It was late summer and it didn't get dark until well after nine, but when it did the crowds seemed to swell and come alive. Sasha, Wade and Velle moved through the sea of people. To anyone else they looked perfectly normal, perfectly human. But one person eyed them from afar – a lone vampire whose presence made Sasha's senses heighten at the possible threat of violence. Meeting others of their kind rarely ended well. Wade felt it too as he stood in front of Velle but she pushed him out of the way, ready to face any enemy head on. Fireworks exploded in the sky above them as they walked towards him. Lincoln stood there, holding his ground. He didn't advance but he held himself ready to fight. In his eyes, Sasha saw resilience but also fear. He would only be a threat if they were. As they approached Sasha smiled and extended his hand. Velle looked him up and down and then winked at him. He looked surprised but no less suspicious.

'You are most welcome, friend,' Sasha said, dropping his hand when the man did not reciprocate. 'Come and hunt with us. This is the finest buffet in the county.'

Despite their friendly welcome, the vampire's face remained serious.

'I would rather not fight, if it's all the same to you,' Sasha said. 'We have come to enjoy the festivities.'

The fireworks soared high above them, throwing out green, blue and red daggers of light across the sky.

'I hunt alone. I'm not a wolf. I don't need a pack,' the vampire said.

'Very well,' Sasha said with a courteous bow of his head. 'Then we shall leave you in peace.' They walked away, but he did not leave. He watched them. How they killed with cunning and skill. How they blended into their surroundings and most importantly how they worked as a team and the genuine affection they had for one another. At two a.m., as they sat among the deserted chairs laughing and talking, he joined them, sitting down slowly next to Sasha, as if he might change his mind half-way and be off.

'My name is Lincoln. You turn on me and I will kill you all,' he said.

'And I you,' said Sasha patting him on the back. 'We will become firm friends.'

'Is Lincoln your real name?' asked Velle, pushing her chair up to his.

'It is my chosen name,' he said.

'It's cool,' she said and kissed him on the cheek.

From that night on, Lincoln stayed with them and as time went by he shared his stories with Sasha. He'd been right.

They would become firm friends. Lincoln's background was also one of hardship but whereas Sasha's had been inside his family home, Lincoln's hardship came from the world outside, and Sasha understood then his assumption that violence was the first and best response for their kind. In the years since he was re-born to blood, he had encountered more vampires bent on destroying their kind than preserving it. There was always a challenge especially from the elder ones who saw it as their right to destroy a fledgling they didn't think fitted their idea of what a vampire should be, which sometimes came down to the very colour of one's skin.

Lincoln had been born of a vampire who imposed his will on those he turned, and those who followed him in the name of freedom. With his band of killers, calling themselves The Whips, they unleashed a wave of terror throughout southern Louisiana turning slaves into immortals and killing their owners. The night he was turned, a thunderstorm raged and lighting crackled through the branches of the trees. He had awoken in his shack to find a group of men standing around him. The leader's face was as white as the moon and he was surrounded by former slaves, all turned to his immortal ways. On the belt of each, was the whip that had been used against them, taken from their former slave master in their final moments.

'Join us,' the pale one said. 'Be a free man at last. I will show you the way.'

Lincoln had no idea how extreme a price he was about to pay for such freedom, but he agreed, and the pale one performed the blood ritual there and then, binding them together. They went from plantation to plantation, selecting others, a few from each, to bring into their gang. However, somewhere along the way, their leader's idea of freedom differed from theirs, as he intimidated and manipulated them into staying with him as one unit. He would not share his knowledge of their kind, telling them only what he needed to control them and have them do his bidding. At night, they would lay waste to the slave owners, but when one of their gang was killed with a blade through the heart, they went underground, afraid for their safety having been assured from their maker that they were indestructible. In the end, they realised that they were still enslaved and turned on their leader giving him the same fate, a stake through his static heart. After that, they had dispersed in search of their own freedom and a quest for knowledge. Lincoln's freedom had come at a terrible price and Sasha understood his friend's complex nature as he too felt the weight of their endless existence.

***

ON THE SECOND FLOOR of the Union Club of the City of New York, four men sat enjoying a hand of poker. The room was thick with cigar smoke, the green velvet of the card table obscured by the gold and silver coins strewn across it, each player comfortably enjoying a nights gambling. A knock at the door announced refreshments and a woman entered with a tray of fresh glasses and a decanter of bourbon. Her presence in the room was startling for many reasons, not least because women were not permitted within its walls.

'Shall I pour?' she said, so sweetly her words dripped with honey.

'Now Miss, this is highly irregular. George, fetch the landing butler.'

'So, you can cheat? I don't think so,' said his companion. 'Just let her pour the drinks, Oswald. She's a lot prettier than that ole butler.'

Velle liked George immediately. He was the eldest of the players and she liked the way his wiry moustache was coiffed into little curls at each end. He took pride in his appearance, his black tuxedo immaculate with his neat bow tie. She walked behind him looking at his cards which he instinctively pulled closer to his chest.

'Did Clay Philips send you up here, Miss?' said Oswald. 'Only Clay would sneak a woman in here, that dog!'

She shook her head, her eyes never leaving George as she dawdled her finger across his shoulder. Bending over, she slid her hands down onto his chest, her breath in his ear. He lay his cards face down, as she kissed his neck. His expensive cologne was sharp on her tongue but when mixed with his blood, it formed a heady cocktail, sultry and delicious. The incision had been quick. To his companions it was no more than a sensual kiss and George was stupefied, transfixed by her charms. It was only when she came up for air and they saw her open mouth, dripping with blood, that they recoiled in horror. She hissed at them, the blood euphoric to her.

Oswald ran for the door. It flew back into his face as Wade and Lincoln joined them. The cowboy grabbed him pinning him to the wall with one hand, taking his time to bring his lips to his neck, his sharp teeth melting into the man's flesh. Lincoln took the other two men down in one go, cracking their skulls together. They fell to the floor, the vampire taking his fill of one then the other. When the dust had settled they looked at each other and burst out laughing. Wade inspected the cards on the table.

'Well what'd' ya know, my guy was winning – a straight flush.'

They left, closing the door behind them as Sasha came out of another room down the hall.

'How many?' he asked.

'Four, a good catch,' Lincoln said.

'Glutton, you got two of them,' Velle said. 'Any you?'

'One,' he said. 'I don't seem to have the appetite tonight.'

Velle linked his arm, wiping a drop of blood from her lips with George's silk handkerchief.

'Take the good that comes your way, Sasha. The plan is set for tomorrow night and you met a girl today and fireworks happened,' she said casting her hand dramatically through the air. 'Immortal or not, it doesn't happen very often,' she said.

'I love you, Velle,' he said.

'I'm special, I know,' she said wiping the last crimson drop from her lips.

23

Ms Rosev was watching Evelyn from the door as she tried to tie the corset, her hands twisted behind her back.

'You need to hurry up, Evelyn,' she said spitting the words at her. 'Mr. Baker wants to address *all* the staff in the kitchen.'

'Could you help me with this?' she asked.

She sighed wearily and snatched the laces out of her hands.

'Lean against that chair,' she said. She knew she'd regret asking, for she'd handed the woman a perfect chance to take out every bit of ill feeling she had towards her. She didn't hold back, putting her foot up on the bed for traction and Evelyn was sure she'd never breathe again without pain. She tied the laces, satisfied with her part, and grabbed the dress from the bed, throwing it roughly over Evelyn's head.

'Say what's on your mind, Ms. Rosev,' Evelyn said, struggling to find her way through the folds of silk.

'You've obviously made an impression on the master,' she said. 'Taken him in hook, line and sinker. When a man spends what he did on a lady as young as yourself, it can mean only one thing.'

She pulled the material together, closing the tiny buttons that ran the length of Evelyn's back.

'You have it all wrong, Ms. Rosev.'

'Don't be so naïve Evelyn. Now are you ready, Mr. Baker's waiting?'

Evelyn held her satin covered slippers in one hand, catching up the hem of her skirt with the other. As they entered the kitchen, Mrs. Osbourne let out a squeal.

'Oh Evelyn, you look like a princess,' she said.

Her gown was a midnight blue, with delicate lace cap sleeves that grazed the top of her shoulders. The fabric ruched across the bodice, clutching her waist, as swathes of silk organza fell to the floor. Pin curls framed her face, the headpiece magnificent in her sweep of dark hair. She had carefully applied rouge to her cheeks, and the softest pink adorned her lips. Mr. Baker smiled, impressed by her transformation.

'Well done,' he said, marking her excellence at a task, that in truth he probably doubted her capable of. 'The Master will be pleased.'

She winced and any feeling of pride in her metamorphosis vanished. She felt like a Christmas goose, glazed and oiled for the inevitable feast.

'You look a million dollars,' Michael said in an American accent, he could take off to a tee. He took her hands. 'Really, you do.' He leant in and whispered. 'Don't worry I won't let him lay a finger on you,' before squeezing her hand reassuringly. Oh God, everyone could see it but her.

Ms. Rosev peered into a box that Mr. Baker had left on the kitchen table.

'He'll burn the house down.'

'Please Ms. Rosev, just do as I ask and light them.'

'I don't even have enough candlesticks,' she said.

'I'm sure you'll think of something,' he said losing patience. He took a ladle, sweeping it through the large pot bubbling on the stove. Scooping some broth, he blew on the ladle before bringing it to his lips as a nervous Mrs. Osbourne watched him, ringing her hands in her apron.

'I followed the recipe exactly,' she said.

'It's perfect,' he said, setting the ladle down with a cough. He turned his attention again to the group.

'Right so, everybody listen well,' he said. 'This evening, there is to be an unusual gathering. It requires all of you to take extra care as you go about your normal duties. Tonight, the Master welcomes some unorthodox guests. Like him they have an interest in the occult and he will conduct a séance of sorts in the study with his guests this evening. Whether you believe yourself in such matters, you are required to take precautions. Mrs. Osbourne, if you will?'

On cue, the cook handed out tiny glass vials of clear liquid.

'Keep this on your person. It has properties that may help to ward off any strange elements that may spring up from tonight's festivities.'

Everyone held their vial, their grip tightening at its description. All except Evelyn who didn't receive one.

'I didn't get one,' she said.

'No,' said Mr. Baker. 'The master said you will come under his protection.'

She could feel their eyes on her. Judging her. Under his protection – what did that mean?

'You can have mine,' said Michael stepping forward. Mr. Baker shot out his hand to stop him.

'No. We must do as he has instructed,' he said, before addressing the group again. 'If you are of a religious mind, you may wish to also wear a crucifix.'

Michael snorted at the notion.

'You have something to say Michael?'

'No, Sir,' he said.

Evelyn knew they were clearly out of their depth. There was more afoot here than a simple reunion and she was to be right in the centre of it. Her gift may be tested again this night. The bell rang once in the hall and everyone jumped. Ms. Rosev didn't move.

'The master wants you to welcome his guests and bring them to the study,' she said.

She thrust Evelyn towards the door, the girl almost tripping over her skirts. Evelyn glanced at herself in the hall mirror, her reflection lit by half a dozen candles placed on the small French table. She would not be afraid and she steeled herself as the door opened to their guests. The first thing she saw was his face. She couldn't speak. She could only stare back at him in disbelief.

'Hello Evelyn,' he said gently. 'Aren't you going to invite us in?'

'Please, do come in,' she said, stepping back to open the door fully. He took her hand again, the same tingle shimmying up to her elbow as he kissed it. She felt lightheaded and cursed the stupid corset pinching her lungs.

'It's good to see you again,' he said.

'You're his brother,' she whispered almost to herself, and she immediately saw the similarities between them. They had the same brown eyes and the same slight turn of their mouth as they smiled.

'Forgive me. I enjoyed your company yesterday. I didn't want to spoil it,' he said sincerely. 'I'm sorry if I've surprised you. Let me introduce you to my friends. This is Velle,' he said.

A woman in an immaculate red dress stepped forward. Evelyn thought she was one of the most beautiful women she'd ever seen. Her hair was as red as her dress, as were her ruby lips. Against her pale smooth skin, she looked like a goddess, her green eyes sparkling in the candlelight.

'It's so good to meet you Evelyn,' she said her accent ringing far south of New York. 'You are a beauty.'

Evelyn felt her cheeks redden. The cowboy had removed his hat upon entering and he ran a hand through his brown wavy hair before he extended it to her. His handshake was firm but alarmingly cool to the touch.

'It's freezing out there,' he said rubbing his palms together. 'I'm Wade. It's a pleasure to meet you ma'am.'

The last man had hung back in the shadows after the door had closed, and he came into the candlelight now, his dark skin beautiful in the half light.

'This is Lincoln, my dear friend,' said Sasha.

He shook her hand with a brisk downward motion and stepped back again, inspecting the high ceilings and glamourous surroundings of their host.

'Forgive me, may I take your coats?' Evelyn asked.

'Hell, no,' Wade said, removing his jacket and throwing it onto the banister at the end of the staircase. Velle linked arms with Evelyn as they walked to the study, Sasha and Lincoln leading the way.

'I do like to watch him walk, you know?' said Velle mischievously eyeing Wade. 'Isn't he delicious?'

Evelyn felt herself smile as she looked at him, but she couldn't take her eyes off Sasha.

'He didn't mean to startle you,' Velle said, as if reading her mind. 'He just wanted to meet you, that's all.'

'Why?'

'The trick with this little soiree, is knowing which side you're on. It's okay if you haven't picked yet but I can kind of tell which way it'll go.'

There was no sign of Vladimir. Only Mr. Baker standing like a sentry outside the study door. As they approached, he went inside. Lincoln gave Sasha an uneasy look. They were talking in low voices and Evelyn wished she was close enough to hear their exchange. Sasha put a reassuring hand on Lincoln's shoulder, but he just shook his head at him. She was trying to work out what it was that made Mr. Baker offer up such precautionary notes.

In the study, the scent was heady. The incense had been burning all day and it changed the air, weighting it with its properties.

'God damn,' said Wade as it filled his lungs. Velle gasped too taking a handkerchief to her mouth in protest.

'Are we to be marinated in this?' said Sasha to no-one. Their host was not here and he didn't seem pleased.

'Please take a seat,' said Mr. Baker pointing to the long dining table and six chairs that had been set up at its centre. 'You are to sit here Evelyn. Beside the master.'

Did she need really need the master's protection? From whom? Wade held out Velle's high backed chair at the far end of the table. The smell had unnerved them both. They could tolerate it but they didn't like it. He sat to her left and she took his hand.

Evelyn sat next to Wade and across from them, Sasha and Lincoln waited expectantly for their host, his chair at the head of the table, empty. Mr. Baker stood by the closed door, his hands crossed. In the candlelight, shadows made shapes and patterns across the walls and ceiling, as if the room were a living thing, pulsating off the energies below. There was a dull thud, followed by the shrill noise of metal on iron, as Vladimir's heavy footsteps descended the spiral staircase. He was using a cane, its silver tip reaching out to the step beneath him, striking the iron as it went. Sasha stood up. They all looked to their host who appeared slow and infirm.

What was he doing? It wasn't until she saw the large crucifix on a gold chain around his neck, that she realised there was no séance to be had here, no conjuring of spirits. No wonder he had seemed so interested in explaining them to her. While she had secretly searched his books for answers to her own condition, he had insisted that they look at the ancient myth of vampirism. She had taken it as a macabre interest but as he came down the stairs, she saw that he believed it with all his being. Vladimir slowly made his way to the table and resting the cane at his chair he embraced Sasha, throwing his arms around him, holding the embrace for a second before releasing him.

'Brother,' he said.

'Vladimir,' Sasha replied.

The manner in which they examined each other, told of lost years and she wondered the circumstances for the distance. Sasha looked at the years etched on his brother's face, the wrinkles by his eyes, the grey in his beard and through his hair. The older man meanwhile marvelled at his little brother, his smooth skin, glossy hair and his brown eyes, the same as his but with so much youth and life in them.

'It *is* you, Alexander,' he whispered.

'You expected someone else?' said Sasha.

'A hoax was not unrealistic, but I see now it is you. Please sit.'

Both men sat down, Vladimir resting heavily on the arm of his chair, labouring to lower himself in.

'Alexander, you have met my companion Evelyn?'

Sasha's expression softened. 'I have.'

Evelyn wanted to correct his use of the word companion, hoping that it did not give off the notion of a romantic interest, when the door opened and Michael pushed in a serving trolley. A large silver bowl sat on top, its ladle slotted neatly into the lid. The scent of garlic wafted in and Velle started to giggle.

'Soup. The weapon of choice.' she said.

Vladimir was not impressed.

'I was not aware I had invited your friends,' he said to Sasha.

'I invited them,' he said. 'They're my family.'

He introduced them formally as Michael began to ladle the broth and Mr. Watson appeared by his side to take them to the table. He had to pull on Michael's shirt sleeve when they were done, transfixed as he was with the unfolding scene and Evelyn's part in it. When the door had closed again, Baker stood before it.

'I wanted you to come alone, so we could talk,' Vladimir began.

'I'm listening.'

'But you brought your friends, these *creatures* into my house and you have changed the very air we breathe. I will not have it.'

'I may look the same but make no mistake, I am not. I will not stand to your orders.'

Evelyn noticed his face change, a darkness creeping into his eyes and she felt it and knew its origin to be true.

Vladimir unfolded his napkin calmly.

'We must compose ourselves. I meant no offence, Alexander. Please, eat.'

'No, thank you,' he said looking at the bowl.

'You don't want some?' asked Vladimir.

'I appreciate the effort but my appetite extends to other more delicate tastes,' he said.

Vladimir's hand crept towards Evelyn's, his fingers crawling over hers, gently at first before his grip tightened.

'There is much to taste here,' he said, raising her wrist to Sasha.

Evelyn tried to pull her hand away but he squeezed it, hurting her.

'Stop it, Vladimir.' There was no fear in her voice. If she had to, she would burn him but it would not do to show her own card too early. She let him retain his hold on her.

'She's beautiful don't you think, and untouched,' he said. 'Just what your kind like.'

'And how would you know that?'

'I have made it my business to learn as much as I can.'

Sasha was amused by this.

'She is a tempting treat, expertly prepared but you can release her. I do not feed for pleasure but necessity and that necessity is borne of my hatred of the men instrumental to my death – you, Rako, Woltacht – and so it is in the blood of men I seek my nightly revenge. The girl holds little interest for me.'

He looked down the table, to the steam lifting from each dish.

'How little you really know, that you would think a little garlic effective?' he said, dipping his finger into the bowl. He swirled it languidly before bringing it to his lips, licking it slowly.

'And this?'

He reached over and touched the crucifix around his brother's neck. Vladimir flinched as he took it reverently in his hand, before closing his fist around it. When he released it, a misshapen orb hung from the chain.

'You may find your homework a little short on fact,' he said.

Vladimir slowly released Evelyn's hand. With her role so clearly defined by her master, she felt foolish. Trussed up for a blood feast, a sacrifice. For what, to appease his brother's hatred? She noted that Vladimir did not appear disturbed by his failings so far. He looked smug even, as if he held a secret inside and would let it out at a time of his choosing. He certainly didn't seem to be afraid of his brother or his friends, even though they outnumbered him. He was clearly waiting for Sasha to make his next move.

'Was that the plan all along? To get me to Castle Valla so you could give me to him?'

'No, of course not,' he said. 'We were both to go. Both of us to have this life that you now so beautifully possess.'

'You lied to me. There never was a treasure to find.'

'Wasn't there? Look at you.'

'There is no beauty in what happened after he took me. No-one would choose that.'

'You get to live forever Sasha. You are stronger and more powerful than any human. You ought to thank me for it.'

Sasha shot his arm out. His hand clamped around his throat, firm but not enough to do damage.

'What did you get for your part in it – this house, your wealth?'

He let go. He was restraining himself and Evelyn wondered just how strong he really was.

'It is between you and I only. This is our business, not theirs,' Vladimir said. 'Perhaps Evelyn can keep them company should they need to feed or are they as fussy as you?'

'Evelyn, you have nothing to fear from us. We are not the ones putting your life in danger here,' Sasha said.

'How very chivalrous of you. You have grown up, little brother. You have finally stepped out of my shadow.'

'Don't patronise me. I saw your face as he took me and do you know what I saw? Relief,' he said. 'My brother, my protector and you just stood there as they gave me to him.'

'I begged Rako to release you, I did.'

'Then, why didn't he? You had so much money. You could have bought my freedom.'

'He requested you. That's what I was told.'

'Rako?'

'The creature. He asked Rako for you specifically.'

'You're lying. Why would he do that?'

'He saw through us, through me. He saw the lie. I don't know how, but he knew I wanted it and who had put me up to it.'

'You could have warned me but you didn't. You knew and you left me to him.'

'I begged Rako to send me after you.'

'Don't lie to me,' he screamed. 'All the time you lie. Did you even feel remorse?'

'Is that what you came for, an apology?'

Sasha stood, as if in doing so he could quell the physical urge to hurt him. He needed to dispense his energy elsewhere. He paced around the back of his chair and gripped the wood.

'How can someone be sorry for what they don't understand? Allow me the grace to tell you what happened, and then you can decide if you're sorry enough for me not to kill you.'

24

THE NIGHT HE WAS taken returned to him. The foulness of that cloak. Cocooned inside, travelling in its innards.

'Rako gave me a blade, did you know that? Told me to hold onto it until the moment I needed it. Not big enough to fend off the creature's attack. Just enough to slit my wrists. He took a risk giving it to me but I suppose it was small enough that I could have hidden it myself. He felt sorry for me.'

He wanted to say something else but instead let his silence speak. He waved his hand.

'No matter now. I tried to cut through his cloak. I'd no idea if I went through it, how far I might fall but it was a risk worth taking. It was sharp, but not enough to even fray the threads of it. And so, I had to endure the journey in its belly until it spat me across the flagstones at his feet. The cloak receded back into him and he stood there, lost in that hood, his hands folded into his sleeves like some sort of holy man.'

He walked around the end of the table, his hand resting on Lincoln's shoulder a moment. His friend had heard this tale once before and had Vladimir been there then, he would not have lived to hear the end of it. To hear it again in his presence, would be a test to them all.

'A bear. A mountain cat. A myth. Do you remember that? Assuring me that's all it was when you knew exactly. I looked at him in that cloak, hidden, the blade pressed in my hand and thought what can I do to him? I didn't know the power he possessed. I didn't even know what he was. Just a monster. Maybe if I got close I could drive that blade into his eyes, one then the other to blind him. But you see he wasn't the only one.'

He caught the look on his brother's face.

'You knew that too,' he sighed. 'He announced my arrival to them by pulling a rope on the wall. One bell after another rang out deep underground. That's when the drumming started. Fists on doors. I imagined hundreds of them, hungry for me. I held onto that blade, I can tell you. Two of them came. A woman, Bethezba and a wolf man called Grom. His lieutenants.'

'A wolf man?' Vladimir said.

'Don't they have them in your books?' Sasha said.

'He was a wolf?'

'You should have come. I would have introduced you.'

Vladimir ignored his sarcasm.

'What did he look like?'

'He was neither man nor beast. He was both.'

He had the stature of a man, yet all his features were lupine. His grey hair, wild and thick. Blue eyes piercing beneath heavy brows. His nose and jaw protruding, his mouth vicious. Sharp teeth. Piercing his skin. He shook the memory away, only to realise that he had opened the door to them. It would only get worse.

'The woman was human once, a warrior.'

Her chest was covered by a dented breastplate, her forearms shielded in thick leather corseted to her skin. Her long hair was braided tightly to her head, streaks of blood and dirt smeared across her face. Green eyes stark against them. On her back, a simple bow and quiver of arrows.

'They took me to the Drain. A place for cleansing, they said, but they wanted to know my character. Test my spirit. Assess its worthiness. The Drain was a circular room of endless height, the floor a grate of metal panels that fit together. They took my coat. Chained my hands high. Left me, though I could hear their voices still. And then they filled it with water. Slowly at first, my feet wet as it spilled from a hole in the wall. I don't need to tell you it was cold – it came off the mountain. Did the creature take prisoners just to drown them, I thought? The water rose, over my knees, my hips, my chest – until it was up to my chin. Then inch by inch until it covered my head. Only my hands were free of it.'

He had Vladimir's undivided attention, his brother looking at him, spellbound. He was studying him, a vessel for scrutiny.

'I kicked my feet out, felt the wall opposite. A shorter man would not have done it but I used it to climb, pushing my hands and feet against the wall, until I was outstretched, my body inches above the water. It didn't rise any further after that. There was a shriek and the floor opened and the water drained away. My chains came loose and I fell into the puddle it left on closing.'

He moved to the fireplace, the chill returning to his bones at the thought.

'They left me there for hours. It must have been dawn I guess, and so they slept, as I shivered there, sure to die of the cold. I tried climbing the wall, but as far as I got, I could never reach the top of it. I was so exhausted that I risked falling if I climbed further. And so, I sat and awaited their return. After dark, Grom returned with dry clothes – a simple tunic. I followed him out, barefoot like a pilgrim. We went deeper into the belly of the castle, to a long gallery, its walls dressed with animal skins and weaponry and a table fit for a horde of men. It was empty save for one seat at the end. I knew he watched me as I was led to him, his hood only a deterrent to my vision, not his. I thought of the blade but it was gone, washed away in the waters that *cleansed* me.

I was put into the seat next to him. Bethezba brought me a plate of food. It was meat of some kind or another, barely cooked, a pool of red juices on the bronze plate. But I was starving. I would have eaten anything. And it was good. She set a goblet of wine in front of me and I grabbed it with both hands and drank it. Woltacht stood. I remember him touching my hair and then a darkness, like a veil over my eyes as the world turned red and then black.'

He caught Evelyn's eye and she held his gaze. He hadn't factored her into the audience for his recollections, but he'd gone far enough already and besides she may understand his motives better if she knew where they came from.

'Did you know he crucified his victims?'

Vladimir looked horrified. If he didn't know that, he didn't know the rest. Good.

'I woke as they drove the first nail into my hand. Bethezba said it was a great honour to be presented in such a way. An honour!' He laughed, its pitch manufactured, unnatural. 'I still have the scars. They didn't disappear when I became 'beautiful'. Come closer and you can see them.'

He moved towards him and Vladimir pressed his back into the chair.

'I could already hear them, the voices of the raiding party ready for their feast. When they raised me to them I could see them all, their faces glowing in the light. Some I recognised from Castle Valla and then I noticed it – the differences between them. The men on the right were skin and bone, prisoners deprived of natural light, the visible scars of torture on their bodies. On the other side were the torturers, men whose paleness seemed reserved for the whitest moon, their skin shining, eyes wide. They salivated at their prey across the room. All fell silent as Woltacht entered, falling to their knees in worship. The tortured reached out to touch his cloak as he passed, a desperate mix of fear and adulation. I was stripped of my tunic, save for a cloth draped around my groin. He beckoned them to stand and they did, pounding their feet on the floor in anticipation.'

He was deep inside it now, the horror untainted by the passage of years.

'They cheered as he rose up before me and I could feel myself falling backwards, the wood resting on some sort of plinth. That's when he took the first bite. His mouth came out from the darkness of his hood, and his teeth broke the skin on my neck. I could feel the blood as it trickled down my body. Then his tongue as he lapped it. He hadn't bitten me deeply. Just enough to begin the ritual. He withdrew then and invited them forward one by one. Bethezba was first, smearing her lips with my blood, a new longing for me in her eyes. Grom's tongue was rough. A grunt of satisfaction. And then the rest. Some licked the blood from my palms. With each one, the group behind them grew more frenzied until Woltacht beckoned all of his vampires to me. Like ants they swarmed, new teeth finding my flesh. That's when I knew I wouldn't die that night. No one wound was severe enough to kill me. It was a taster. Another test.

Woltacht cried out to signal the end, as the blood drinkers' attention turned to their slaves. They had formed a long line opposite them, a parade of living decanters providing the very best the human body had to offer. They selected their victims, found new skin around old scar tissue, took just enough blood to sustain them while keeping them alive. Some argued over the same person, neither relenting until they both just decided to feed. I passed out and so it continued, night after night. New places on my skin to taste and I realised that Grom and Bethezba were debating with their master, deciding ultimately which side of the room I would end up on. I wished for Rako's blade so badly.'

He took a deep breath in, exhaling it slowly.

'When they took me down, I thought I would die. I saw it, was almost at its door. They dressed me. This time not in a tunic but a heavy robe and I knew.'

He could feel Evelyn's eyes on him but he daren't look at her.

'He'd decided. I would join them. He spoke to me, told me how impressed he was with my stamina, my strength of character. He said it was my destiny. Do you believe in destiny, brother? Was it destiny that brought me to Castle Valla? Or was it you? He said I would make a worthy lieutenant to stand with Grom and Bethezba and so she put me to my knees in front of him. She pulled the robe back off my shoulders and whispered in my ear. 'Only a few of us are borne of him. You should be honoured.' And I thought again, with honour? This was no special gift and I tried to take my mind elsewhere, to leave the chamber and its monsters. And do you know what I thought of, what came into my mind? That winter we went to stay with babushka and we fished through the ice on the lake by her house. Do you remember?'

Was it painful for his brother to think of it? He hoped so.

'You'd cut a hole in the ice and sunk the line in, both of us waiting for the fish to bite. But when it did, we couldn't get it out of the hole. It was too big and you were trying frantically to break more ice and when you couldn't, you put your hand in to grab it out, to force it and your hand got stuck. And there was a loud crack and the ice broke and you went sliding in. I helped you out, pulled you back onto the solid ice, the fish clutched in your hands and you laughed so hard.'

'I remember,' Vladimir said. 'I almost froze to death but that fish was worth it. Babushka scolded me for bringing you out there.'

'What is life without the risk, you said. I thought of you in the ice. Our laughter. The taste of that fish – the finest meal we ever ate. But it wasn't enough. Woltacht found the deep sanctuary he longed for in me and he drank, taking my skin to his ruined lips until my insides burned with death. And then it was quenched by a vileness on my lips as he forced his bloodied wrist to my mouth. I was powerless to stop him. It wound itself like tendrils down my throat and it was too late. I felt it approach as the sky does a storm, dark and grey and without mercy.'

He paused.

'You look shocked brother. Did you think his immortal gift came by other means? It is a vile, monstrous thing and you think me the lucky one.'

'How did you escape? What have you been doing all these years?'

'Killing. I'm very good at it.'

'I imagine you are.'

'You don't seem afraid.'

With the aid of his cane, Vladimir rose and poured himself a large glass of whiskey.

'Am I to beg for your forgiveness,' he said, taking a gulp, 'cling to your feet and weep?'

'A man can change.'

'You think I didn't lose anything. But I lost you. I thought you were dead. What would you have me do? Storm the castle alone and drag you out, despatching vampires as I went? I'm sorry for what happened. I am. And I know that's not enough to make up for what you've been through but does it have to be a battle?'

'It is too late for anything else,' Sasha said. 'I am not the person you knew and neither I think are you. I gave you time to prepare. I wanted to see what you would do with it. But I must admit I'm a little disappointed. I expected more than old superstitions and to offer, yet again, to another monster, the innocent blood of another, is unforgiveable.'

'She's a servant girl,' Vladimir said draining the glass. 'They're ten a penny.'

The glass flew out of his hand as the full force of Sasha's body came crashing into him. He hurtled backwards into the glass cabinet. As one hand reached for a broken shard, the other came up with a vial of liquid, smashing it into Sasha's face. Holy water. Did he really think that would work? It had no effect, but splinters of glass cut into his eyes and he loosened his grip. Vladimir grabbed his cane. From the handle, he pulled a long silver blade. He *had* prepared. But Sasha was not without help and Lincoln swept in, knocking Vladimir sideways. The blade flew out of his hand and fell beneath the staircase as the deafening blast of a pistol filled the air. A bullet whizzed close to Lincoln's ear. Everyone looked to Baker, the gun smouldering in his hand. Wade took the pistol from him.

'Gimme that,' he said.

He opened the chamber and emptied it into his hand. Lincoln was holding Vladimir by the neck, ready to despatch him if needed.

'Should I shackle you, as you await your fate?' Sasha said, the last of the shards clearing from his eyes. 'A re-enactment perhaps?'

Someone was trying the door handle but Mr. Baker had locked it from the inside. Sasha leaned in to Vladimir.

'Will you taste as horrifically soured as your soul suggests?'

Pounding on the door, voices demanding to be let in. He moved in, the space intimate between them as he brought his hand around the back of Vladimir's neck. His brother was calm, waiting. He pulled him close, the movement swift and brutal and it was only when his brother felt his lips on his skin that the fear really began to dawn.

'Help me!' he cried out. 'Help me!'

Sasha withdrew and rose to face him. He would enjoy this.

'Who do you call on?'

'I have friends that will come to my aide and they will tear you apart, vampires or not,' he said.

Sasha took a step back, arms outstretched. He turned to Velle and Evelyn now stood by the fire, to Wade and Baker by the table, and back to his brother. There was more pounding on the door as the others tried to break the lock. Ms. Rosev was shrieking.

'Is that them?'

'Don't be ridiculous.'

'Alas they do not come. Or choose not to hear you.'

'Gabriel!' Vladimir screamed louder.

'Gabriel is not coming.'

Vladimir froze. At last his face bore the expression he had longed to see – fear and panic.

'Who do you think granted me permission to seek my revenge in this metropolis? He does not come. You are no longer useful to him. I, on the other hand, well…'

Vladimir's eyes darted around the room, falling on Baker who had hunched down by the wall.

'Baker, get up off your knees,' he said desperately. 'We're in this together.'

Baker slowly rose to stand, his bones cracking as he did. Outside, the sound of cartridges being loaded into a shotgun by Mr. Watson. Michael shouting at him to hurry up.

'You have no help in this room,' said Sasha. 'Mr. Baker and I are well acquainted. We met through our mutual friend. He has proven a great help to me, though he did very nearly shoot me just then, playing his part as your loyal servant. I won't hold his poor aim against him. I have promised him a nice bounty when we are done here – one he was very happy to accept. Of course, he also gets to live so that helps his cause too. Everything you own is now mine, brother. It's over.'

He nodded to Velle. She knew what to do. He didn't want Evelyn to see it. The act, the monster he was. On the other side of the door, there was a click as the chamber of the shotgun snapped shut.

'Protect her.'

'Go,' Velle said. 'I can handle it.'

Vladimir offered no resistance as Wade and Lincoln took hold of him. He seemed lost in reflection, registering the turn of events, calculating the angles and if he had any left to play. He didn't. Sasha knew it. In a blast of cool air, they left, a flight of lace as the curtains flew out the open window after them.

25

EVELYN FELT VELLE PUSH her down as the shotgun blasted a hole in the door like thunder. An angry scream as Velle met it head on; the thud as she fell to the floor.

'Jesus Christ, you shot her,' Michael said.

He pushed aside the broken door, followed by Mr. Watson, the smoke rising from the barrel of his gun. Velle writhed on the floor, a large hole gaping in her stomach.

'Get a doctor, Ms. Rosev,' Michael shouted.

'No,' Baker said. 'Just wait.'

There came a laugh from the floor, the blood gurgling in her throat, as Velle sat up slowly, curling her shoulders.

'Who the hell pulled that trigger? You almost killed Evelyn here,' she said.

They all stared at her. Slowly the hole reduced, flesh building on flesh, until all they could see through a ravaged hole in her dress was her pale skin.

Ms. Rosev grabbed her vial of holy water, blessing herself. Watson raised the gun again forgetting that he had not re-loaded.

'Where's the master?' he said.

She ignored his question.

'That shit hurts,' she said. She stood up, Baker helping her as she rubbed her stomach. She walked towards Watson, his mouth agape as she lowered his gun. Taking his right hand, she sprinkled the buckshot into his palm.

'Souvenir for you,' she said clasping his hand over his prize. 'Now I'm sorry to say that this night has come to an end.'

Baker looked uncomfortable. He knew what was coming. Mr. Watson, who stood a foot taller than Velle's petite frame, stumbled back a few steps as she reached her arms up around his neck, lacing her fingers to pull him down. He tried to tear her arms away but couldn't. She bit him, almost graceful in it, a lover's kiss to his neck where it not for the fear in Watson's eyes.

The fire in the hearth swelled behind Evelyn, its flames licking higher, escaping the grate. She felt its power and the familiar feeling of it growing inside her as her defences readied themselves. Michael ran to the serving trolley, the dish still warm and emptied it like a bucket over Velle's head. She let go of her charge. Watson fell to the floor. He was dead already. It had only taken seconds.

'You'll pay for that,' she said.

She hurled the empty bowl back at him. He ducked behind a dining chair, the bowl crashing against it. Ms. Rosev ran for the door, making it out into the corridor, running for her life now.

'Catch her, Baker,' Velle cried.

'I have done my part, Madam. The rest is up to you,' he said.

'Nice,' she said sarcastically, sweeping out the door to the hall. Evelyn could hear the sound as Velle caught her, and the thump as Ms. Rosev's head met the front door. Silence. Was Velle feeding on her? Was Ms. Rosev's blood spilling out across the chequered tiles?

'Michael, you need to go, now,' Evelyn said. 'Out the window, quick.'

He grabbed her hand, but she pulled away from him.

'She won't harm me.'

'What are you talking about?'

'I can't explain it, but you need to go.'

Michael looked at Baker who nodded in agreement.

'She's right. I have no wish to see you die at the hands of such a creature. Your sister is under their care and mine.'

'I'm not leaving without you.'

Then she would have to protect him. She encouraged the fire within her when she felt a presence she had not felt since the voyage. His voice whispered to her.

You can save your brother without showing your gift. Trust yourself. Trust me. You must keep it a secret.

Velle entered the room. Her complexion was rosy as if sat beside a warm fire but her dishevelled hair, dripping with soup and the large hole in her dress, had dented her jovial outlook.

'C'mere,' she said.

'No. Not him, please,' said Evelyn stepping between them. 'He's my brother. I can't have you harm him. I wouldn't be here without him and I won't survive if he is not with me.'

Brushing her hair off her face, Velle appraised the situation. 'We don't leave any witnesses. We can't. There are rules.'

'You're leaving me, aren't you? Why not him?'

'You're special,' she said. 'Sasha's never wrong about anybody.'

Evelyn felt her pulse quicken at the mention of his name. She didn't know what these vampires wanted with her but she had to trust the voice of the man who had guided her this far.

'I would hate to distress your sister here,' Velle said to Michael, her vampire teeth receding. 'We are to be firm friends and killing you is not a good way to start really, is it? Wade likes you too, you know, but you need to stop with the garlic throwing. You've seen for yourself that we can't be destroyed.'

Michael looked to Evelyn. 'As long as my sister is safe,' he said.

'Look, I know how hard it is to see this and be afraid. But we're the good guys. Vladimir was giving your sister to us for food. I dare say he won't be a loss to anyone.'

He looked to her for confirmation and she nodded. Exasperated, he reached for the decanter, not bothering with a glass. He sat back on the steps of the spiral staircase, and took a swig. Evelyn sat next to him.

'What do these people want with you?' he whispered.

'I don't know, but I don't think they'll do that to us,' she said looking at Watson's body lying on the rug.

'This is a dangerous game,' Michael said. 'As soon as we can we need to get away from them, do you hear me?'

Biting her lip, Evelyn nodded and Michael saw the glint in her eye.

'Oh my God, you like him, don't you?'

'Who?'

'Sasha, I knew it. I saw the way you were looking at him.'

'Don't be stupid. I met him on the street yesterday. I didn't know who he was.'

'Maybe he cast a spell on you.'

'I don't think they can do that,' she said.

'Michael, help me, will you?' said Baker as he tried to lift Watson's body.

'Jesus Christ,' Michael sighed taking another swig. 'What are you going to do with him?'

'Not our department, thank goodness. Let's put him in the hall with Ms. Rosev and they can sort them out themselves.'

'What happened to Mrs. Osborne?' Michael said.

'I fired her tonight. Gave her her wages and dismissed her. She was upset, tears and all, but I think she knew that her time here was finished one way or another.'

'You have a heart, Baker,' Michael said.

'Well, keep it to yourself,' he said and they lifted Watson's body over the top of the serving trolley, before wheeling him to the hall.

26

THIS WAS WHAT SASHA had waited for. His waking thought every night for so long. He had driven himself mad with it, imagining his brother out there in the world and his reaction when he would finally meet him again. Twenty years, over seven thousand days and who knew how many hours. And now the end was in sight, his vengeance but a last embrace away. He had dreamt so long of prolonging Vladimir's suffering over endless nights of bloodletting, but now that he had him, he just wanted it to be over. It was a peculiar feeling and he felt cheated by it. Was it the girl? Was it that Gabriel had given him another task after this one? One so important that it made him look beyond his revenge to the start of something new?

The distant lights of Bergen County flickered across the water. The Hudson was at high tide, the current circling amidst the choppy waters. Wade and Lincoln had dropped Vladimir in the long grass on the riverbank, where he lay, afraid to move.

'Please. I don't want to die.' His voice a whimper.

'No-one ever does,' Sasha said. He circled him like an animal, his eyes never leaving him.

'You could show mercy. I beg you,' he said. 'Please Alexander. I'm sorry for what I did. I could not reverse it but you must believe me I never wanted this for you, not like this.'

'Not without you to guide me?' he said.

'I have only ever tried to protect you. Gabriel said that I would be forever young once the creature turned me. I couldn't do that and watch you age and die before my eyes. I had to take you with me.'

'I'd forgotten how much of a burden I was to you.'

Vladimir got to his knees, his hands clasped.

'I'm begging you, please.'

He had wanted him to beg, yet it was strangely unsatisfying.

'You should have told me the truth.'

'Would you have come?' he said. 'I needed you with me. I had no idea the creature would choose you. You can't blame me for that. I am guilty only of my selfishness. I wanted us to share in it together and I lost you because of it. I have never forgiven myself…and you return to me, borne of a creature that terrifies me even still, and you think me lame to take precautions. I am the mouse to your lion. The greatest gentlemanly honour you can do is spare me.'

Sasha bent down, gripping Vladimir's face in his hands. His brother looked old. Time had not been kind or was it the shock of seeing him again after so many years?

'Were you not listening? That is a not an option.'

Vladimir began to weep and Sasha held his wilted body. A monster comforting his victim.

'Then show me,' he whispered. His fingers grasped Sasha's coat. 'Make me like you.'

He considered his plea. What if they had a proper reunion, one that would give his brother a true understanding of the pain of such an existence, and thus a new start? Perhaps that's why he had felt so untethered all these years. He had been without his brother, his mentor. The only other person in this world who knew all that he'd endured in his human life.

'My brother,' Vladimir whispered, putting his arms around him. 'Please Alexander.'

Sasha leant in closer, his face almost touching his.

'My name is Sasha.'

He bit him. Quick and vicious. His teeth opened the jugular, a fountain of blood spraying the air, covering him in scarlet rain. But he did not drink. He pulled back and watched as his brother gasped, his eyes wide, his hand reaching for him. The life he had made for himself was enough. In fact, it was more than that. He had found a new family and without the burden of revenge, could he, dare to think, enjoy it? Vladimir was not a part of that.

He put his hand to his chest, a final goodbye before he lifted him, taking his body to the water's edge. Without hesitation, he cast him out into the night. The water ebbed to meet him, taking him down into its swell until not a trace of him remained.

'Your grave is water, brother. I would not taint the soil of this earth with you.'

He hadn't cried in a very long time, didn't think he could, his emotions so twisted by vengeance but tears filled his eyes – ones of relief as his desire for revenge had finally been sated, but also tears of grief and self-loathing. An image of his creator came to mind and he shook it away, a distant memory brought to bear in the moment. Maybe it was a goodbye to his past but it rippled across him like the current. Wade and Lincoln came to his side. The only brothers he would ever need and together they disappeared into the night.

27

'How're you holding up?'

'Okay, considering you just killed two people.'

'Yeah, sorry about that. It's not pleasant but I guess you get used to it pretty quickly.'

Aside from being visually striking, Evelyn couldn't help but be taken with Velle's spirit, her enjoyment of her form and the ease in which she accepted it.

'How long have you been with them?' she asked. 'Was it the same for you, as for Sasha?'

'Oh, God no, Sasha had it bad. The worst. No, I had a choice. Wade asked me and I fully accepted.'

'Wade made you?'

'Not all of us have horror stories. But Wade saved me long before he made me a vampire. He took his time after that, let me fall in love with him, the bastard, and after that it was an easy decision. You ever kissed a man and felt the world fall around you? Lose sight of everything but that kiss?'

Evelyn blushed.

'Yeah – exactly. It's a rare and beautiful thing and it took a hundred-year-old man to knock me off my feet. Before that, well, let's just say I didn't think that ever existed. He's a good man Wade. So are Sasha and Lincoln. Just because you're a monster, doesn't mean you're a monster. I've met more human ones than any other kind.'

Evelyn thought of Corcoran, his cruelty, his hate.

'You've met them too. I can see it in your eyes. We're not that different, you and I.'

Maybe she was right. Who was she to judge Velle anyway? She was a killer too.

'Where are you from?'

'Athens, Texas but I grew up just outside it on my Grandpa Emery's farm after my folks died. I was thirteen and ole Emery introduced me to a new working life that year. He was a soldier, injured in battle, not able to run the Indians away anymore so he put his skills to running girls instead. Biggest brothel for miles. Popular.'

She tucked a wet strand of hair behind her ear and for a moment Evelyn saw a glimpse of the little girl she once was.

'My Grandpa Emery loved my red hair. Said he could charge extra special for me. He had a woman, Kate McCross, crueller than him – Crazy Cross we called her. He'd been paying her for years to take care of him and I guess they grew themselves a little business. To them I was just another orphan, or one of their runaways that ran in there and never got out. I was nineteen before I saw a way to escape. You have to understand, they convinced us so young that there was nothing out there for us. The world wasn't meant to serve girls like us. We served it. And we had food and a roof over our heads. Nobody outside of there was gonna do that for us. And if you saw the men who came, you'd believe it. They made us believe we were safer there than anywhere else. Sure, I dreamt of escaping but the fear of the unknown… better the devil and all that.'

Her voice trailed off.

'Did Wade rescue you?'

Velle smiled. 'On a white horse? No. It was up me to change things or at least try. I knew it wasn't right. Guess I just needed a place to start and that's when I found the map. I liked to rummage through the drunken ones' belongings when they passed out. There'd be hell to pay if we took anything but I liked to look, you know. Anyway, this map was big, like a jigsaw of states, Texas folded to the front. He must have been a salesman or something but he'd drawn a line all the way to the east coast.'

She traced her finger along her skirts.

'And I thought, I could go there. How much worse could it be? Even though Cross kept us in rotation depending on when we bled, it was only a matter of time before I got pregnant. It wasn't fool proof and what would I do then? I was already at the crossroads. That map just gave me the shove I needed to try. But before I left there was one thing I had to do.'

She smiled as if the memory were a nice one.

'He had a name, a real one I guess but I called him The

Blade on account that Emery let him use one on me. He told him he could do what he wanted once he didn't affect my 'saleability'. He liked the extra he was willing to pay. He would cut me in discreet places, watch me bleed. Each time he was getting more agitated, he wanted more. He joked with Emery that he was gonna come there one day and put a bag of gold on the table and buy me outright. Then he could do whatever he wanted with me. More than running away from Emery, I was afraid he'd come after me too and so I needed to make sure that didn't happen.

He liked to intimidate me and he'd take his knife and ram it into the wooden post, fly the flag for the adventure to come. I guess I'd normalised it 'cos I used to let him but the thoughts of that map, the world denied to me, made me brave. I seized the knife and dropped, stabbing him in the foot. It went clean through his boot and he started to curse and hop. That's when I pushed him back onto the floor, a little rough and tumble and I sat on his chest as he tried to push me off. But I had that knife in my hands and I threw myself down on the handle. It melted into him like butter. I could hear the tip strike the wood underneath. And he didn't move after that.

I took what I had and ran. I needed to get as much space between me and Emery as I could, or he would be dragging my ass back there. I ran some of the way north east, left my shawl snagged on a branch on the road to Kaufman. Maybe he'd think I'd gone to Dallas. Then I doubled back for Frankston and then Jacksonville. I was so exhausted I crawled under the pilings of a hotel and slept there in the dirt. Best sleep in years. As the people of Jacksonville bustled through the streets, I bustled their wallets. Texas was at the business of fighting the Mexicans at Santa Anna, soldiers marching through the streets. No-one was gonna ask me any unwanted questions. I bought food, new clothes, kept moving – Texarkana, Memphis, Nashville, Louisville. It wasn't until I reached Cincinnati that my luck began to change. I was surviving hand to mouth, fare to fare, but I needed more than that, enough to set myself up when I reached the coast eventually.'

She let out a sigh. Evelyn had forgotten the room, the dead, everything, her attention held on every word Velle said as if she were there, in Cincinnati with her. As Velle described what happened next, Evelyn could see her in her mind's eye, perfectly poised as she sat in the bar of the Shelding's Hotel.

***

SHE HAD MADE THE extra effort, wore her finest dress with the green velvet sash, her hair braided and swept back off her face. She'd spotted the handsome man immediately when he walked in. He was tall and strong, his shirt sleeves rolled up to his elbows, his waistcoat open. He joined two other men sitting at the bar, as they offered him a whiskey shot. The men were laughing and as she stared she caught the man's eye and he raised his glass to her. The other men followed his gaze, one of them saying something that made them all laugh raucously. The man moved off his stool and walked towards her, his stride confident, two glasses of whiskey swimming in his hands. She smiled coyly at him.

'Mind if I join you?' he said handing her a drink.

'Be my guest,' she replied. 'Something funny?' She nodded to the other two men.

'They reckon you're a young widow looking for a bit of love in this godforsaken world and that I may be the one you've been searching for?'

'Really? I think you've made a wager, is what I think?' she said taking a drink.

'They bet me a day's wage on how quickly I can make you leave with me' he said his smile disarming, his confidence not diminished.

'I'm shocked,' she said, the liquor burning her throat.

'So was I. They obviously can't tell you're not interested unless I have cash to spend.'

He looked at her knowingly, a secret shared between them, an advantage on his bet.

'I knew you were a whore, the second I saw you.'

She bristled, the smile slipping from her lips.

'Aw heck I've offended you now. I'm sorry. Look I have a habit of putting my foot in my mouth. It's how most of my conversations with women go.'

'And there was me wondering why a nice guy like you, would have to pay for it. That mouth must get you in some trouble.'

'Like you wouldn't believe. What do you say we start over?'

'So, you can win your bet?'

'Ah, I already lost it. They bet a minute flat.'

'That's some record…especially with that mouth.'

'You wanna get out of here? Come on," he said, taking her hand. 'Promise, I'll behave like a gentleman.'

Velle had broken her own rule. Men on their own were discreet and as they walked by the other two men, they slapped their buddy on the back and whooped for his success even though the bet was lost. A distant alarm bell rang for her but so too did the one for the morning's stagecoach to Columbus and her need to be on it.

'You need to pay me up front,' she said as he opened the door of the hotel room.

'Sure thing,' he said taking out a silver money clip, its many bills neatly folded. He handed her the money and she put in it her purse. Kissing her on the cheek, he opened the door for her. It was a nice hotel room, with curtains on the window and a proper eiderdown on the bed. She'd been in a lot worse.

He asked her to undress slowly as he watched. She removed her clothes, item by item, her fingers fumbling with the strings of her corset. She felt woozy suddenly, as pain spiked in her head and she sat down on the bed, disorientated. A light knock sounded on the door and the man answered it, his two friends coming into the room. She tied to sit up again but the room began to spin.

'I don't feel well. I think I'm going to be sick,' she said, trying to get off the bed.

'You'll be okay. We just gave you a little something to relax you.'

She looked at him, seeing double.

'You...' Her words faded and she slipped out of consciousness, coming too again with a sharp pain in her cheek. One of the other men had slapped her face.

'Jeez, Robert you gave her too much. It's never fun when they're unconscious.'

'I don't mind,' said the third man, unbuttoning his bitches. She opened her eyes, the man looming above her and moaned a groggy 'No'.

The next thirty seconds, were a bizarre blur of noise and images. The man was on top of her for only a second before he suddenly flew upwards, slamming into the ceiling and falling backwards to the floor. The second man let out a gurgling cry, as a spurt of blood erupted from his neck. The first, had made it to the door but was yanked backwards, his body meeting the wall with a loud crack. She heard the stranger's voice as he leaned into the fallen man.

'That ain't no way to treat a lady.'

She tried to get up but her hands felt numb, and then the blanket was covering her, her clothes wrapped in with her in the eiderdown. Carefully, he carried her out of the room, her bare feet dangling over his forearm and down the back stairs, his grip never faltering.

'Don't worry, it's gonna be okay.'

She rested her head into his shoulder and allowed the tears to flow.

***

'He put me to bed somewhere dark,' Velle said, 'the covers warm, and when I woke up I was alone, the sun streaming in through the curtains. On the bedside table, was a note.

Know that you are safe here. I'll be back tonight if you choose to stay. Wade.'

Evelyn could feel her heart beating faster.

'How's that for a rescue?' Velle said. 'Speak of the handsome devil, they're back.'

28

WADE TOOK ONE LOOK at Velle and put his arms around her, pulling her into him.

'Don't, I smell awful,' she said.

'Smells like chicken,' he grinned. 'I'm gonna take you home and wash that right out of you.' He rested his hand inside the hole in the front of her dress, finding her waist as she kissed him. Evelyn watched them, envious of their intimacy. Michael and Baker had also returned and while none of them expected to see Vladimir again, the room seemed strangely empty without him, his books and treasures now orphaned. Lincoln recounted Vladimir's demise to Baker, as Michael listened in.

'Are you okay?'

Sasha had come to her side. She felt awkward, unsure how to proceed. Did she condone his revenge?

'He didn't suffer,' he said, sensing her discomfort.

She knew it was a lie. His coat was blood soaked but he was trying to make her feel better, dim the horror of what he'd done.

'You have nothing to fear from me Evelyn.'

'What do you want from me?'

'He will tell you when the time is right.'

'Who?'

'Gabriel.'

'Is he a vampire too?'

'No. He is much more powerful. He is the gatekeeper of this magnificent city and more.'

Of course. Her guide along this merry path thus far. It had to be. She waited, hoping to hear his voice, to confirm it. But there was nothing.

'I want to see him,' she said.

Something caught her eye outside. Movement, then a pair of glowing eyes peering through the window. Sasha drew back the lace curtain. He undid the latch and in slipped the most beautiful and unusual animal Evelyn had ever seen. A large cat, its eyes ringed in black fur that streaked from each corner to the tip of its long ears. Its coat was golden, dotted here and there with traces of black. Sasha bent down to pet the cat's head, its bright eyes closing, thankful for the welcome.

'This is Mafdet. She belongs to him,' he said. 'Beautiful, isn't she? Has he sent you my lovely?'

Mafdet purred arching her back as he ran his fingers down her spine.

'Very well,' he said.

With that Mafdet left him and went to Evelyn, sitting back on her hind legs at her skirts, like a sentry guarding her queen.

Evelyn was almost afraid to touch her. She eased her hand towards her, the spiked fur of her ears touching her hand, as she rested it softly on Mafdet's head.

'You will see him tonight,' Sasha said. 'Mafdet will accompany us, just you and me.'

'I don't want my brother harmed,' she said.

'Are we safe from him?' Sasha said, looking at Velle.

'Probably not. Do I have your word?'

'He will be safe, once he behaves.'

Michael was half-way through the decanter of whiskey, his eyes heavy as they followed Lincoln around the room. She could imagine all the scenarios flicking through his head, all ending in bloodshed, namely his own. Baker too was taking caution. Vladimir's sword lay under the staircase and he picked it up, slipping it back into its casing.

'He's not going to let me leave on my own.'

'I wouldn't worry. Baker's taken care of that. There's more than just whiskey in that bottle. A little laudanum, enough to subdue any notions he might have. For his own good. He is a danger to himself drunk, I think you realise that. He will be trouble and will find himself in trouble because of it. Let him sleep.'

When she looked, Michael had already passed out, the remains of the whiskey trickling onto the floor.

'Wade will look after him. Now, we must go. We shouldn't keep him waiting.'

Evelyn could feel the fingers of manipulation beginning to

tighten around her and she didn't like it – even though she knew the importance of her going alone. She'd kept Michael out of everything so far. Where would she possibly begin now? She would meet with Gabriel and at last find out what was expected of her and her gift. Then she would tell Michael everything.

Outside, Mafdet led the way, a few paces in front. A couple walked towards them, saw the lynx and swiftly crossed the road. Mafdet was quite the sight.

'Do you mind?' Sasha said taking her hand.

'No' she said, though Mafdet cast her head back to them and quickened her pace.

'Why are you not afraid?' he asked.

'When you have nothing left, you have nothing left to fear,' she said.

'Not even death?'

'You're dead, you tell me,' she said with a half-smile, as he laughed.

The streets seemed to go past them in a blur as they spoke and as he let go of her, she realised that by holding his hand she had moved at a preternatural speed and they stopped now in a darkened alleyway, miles from the tree lined corner they had left. As Mafdet approached the door it swung open and she turned to look back at Evelyn, her stare transfixed, green speckles like stardust in her golden eyes. Evelyn felt *him* beyond that stare, looking at her. She could feel him. And he was pleased. Maybe even a little excited.

Inside, they descended a staircase into the basement below. It was vast, a catacomb of tunnels and caverns that stretched out beneath the city like a spider's web. The walls leading to the main chamber were a blur of yellowing round stones, lit every so often by torchlight and it was only as Evelyn reached out to touch them that she felt the coldness of the bone. Skulls with long lost eyes, compacted side by side and top and bottom, building blocks for another world. She had left the Earth she was sure, for she'd never seen a place such as this and that music – with notes so low they made the ground hum beneath her feet, like a secret world hidden under theirs. Soaring strings mixed with instruments her ear couldn't identify, their strain charged and powerful and a voice, male, deep and sultry. In a wide cavern, she looked everywhere for its source, for the group of musicians creating such a powerfully seductive overture, and yet they were nowhere to be seen. As the music swelled so too did the inhabitants, the walls lined with its nocturnal residents moving to its chorus, their bodies twisting inwards, their hands treading the air.

Sasha took her hand protectively as they came closer to investigate. Her humanity was a beacon in the darkness, the smell of her filling their senses, the curiosity of their human visitor luring them closer. She felt a sharp prod in her back and turned to see a cloaked creature, half her size, retract a wizened hand, its black fingernails curling back in. Sasha pulled her through them and they left the cavern, travelling down a narrow tunnel into the darkness until the light ran out and Evelyn could see no further. Sasha led her onwards, his vision clear but the sudden loss of hers was unnerving and she felt the first tiny drops of fear start to invade. Sasha stopped and she grabbed his arm as he turned back to her in the dark, putting his hands to her face. Her eyes searched in the darkness catching the tiniest glint of light from his as he moved closer to her.

'Don't be afraid,' he whispered, his lips brushing her cheek.

'Where is he?' she said, his lips finding hers as he kissed her softly.

Sasha didn't answer, his lips parting to kiss her again. She felt every cell in her body react, accelerated by desire and for a moment she lost herself, forgetting their surroundings and the purpose of their visit. Her heart leapt as his lips moved over her cheek, into her hair, softly skimming her ear before finding the soft flesh of her neck where he kissed her hard, catching her body up in his arms. She gave herself away in that moment, not realising until she felt the sharp pain, that his desire was of another kind. She could feel his tongue drawing the blood from her, his hold strong as she tried to push him away. In the darkness, Mafdet's eyes glowed at her and she knew *he* was watching.

Through the murky blackness, all her fears were suddenly given form as invisible hands sought to grab at her, pulling her clothes. Decaying faces loomed out of the shadows, as they begged for their lives. The face of her father, soil resting in his eye sockets, Corcoran's spectre beside her, his tongue extending to lick her cheek. Cries of starving children filled her ears as they crawled on the ground beneath her – and Sasha, in a blur now as she swooned into unconsciousness, the loss of blood too much for her as he pulled back, sweeping his hands up to her face. Through half-closed eyes she saw him but gone was the handsome prince, replaced instead by a red eyed monster, his skin a slick of black oiliness, his long teeth jagged hacksaws dripping with her blood. His hands felt like leather on her face, his nails curling as they extended, gripping her and threatening to pierce her skin. He was silent, holding her as she tried to cry out, the noise crushed in the small space and as she lost consciousness, she saw Mafdet's eyes, the gleam swirling before disappearing into the black.

The tunnel exploded with the flames of torches along its path and Sasha carried her to a small chamber – Mafdet gone, returned to her master. Animal furs lined the floor like some prehistoric dwelling and as she came to, Sasha was bent over her, pulling at her corset. She felt her lungs expand and the agony with it, her insides no longer able to bear the pain as her veins ran empty, a million tiny tributaries with nothing to offer her slow beating heart. His hand brushed her cheek, the leathery touch now warm and soft, and she felt a trickle of liquid touch her lips. He pressed his wrist to her mouth.

'Drink, Evelyn,' he said as her body convulsed, spitting it out. 'Drink. You have to, do you hear me?'

She looked at him, the prince returned, the concern etched on his face, and her tongue slid involuntarily over her lips.

'That's it. Your body knows what to do. You just need to let it.'

She found his wrist again and drank gently at first, the flow increasing as her pull became stronger. When he eventually pried it away, she glared at him with wild eyes. Her humanity ebbed away as his blood ran into every fibre of her body. It wrapped around her organs, remoulding them for immortality and when it reached her mind, it engulfed her in its immortal fire. It was a different fire though – not hers. She couldn't feel hers anymore. It had fled, a distant human memory, and she knew that it was lost to her. Everything was different. Everything had changed. He tried to take her hand and she pushed him away, surprised that in her state she was strong enough to do so. When he tried again, she pointed a finger in accusation.

'Stay away from me. Don't you come near me.'

She was listening to her own heartbeat fade away, its drum beat faint and then it was gone. She waited, but it was silent, settling into its eternal stillness. She wished for death to come quickly but nothing happened and as she lay there she felt all pain leave her, her limbs tingling as Sasha's blood finished its act of fortification.

Sasha waited, his back to the rocky wall, his head in his hands. Was that guilt or just the reminder of what he'd endured himself on his own transformation? The most visceral of reminders. She could hear Mafdet approach, her paws soft on the earthen floor and Sasha stood up. It was time. Her legs felt strange to her, as if the muscles were not yet strong and carefully Sasha slid his arms underneath her, lifting her easily. There were no torches in the dark passageway and yet she found it to be filled with light, her vision clear, every shadow transparent. By the time they reached the chamber, she was confident of standing and she demanded that Sasha let her down. In front of them on a table was a piece of folded cloth, a cloak that she swept around her bare shoulders where her open dress had slipped, no longer held in check. She pulled the pin from her hair and it fell past her shoulders in waves, shiny and dark and though she could feel Sasha's eyes on her, she focussed ahead, half afraid of seeing the monster again in the darkness.

'Welcome my dear.'

His voice, from all around her. Then with it, Gabriel himself, out of the shadows, his arms outstretched, reaching for her embrace. It *was* him and despite herself she was glad to finally meet him face to face.

'How are you feeling?' he asked.

'Betrayed. I was told I was safe. *He* told me I was safe.'

Sasha lowered his eyes.

'You mustn't blame him, Evelyn. It was I who gave him his instruction, in return for his revenge. It is a price which bears heavy on him.'

'Am I dead? Like *him*?" she asked her eyes remaining on Gabriel.

'Yes, my dear.'

His words cut her more sharply than Sasha's assault.

'It's okay to grieve for your life, Evelyn. Like all grief it will diminish over time but it is important to let go of your human sensibilities. You will eventually.'

'You want to make me a monster,' she said, finally looking at Sasha.

'That is not my intent,' Gabriel said. 'But you need to learn from Sasha about his kind and how to survive, how to feed and we will talk again, when you are ready.'

'I'm not going with him,' she said flatly.

'You must,' said Gabriel. 'Don't you wish to see your brother again? Please, Sasha is not your enemy. Believe me we have many enemies here. Sasha is not yours, so let him help you. Mafdet will stay by your side and watch over you.'

'I am trapped then.'

'It is a mere question of perspective. You will be glad of your new vampire family. They will take care of you. You are angry and I understand that believe me, but have patience.' He turned to Sasha, 'It is almost dawn, my friend. You should both rest here.'

'You can take me back home,' she said. 'I won't stay here. I want to see my brother.'

'We'll make it back,' said Sasha to him. 'Lincoln was making provisions for us to rest there.' With a short bow, Sasha turned to go.

'Thank you, Gabriel.'

'How tasted your revenge?'

'Bittersweet,' he said as Evelyn glared at him, her eyes a bright sapphire blue.

Gabriel took her hand as Sasha left the cavern.

'Trust *me*. Trust *him* and all will be well, sweet Evelyn. And try not to kill him,' he said.

'I don't know how,' she said, 'but perhaps I'll learn' and with a turn of her cloak, she disappeared into the darkness after him.

29

MICHAEL HAD AWOKEN ON the sofa, where he'd slept sprawled, one leg hanging to the floor. He forgot where he was for a moment, his eyes blinking, head thumping, as he looked up at the ceiling. Slowly he moved his eyes from side to side, his brain sending a fork of pain across his temples and he winced, rubbing them with his hand. He was no stranger to the after-effects of too much drink but he hadn't felt this bad since Jack O'Keefe's emigration wake when he, Jack and his six brothers, had stayed up all night drinking poitín. When light dawned, five of them had black eyes, him included, one was missing two teeth and another two were found asleep in the fields, a fresh trail of snails shuffling over them. It was wild stuff that crumpled their minds into a mess of laughter and violence and Michael had never seen a man look as green in the face as Jack did when he left the next day.

His mouth was dry and he sat up, startled to see Wade looking at him from across the room. Damn it, it was real. All of it. His mind could have quite easily convinced him that it was a dream, a product of the whiskey filling his mind with fantasy but here he was. They were alone and he immediately realised his sister was not there.

'Don't worry Michael, she's with Sasha. They'll be back shortly. You my friend, look like you could do with some coffee.'

He handed Michael a cup, the sides hot, a wisp of steam trailing from the top.

'Where is she?'

'They won't be long. You should drink that. You look like crap.'

'Yeah well, I feel like it too,' he said, the coffee warming his insides. He sighed. 'If you're giving me coffee I'm guessing you're not about to kill me.'

Wade sat back.

'I like you Michael and I'd hate to kill you. Me, I'm fine with humans if they're fine with me and they generally are. I'm an easy guy to be around, as long as people behave. Sasha on the other hand, well he has a general low opinion of mankind. He doesn't like to engage too much. For him, it's easier to just think of them as food. Take the emotion out of it, you know. We are what we are and you, well you are what you are.'

'He killed Vladimir.'

'He sure did,' Wade said. 'But his brother tricked him into a scheme that left him in the hands of the most ruthless vampire that ever lived and for that he had to pay. I feel bad at what Sasha's been through but if he hadn't, me and Velle would never have met him and we're all the better for that, and for

Lincoln too. Sometimes you can't help the cards you've been dealt. You just have to make the best of it.'

'What does he want with Evelyn?'

'He likes her that's all you need to know. Never seen him like that about anyone. Like I said, he tends to keep emotions out of it.'

'She won't be with someone like that.'

'A vampire?' he laughed. 'Well we'll see huh? Be smart, Michael. You might wanna finish that coffee before they return.'

***

SASHA HAD KNOWN BETTER than to speak to Evelyn on the way back. He took her hand as again they moved at speed, arriving at the steps on Fifth Avenue a few moments later.

'I will teach you, so you can do that yourself,' he said.

She realised that in all of Vladimir's books in the study, not one would tell her how to behave as a vampire. No one text embraced it as a living, breathing entity, only a creature, born of superstition that must be repelled at all costs. Pages devoted to the power of religion and defences built on old wives' tales of garlic and crucifixes that she knew first hand were useless. Perhaps no one had ever gotten close enough to such monsters to document them. She could understand that perfectly. The only thing she did know from her studies, was that the night was their friend, the sun their enemy. She did not know why but she supposed the beautiful golden light of the sun was akin to the kingdom of heaven, while the dark night swerved the corners of hell where such abominations flourished. Their place in this world was set and she would have to rely on Sasha for any answers she sought. He watched her as she looked at the slow break of daylight in the east, turning the dark skies a navy blue as it brought the dawn.

'The sun will burn your flesh as hot as any funeral pyre and you will suffer a horrific death at its hands,' he said.

She scoffed at the horrific death she had already endured thanks to him.

'We sleep in protected darkness while the sun shines and when it has set, the night is ours.'

'What if I just stayed here,' she said, 'and let it take me.'

'You could do that but there are plenty of reasons not to, as well you know. Your brother, for instance. What would become of him?'

'Don't threaten me, or my brother' she said. 'I won't be held to ransom.'

'I'm merely stating what you already know. If you are destroyed, he will be too. He has seen too much.'

'And the other reasons?' she asked.

'I think you want to see what Gabriel has planned for you. He believes in you and I haven't yet put my finger on exactly why that is. But *you* know and you're curious. The last reason is me. Gabriel brought us together. In time, I hope that you'll forgive me and look at me the way you did when we met.'

It had been not two days previous and already it felt like a lifetime to her.

'That girl is dead,' she said. 'She was killed by a monster.'

The front door suddenly swept open behind them and Velle stood there excitedly waiting to greet them.

'We thought you weren't coming back. It's almost dawn. You can't keep her to yourself all night Sasha. Oh my,' she said looking at Evelyn's transformation. 'You are exquisite.'

She examined her as one would a museum piece.

'You knew he was going to turn me.'

'Yes, and I for one am glad,' she said. 'But look at your dress. We must rectify that immediately.'

'Where's Michael?' asked Evelyn.

'Talking to Wade in the study.'

'Does he know?' she asked.

Velle shook her head.

'Good,' she said catching sight of herself in the hall mirror. Velle was right. She did look different. Her skin was devoid of the sun's freckles that had dotted her nose and cheeks, as if polished and buffed away. Her complexion was pale, luminous. He would know. There was no concealing it. She opened her mouth half afraid at what might greet her but her teeth were as they had always been, if a little whiter. Velle came to stand beside her, her reflection nothing more than a silver shimmer of light.

'By nightfall tomorrow, yours will be gone too. It's like a light dimmed until it loses all the contours, a memory of a person that's ceased to be.'

'We need to rest now,' said Sasha interrupting. 'The sun is rising. Lincoln is everything ready?'

Lincoln was coming down the stairs with Baker, who was carrying a small toolbox.

'All the necessary windows have been sealed and extra locks put on the doors,' he said.

'I need to see my brother,' she said walking past him to the study.

Inside Michael and Wade sat by the fire. Wade stood as she entered, patting Michael on the shoulder.

'Could you leave us alone please?' she asked.

Wade nodded, taking in the changes in her appearance before looking back to Michael sympathetically.

'Go easy on him. He's had enough liquor to sink a small ship.'

He didn't envy either of them the conversation that was about to take place. Even Mafdet stayed at the door, not following her mistress inside. When Wade closed it behind him, Michael rushed to the window, opening it just enough so that they could climb out.

'Quick, we don't have much time,' he said.

Evelyn stood still, brushing a silky strand of hair behind her ear.

'We can't stay here,' he said motioning to her to hurry. 'What's wrong with you?'

His eyes slowly registered the changes in her appearance.

'I'm so sorry,' she said reaching her hand to him and even that small movement was different as if her body had learned a new rhythm in how it moved. Quicker, more fluid.

'Fuck,' he said, taking a step back from her. 'You look like Velle. Fuck.'

'I didn't choose it. He lied to me.'

She was trying to be strong for him, but her voice was thick with the betrayal, the shame of what they'd done to her. Moreover, she lamented the loss of her power. There was no need to tell him that now. Tell him what had led them to her in the first place. How she had brought this down on them.

'We'll figure something out okay but we need to go. C'mon.'

'I can't leave now,' she said. 'You've seen what they are. They won't let me go and we can't outrun them. But you, on your own, have a chance.'

'I'm not afraid of any of them,' he said. His eyes flickered to the door.

'If you fight they will kill you, Sasha said as much, so this is your chance now. Your chance to get out.'

'What if we fought them together?' he said.

'I don't know how.'

'I'm not leaving you.'

'You have to. There's nothing else they can do to me now. It's done.'

'Really. So, you're going to just stay with them, without me?' He paused. 'I knew he'd done something to you. How could you trust him?'

'You don't understand.'

'Jesus, the first man to turn your head and look what you get into?'

'That's not fair. Besides with you around to bat them away, it's a wonder he got close at all.'

'Yeah well, I've never had to bat away a vampire before have I? Jesus. So, I stay and what?'

'You won't be safe.'

'You can protect me.'

'From them? Michael, I died tonight. Do you understand that? I know no more about the strengths and weaknesses of vampires than you do.'

'Well I'm not leaving without you and I'm not joining their…I don't know what you call it…their coven of whatever… and neither are you. They killed innocent people tonight.'

He went to drag her by the arm, the first light of dawn creeping low through the open window, the air cool, their escape waiting. Evelyn knew it was already too late for her, the first glimpse of the sun waiting to welcome her.

'You are just a toy to them, another trinket like her.'

'Stop it,' she said.

'You did this, you brought this on us. It was you who wanted to come here. We could have gone anywhere. We could have stayed in Liverpool for God's sake.'

'You go. Disappear. Build yourself the life you deserve, have the chance you wanted. You're not bound to me.'

'But you see I am. This is it now. You and me.'

He wasn't going to give up, was he? What if he stayed? He would never forgive Sasha and where would that leave him? Did they even keep humans with them? Would his blood become a temptation? No, he was in danger if he stayed. Getting out was his only chance. She saw no other solution.

'The truth is Michael. I don't want you here with me.'

'Don't say that,' he said.

'Your sister is dead. I belong to Sasha now. You were right. I do like him. From the moment, I saw him. He tells me that soon I'll leave my humanity behind, become that creature that wants only the blood of humans, a killer. That's what I am now – a killer.'

'Stop,' he pleaded.

'I won't need human connection anymore. Sasha's blood is inside me, changing me. I don't need you. The only thing I will ever need from you now, is your blood.'

She grabbed him and flung his body to the floor, using just enough force to scare him. She was different now. Something else. His sister gone. But he didn't run. He just lay there, in confusion.

'Go, before your beating hearts tempts me. Even now,' she said panting, 'it calls to me, drawing me close. I can almost taste it.'

A pain began to build in her sinuses, the bones shifting in her face to allow the first emergence of her supernatural form. Her cheekbones ached and she stretched her mouth open as two knifelike teeth cut through her gums, bringing with it her own blood spilling onto her tongue. She let out a cry of pain as Michael recoiled from her in terror.

'This is what I've become and this is all I want now,' she said, putting her hand on his chest. She brought her mouth close to his, her blood dripping from her lower lip. In his eyes she saw the belief, the horror of what she had become.

'If I ever see you again, I don't know that I could control it.'

She released him and he crawled backwards away from her, finding his feet, clambering for the open window. He took one frightened look back at her before disappearing, his feet scrambling to gain speed, her ears picking up every footstep, as he ran farther away. Gradually her teeth receded back into her gums and she collapsed on the floor. The taste of her own blood had awakened something in her and she was glad he was gone, for she'd spoken the truth.

'Are you happy? Did you get all that?' she said as Sasha came into the room.

He said nothing but took her hand, the journey a flash as seconds later, he tucked her under the covers of the four-poster bed. He pulled the deep red curtains around it as Mafdet curled in beside her. The shutters on the window had been sealed, the room in darkness and Evelyn felt herself give in to her first preternatural sleep.

***

WHEN SHE AWOKE, SHE found Sasha lying beside her. His eyes were closed and she propped her head up on her elbow as she looked at him. She thought of the kiss, the feeling of his lips on hers in the darkness, when he opened his eyes.

'You slept here,' she said.

'I wanted to take care of you.'

'More like, make sure I didn't run away.'

'That too,' he said. 'It's better that Michael left, you know that, otherwise you wouldn't have scared him away.'

'He was so afraid,' she said, falling back away from him.

'That is why we cannot exist side-by-side with them,' he said. 'They are our food when all is said and done and they know it. Are you hungry?'

His question hung in the air as she tried to gather an answer. She was not hungry in any sense she'd known before. There was no growl from her stomach or emptiness in her that yearned for sustenance, but there was something else. She felt a pang in the empty chambers of her heart and she knew she wanted blood, that it would nourish her in ways that food never could. The more she focussed on it, the more she wanted it.

'Show me,' she said.

'Get dressed,' he said hopping up. 'Velle left some clothes for you. We'll hunt alone. I don't want us overwhelming you on your first night.'

When she came down the staircase, he was waiting for her. He wore black tie with an opera cape and top hat and she was glad she'd made an effort. Velle had left three dresses in the armoire for her and she'd chosen a purple gown with a high collar and fitted sleeves that ended in a point on the back of her hands. It was stunning and she felt herself channel some of Velle's confidence as she moved in it. Sasha was lost for words as he swept the cloak around her shoulders and she knew she'd had the desired impact. She squeezed her slender hands into a pair of soft purple gloves and they made their way to their waiting carriage.

'It doesn't always do to whisk about at our own speed,' he said as they passed through the busy streets. 'It is early in the night and we do well to blend in where we can. Also, if you take the pace of humans you are less likely to miss something in observing them and choosing your kill. The choice is so vast Evelyn and you must choose carefully. You will not always crave the same meal. Sometimes it's fine-dining on the decadent and sometimes it's a fast bite of nourishment wherever you can get it, be it the soup kitchen or the tenements. It's the variety that's interesting.'

'What will it be tonight?' she asked, feigning interest.

'Someone deserving of this fate. They are easily plucked off any street. The evil-doer, the thief, the murderer...'

'One murderer killing another,' she said.

'You won't always see it like that,' he said not rising to her cynicism. 'Think of it as ridding this great city of its vermin.'

He tapped his cane on the roof of the carriage and it came to a halt. As he stepped onto the pavement, he reached for her gloved hand, delicate in his own and he held onto it, curling her hand around his arm as they walked, a couple

out for a romantic stroll. At the next corner, two munici-
pal policemen stood with a local merchant, his frock coat
swinging with gusto as he recounted the details of a story,
the two officers rapt with smiling curiosity. Opposite them,
a man was walking but when he caught sight of them, he
swerved into the shadows.

'Him,' Sasha said.

The man had disappeared down a side street but when
they followed, they found nothing but a dead end. Evelyn
could smell him though. She could even hear him breathe.
Close by, hidden. Was he behind her? She was about to turn
when she felt the cool metal of his knife at her neck. The
scent of dried blood rose like nectar to her.

'Don't scream Miss, or I'll slice your throat. I'll be having
your purse now. Sir, your pocketbook too.'

Sasha's hand was on his arm before he knew what was
happening. With a quick twist and kick to the man's legs, he
was on the ground, his knife flying out of his hand. Sasha
held his throat, his body immobilised, his voice unable
to make the scream it wished for. His face was a million
regrets. He had met a foe he should never have troubled
with his petty thievery. Sasha took off his top hat, handing
it to Evelyn, who subconsciously took a step back, hugging
it to her chest.

He picked the thief up and slammed him against the wall.
The impact crumbled the bricks, dusting the air in fine red
powder. He bid his pupil to come closer and she did, the

hunger beginning to rise within her as he quickly slid his hand up to the man's neck. He bit the tender flesh, a flash of blood visible for only a second, before it disappeared into his mouth. The entire world seemed to go quiet and the only sound that Evelyn could hear was the steady loss of a human life, a heartbeat that was only moments before beating rapidly, now slowly succumbing to a dull thud as Sasha drew away its lifeblood. Evelyn felt her own teeth want to burst through but she fought it, her human instinct telling her instead to intervene and save this man from the hands of a monster. But it was too late.

The man's body went limp, as Sasha at last drew back from him, his eyes closed, licking the last of the blood from his lips. He let the body slump to the ground and when the rapture of the kill left him, he looked at her dreamily.

'For such an ugly act, the reward more than overcomes it.'

He gestured for his hat and she gave it to him stepping over the man's body.

'I'll never do that, you know. I'd rather die.'

'Therein lies the problem. If you don't feed, you won't die as a result. You will just grow weak and the hunger will break your will in a never-ending spiral. You will have to face it. You have no choice.'

'You can feed me.'

'We can't feed each other. We can only offer our blood in making you one of us. It is living human blood that will sustain you.'

They walked back onto the street. The policemen were still there and one of them looked their way as Sasha bade them good evening, taking her hand.

'Are you repulsed?' he asked her.

'I am,' she said quietly.

'You're more composed than I thought you would be. You do surprise me Evelyn.'

'You're not the first man to think that,' she said.

30

FOURTEEN NIGHTS PASSED AS Evelyn refused to drink. The night after the killing, she simply refused to leave the house and Sasha went with the others, returning minutes later, fresh blood spilled on his shirt, the result of a rushed feed or perhaps a ploy to have her smell the richness of it and want it for herself. His care of her was straining on the group and as she lay on the bed upstairs with Mafdet, she could hear them discussing her fate as if in the same room.

'It's not normal for a fledgling to refuse to eat. She must be starving. How is she able to resist it?' Wade asked.

'We're all different,' said Sasha. 'Give her time. How long did it take you Lincoln?'

'About five minutes,' he said solemnly. 'But I welcomed the change. She did not. That's the difference.'

'She's holding on too hard to the person she was,' Velle said. 'You have to embrace this otherwise you may as well be dead.'

'She'll come around,' said Sasha hopefully.

'What about Gabriel? Surely he'll intervene?' she said.

'He hasn't so far so he's waiting, like us, to see what she decides herself. If she chooses not to feed than I have no doubt he'll take her and force her to do it. He wanted her a vampire. He's invested in her and he needs her for something. He won't just let her go.'

Mafdet's ears pricked up at the mention of her master's name and Evelyn pet her side gently as they lay together. The lynx turned her head back to her as if to second the thoughts of the group below. As her delicate hands moved through Mafdet's coat, she knew she would have to feed sooner or later. Each night she pushed the desire away, banishing it, but it was getting more difficult as time went on and she knew that she was weak, the strength from Sasha's blood slowly fading. When he appeared in the room a moment later, he read the look on her face.

'Come, I can look at you no longer. You must feed.'

She sat up as Mafdet climbed off the bed, welcoming it after many nights of lying patiently waiting for her mistress to rise.

'Let me take someone who will welcome it,' she said. 'Someone who is waiting for it, the door to the next kingdom already ajar.'

'As you wish,' he said taking her hand.

'I think I know the place,' she said. 'Can we travel over water?'

'We can go where we please, once it's within the hours of night.'

'Take me to Staten Island,' she said, rising swiftly.

31

MICHAEL HAD SLEPT MOST of the journey south, curled into the corner of the stagecoach, his belongings tucked up in a small suitcase beside him. When night came he would wake, watching and listening for them, looking out at the blackness as the carriage rolled on, taking him further and further away from New York. He had no doubt they could use their preternatural senses to sniff him out if close. His only hope was that he had given them the slip and that they like Baker believed he was on a ship back to Ireland. When he'd seen Baker waiting for him at the corner, his immediate instinct was to run from him too, but then he saw the suitcase and the look on Baker's face, almost envious, and he knew he was not there to foil his escape, but to aid it.

'Quickly,' he'd said, hailing a carriage.

Michael climbed in, Baker following close behind.

'Why are you helping me?' he asked.

'Because you are not meant to be around these creatures. You've seen what they are, what they do. They'll kill you, don't think that they won't.'

Michael stuck his head out of the carriage window looking backwards and to the skies.

'I am assured of it Baker, believe me,' he said, his hands shaking as he patted the suitcase on his lap.

'There's a ship sailing tonight for Liverpool. Go back to Ireland and make a life for yourself. Forget this ever happened.'

'Without her?' he said.

'I'm sorry, but you are best to consider your sister dead.'

Michael thought of the blood and her teeth, so close to him.

'Is there any way back for her?'

'To be human again? I'm afraid not. There is no reversing it. It is not a spell of magic. It's a transformation.'

'Can they be killed?'

'Michael, I am giving you an opportunity here.'

'Why are you helping them? Maybe you're hoping they'll change you too, are you?'

'I have my reasons,' he said as they made their way to the port.

Baker bought him his ticket and though they parted with a firm handshake, he did not leave. He waited until the ship's anchor was raised and then satisfied, he left. It began to move slowly away from the pier and Michael saw his chance. He ran across the deck, his case in hand and leapt over the edge. His feet landed inches onto the wooden pier, the weight of his case almost tipping him backwards into the water. He cashed in his ticket at the office, stuffing the bills into his jacket.

He had no intention of leaving America. That was exactly what they wanted, to be rid of him for good. Terrified as he was, he knew he couldn't leave. Baker wasn't going to share any knowledge with him, but not one of these vampires was from New York. They had travelled across America and so would he, until he found the knowledge he was looking for. And so, he found himself journeying by stage to Philadelphia and onwards to Washington, then to Richmond, Virginia through to Greensboro, North Carolina. By the time he reached Georgia, his money was almost spent and he arrived in the thriving city of Atlanta, in the hope of finding lodgings and a hot bath. That night, he sat by his hotel window on Peachtree Street, watching the people below, the sounds of the train whistles echoing as they came into the terminus. As the sun came up, the train workers arrived in their droves, the streets full of carts carrying coal and cargo to the busy station. He walked among them, eating a slice of cornbread, watching them as they scurried about, oblivious to the darkness that prevailed around them. He almost wished he was one of them, carefree and with no knowledge of what lurked in the corners of the night. He longed for the simplicity of his farming life and the sweat and satisfaction of a hard day's work. A sign in the window of a local trading post caught his eye, and instantly he knew it was just what he needed.

LABORERS WANTED.
OAK HILL PLANTATION. (32 Miles).
ASK INSIDE.

The store keeper was a friendly man in a pristine white apron. He said he was in luck, as the plantation's weekly supply wagon would be in town that afternoon and he could talk directly to Oliver Kempner, who looked after the provisions and hiring. Michael liked the look of Kempner as soon as he saw him. He was in his forties, his skin permanently reddened and wrinkled by the hot summers, his hands, like shovels, calloused and coarse skinned as he shook Michael's hand. Within five minutes, Michael was helping him load cartons and boxes into the wagon and the two chatted all the way back to Oak Hill as the sun began to dip into the horizon. The wagon pulled off the main road and down a long path lined with oaks, their branches haunted by the Spanish moss that clung to them like a veil. Michael caught his first glimpse of the house, its white portico columns running the length of the façade. The colonial mansion was like a jewel sitting in the sceptre of a king, the winter sun hitting the windows of the first floor, reflecting its light in beams across the wide balcony overlooking the gardens.

Kempner drove the wagon around to the back. Cotton fields stretched as far as the eye could see, cabins dotted here and there between clumps of trees. The sky was a bruise of deep red and purple, the sun almost gone and as they unpacked their cargo, a man rode up on horseback.

Kempner turned to introduce them.

'Mr. Yates, this is Michael O'Neill,' he said, his southern accent drifting lazily on the evening air. 'A new pair of hands.'

Mr. Yates looked down at him from his horse, sizing him up.

'You're a ways skinny. You got farming experience, boy?'

'Yes, Sir.'

'How long you been in America?'

'A couple of months, Sir.'

'You're in danger of losing that Irish accent of yours,' he said. 'Fella I know, name of Geraghty, forty years in America and never lost his Irish accent, a Cork man …great fella,' he smiled.

'I guess it's leaving me whether I like it or not,' Michael said. 'That's the effect your America is having on me.'

'Show Michael to his quarters. Pay is a dollar a week plus keep.' He nodded his head, clicking his heels into his steed as he headed in the direction of the stables.

'Welcome to Oak Hill,' Kempner said. 'Mr. Yates expects hard work but he's one of the best in these parts. A gentleman.'

Michael's quarters were in a house at the back of the property. He shared it with eight other men, including Kempner who had a room to himself. That evening as they ate a stew of winter vegetables and a chicken, roasted on the open fire, he listened to them talk of his new master.

'God bless Mr. Yates. At least we have our jobs long as he doesn't take them negroes,' said one, his hands grabbing for a piece of bread, the dirt from the fields still under his fingernails.

'Mr. Yates doesn't believe it's right,' said another to Michael 'keeping people like cattle, chaining them up. He's rich so he ain't got the worry of not being able to pay for workers, but some of them plantation owners, they don't got that sort of fortune and they will take that labour from the slaves or hell, they think it's their right to.'

'Count yourself lucky boys, you have the freedom of this fine country,' said Kempner raising his cup of apple cider. 'Here's to freedom.'

'To freedom,' Michael said, raising his cup high into the air.

32

EVELYN FELT THE SOFT earth under her feet as they came to rest on the rain soaked grass of Tompkinsville. Before them loomed the gates of the Quarantine Maritime Hospital, a walled compound of twenty or so buildings containing over a thousand sick and dying souls, who never made it into New York Harbour.

'It's perfect,' said Sasha.

She realised she was still holding his hand and she let go. As they had glided over the waves, she was pretty sure she knew how to keep herself above the water without his help, but she was hungry and didn't want to let go, for fear her weakness would cause her to tumble into its icy depths. Inside the gates, the grounds were quiet and Sasha moved to an open window, quickly disappearing inside.

She joined him as they moved through rows of beds. Most of the windows were open, in the hope of cooling the feverous. Patients stirred, groaning through their agony as others slept soundly, glad of a night's respite, free to dream that soon they would leave there with a cheery goodbye and be on their way – though the potter's field, not far from there told another story.

A nurse sat at one end writing up her records, every now and then glancing down the room. They kept to the shadows, disappearing through a door at the far end. The smell of soap and camphor filled the air and Evelyn paused, allowing her vampiric senses to guide her. Two doctors passed them consumed in conversation, oblivious to their night time visitors hiding in the gloom. When they had turned a corner, she stopped at a set of doors, her fingers running over the letters painted there – *Critical Care*. Could it be? She slowly opened the door, her hand trembling.

Three beds lay against the wall. Two were empty, as if recently stripped of their bedclothes, the stained mattresses telling a thousand tales, while the far bed was a mini fortress, a framed green curtain fencing it off from the rest of the room. She felt the tiny muscles in her gums flex, her teeth yearning to come through. Her fingertips brushed the fabric, pulling the screen away and there in its protection lay Lawrence Sherlock. The young man's skin was the colour of spoiled milk, his eyes sunken into the dark circles that swept under them. He had lost weight and his bony arms lay either side of him, on top of the hospital blanket. His chest barely moved as he breathed, the air no more than a harsh crackle as he exhaled, his chin lopping downwards on his chest. Evelyn could hear the rumble of each expiration, his lungs laboured, his weakened heart slowly beating its way to the end. She touched his forehead softly and he stirred, his eyes opening for a moment trying to focus before giving in and closing again.

'Don't be afraid,' she whispered. 'God will welcome you into his kingdom this night,' she said, the words heavy to her, her own dismantled faith making a liar of her. He tried again to open his eyes, seeing her this time and a single tear rolled out of the corner of his eye. She was helping him. She just had to focus on that. Her lips brushed against his cheek and she kissed him – an apology for what she was about to do. She moved to the soft flesh of his neck. Her sharp teeth projected from her gums at the feel of his skin and then they were inside, cutting deep with very little effort. She felt the blood rush into her mouth, warm and metallic, her body savouring it, allowing it to find those parts of her that needed its strength, building the new vampire, making her strong. As she drank, an image of Lawrence came into her mind, of him sat on his bunk on The Eleanora, telling stories from home. A happy, hopeful young man with the sweetest smile on his face. She gagged as her mind took over the act, her repulsion overpowering her body's yearning for it. His blood caught in her throat, and she spat it out, a red pool on the floor. Panicked, she took a cloth from his bedside to clean it up.

'Don't waste it!' said Sasha incredulously.

She brought the blood-soaked cloth up from the floor and threw it at him.

'Here,' she cried 'you have it.'

Lawrence let out a sudden groan that startled them both.

'Finish it,' Sasha said. 'You owe him that.'

She turned her back to him, leaning in towards the wound. She allowed her desire for his blood to rise. She must end his suffering, and her own. This time her body welcomed every drop and she drank until she felt his heart take its last leap and she withdrew, knowing he was gone.

'We need to leave,' said Sasha still holding the bloodied cloth. 'You will learn that it's best not to leave evidence of your visit.'

She stood back. Her legs felt like jelly and Sasha caught her arm, before they failed her.

'Steady yourself. It takes a little while for it to work its magic the first time until you get used to it,' he said.

'Monster,' she said as he grasped her hand.

The hospital disappeared and just before sunrise, they were back in their room, safe from the sun's gaze.

'Now you sleep,' he said, 'and tomorrow night, we will try again.'

Within ten minutes he was sleeping the sleep of the dead beside her, Mafdet curled into a ball at his feet. Evelyn couldn't contemplate rest. She could feel Lawrence's blood in her veins, like a poison infecting her with this immortality and she hated how her body had welcomed it. Michael had been gone two weeks and every night she thought of him, alone on his journey back home. Baker had told her that he'd followed him to the docks, where he'd stowed away on a ship bound for Liverpool and her heart sank as she thought of him alone and scared, fleeing a country that was to be a dream but had turned into a hellish nightmare.

She wept at the memory of his terror-stricken face and the thoughts of never being able to make that journey across nights and days to see him again. The taste of blood rose again in her mouth and she despised herself for it. She swung her legs off the bed, an idea forming in her mind, seducing her with its simplicity. Silently she lifted the drape around the bed and stepped onto the floorboards, hoping they wouldn't creak under her bare feet and give her away. She slipped out onto the landing, where she stopped.

The sun was rising and it streamed a long rectangle of light towards her from the window. She tiptoed down the landing towards it, edging forward until her toes met the shaft of light. She wriggled them in its warmth, waiting. When nothing happened, she took a step boldly into it, drowning herself from head to toe in the warm bright sunlight. Still nothing. Confused she waited there a few seconds more and then scampered down the stairs to the front door, throwing it open and running out into the street. How was it supposed to begin? She imagined the warmth would start to intensify, then her flesh would redden and perhaps blister before bursting into flames or instantly turning her to ash. But none of those things happened. The sun's heat penetrated her skin but no more than she felt on any other normal day when she was alive. She looked back to the house. Had Sasha told her the truth? He must have for that's the way he lived, out of the sun's glare for fear of destruction. The others too. She wasn't going to die in that moment – not that way.

She hurried down the avenue, the road busy with morning traffic. In desperation, she flung herself out in front of a carriage. Her body slammed into the two black horses with such force, that it broke the legs of both animals. They fell onto the cobbles, crushing her underneath as the carriage overturned, throwing its driver to the pavement. Passers-by screamed. Anyone else would have died there and then, yet all that Evelyn suffered was the painful truth that she had caused harm where there was no need. She was truly inde-structible. And she had injured two horses in the hope of defying it. She rose from under them, horrified and ashamed. A crowd were gathering and she knew that she had to flee. She moved quickly, vanishing from sight and soon she was miles away, standing at the water's edge, as the morning sun glistened on its surface.

When she returned to the house, Mafdet was waiting for her and they slept together curled up beside Sasha, Evelyn's tears soaking into her soft fur. When darkness came, Sasha awoke with a start. His hand sprung across to feel her beside him. She opened her eyes looking at him.

'I dreamt you had been killed,' he said disorientated.

'Do we still dream?' she asked.

'Every day is a dream,' he said. 'Come, let's hunt.'

33

'Oh, my dear Louisa, it's simply divine,' she said, the fruit cake shifting slowly back and forth into the corners of her mouth. 'You must give me the recipe and I'll get Annie to make it for me at once. I don't know where you find the time for baking yourself – and the mess, well you must be covered in flour by the time you're done.'

'I don't mind, Ashleigh. I like baking,' said her friend, delighted with such fine praise.

'Well, you're so good at it,' she said. 'And I only brought you a jar of Annie's pickles. What must you think of me?'

'Annie's are the finest in the county. Everyone knows that.'

'Yes, we're lucky to have her. Such a fine cook. Well, I'm afraid I must get on. Father will be wondering where I've gotten to. Merry Christmas, my dear friend,' she said grasping her hands.

The girls stood, the bustles on their dresses falling in layers behind them as they embraced, and Louisa Yates knew that the best of her day was already behind her. Not even a present from her parents could equal the joy of a visit from

Miss Ashleigh Boudreaux. She was one of the most popular young women in the county and the prettiest, known for her beaming smile and signature blond ringlets that bounced as she walked. They swung merrily either side of her head as she waved an enthusiastic goodbye, holding the pound cake, as a large negro man helped her into their cart, before taking the reins.

Ashleigh sat quietly and patiently at his side as they left the grounds, her feet tapping ever so slightly up and down and when they had cleared the house from view, she tossed the cake high into the passing trees where it landed with a thud. Free of it, she broke her silence.

'I almost spat it out, Bailey. Right there in front of her. An odious thing. I don't know who told that girl she could bake. You wouldn't feed that to anyone. Not even you,' she said, nudging him, a joke just between them. 'Now hurry up, I want to get home,' she said.

Bailey didn't respond, his eyes forward on the road, flapping the reins to hasten their journey. He had learned very early on not to engage in conversation with his owners, lest you find yourself at the wrong end of a whip. So, he did what he always did. He simply shut out her voice, pretending she wasn't there. He'd been at the Boudreaux plantation for all seventeen of her years, watched her grow from a beautiful baby into a horrible child, and then a nasty young woman. Perhaps Miss Louisa had tried to poison her. Wouldn't that be nice?

Lost in thought, he only saw the flash of fur at the last minute, as an animal darted out in front of them. He pulled the reins to the right, the cart swerving but their speed coupled with it, sent them into the rocky roadside. Wood crunched on stone as the front wheel splintered then broke, sending the cart over on its side. Bailey and Ashleigh were thrown forward, Bailey out onto the road, Ashleigh held captive, her dress caught, pinning her to it.

Along the road, Michael was on his way back to Oak Hill, having delivered a Christmas goose to the Reverend and his wife in town. The first thing he heard was a high-pitched squealing, like a wild animal in distress. Then it took human form in the words, 'Bailey! Bailey!' yelled at the top of the squealer's voice. The tone was one of anger more than peril, and as he came upon them, he saw the young woman or rather part of her concealed beneath an upturned scarlet dress, her white bloomers and stockings exposed. Her foot was trapped and a black man, Bailey, he presumed, was trying to free her.

'Get your hands off me, Bailey,' she screamed. She stopped when she saw Michael, her eyes lighting up at the prospect of some real help. Climbing quickly into the upturned cart, he freed the piece of broken wood that held her captive, slipping her foot out as Bailey grabbed her under the arms. When she had two feet planted firmly on the ground, she struck the man, not with force but with feeble dissatisfaction.

'Bailey, you idiot. I could have been killed.' Her gold ringlets bounced wildly as she hit out at him and though a foot taller than her, he appeared to cower from her touch. It was obviously an accident, the man visibly shaken.

'I can take you home?' he suggested to them both. 'Miss, are you hurt?'

'Oh, nothing a hot bath won't sort out,' she said with mock bravery. 'One of these days Bailey will kill us all – just to avoid the local beasts on our roads. Sir, your offer is kindly accepted. I don't suppose I'm going home in this.'

She kicked the cart hard with her good foot like a spoilt child. She winced in pain and for a moment Michael thought he saw a glimmer of a smile pass across Bailey's face.

'Bailey, stay with the cart. I'll get one of the others to come back for you. Father won't be happy you know.'

Turning to Michael with a demure smile, she said: 'My name is Ashleigh Boudreaux. May I lean on you, Sir?' she said taking his arm, limping on her sore foot. 'I don't know what I would have done if you hadn't come by.'

Michael helped her into the cart, sure that it was a relief for her man servant not to have to listen to her whine any longer. As they rode along, she continued her rant.

'My father will be livid. That Bailey – a useless aide if ever there was one. He'll get fifty lashes of the whip for this one.' Michael resisted the sudden urge to push her out of the moving cart. He allowed himself the daydream of it and then realised she was asking him something.

'I said where are you from? Your accent. Are you a northerner?'

'New York,' Michael said.

'Ah you see I knew it!' she exclaimed. 'Are you passing through?'

'Actually, I'm working at Oak Hill,' he said.

'Oh.' Her interest dropped immediately and he sensed she was sorry she asked.

'Not quite the knight in shining armour you were hoping for?' he said.

'This is just the worst day,' she sighed.

It was only when they pulled up to the Boudreaux plantation of Raven Wood, that she quickly re-evaluated her rescuer. Her older sister Marianne came out to greet her and was unable to hide her excitement on meeting the attractive stranger who had come to her sister's aid. She blushed as he extended his hand to her in greeting, his clear blue eyes meeting hers. Rugged and a little rough around the edges perhaps but Ashleigh had to admit he was handsome and his value once again began to rise, labourer or not. She regaled her sister with her terrifying ordeal and the bravery and chivalry of her dashing saviour. Near hysterical with both horror and excitement at the story, Marianne ran inside to fetch her father, Alfred.

'I shall ask my father to give you a job,' she said. 'Mr. Foster, our overseer, can always do with another pair of hands where the slaves are concerned.'

'I like to find my own way, thank you Miss Boudreaux.'

'Don't be silly. I shall insist upon it.'

'I already have a job,' he said.

'Nonsense, now come inside and meet my father,' she said grabbing him by the arm and marching up the porch steps. As they did, a shriek came from inside and Michael thought to himself that the apple hadn't fallen too far from the tree. Mrs. Boudreaux came flapping down the hall, clutching a lace handkerchief to her mouth, followed by her husband.

'Oh Mama, the fool crashed the carriage,' Ashleigh squealed, her pitch even higher than before.

'My dear child, are you hurt? Who is this young man?'

As Ashleigh explained the circumstances again, adding extra flourish to every detail, Alfred Boudreaux shook Michael's hand. He shouted to the young farm hand, who had come to tend to Michael's horse.

'Thomas,' he barked, 'you go now and get Bailey and that carriage back here, do you hear? And be quick about it.'

Michael saw the look of concern on the young man's face.

'He's okay,' Michael offered to him. 'Probably just a little bruised.'

'He'll be black and blue by the time I've finished with him,' snorted Mr. Boudreaux.

'He'll need a new wheel too,' Michael said ignoring the older man's comments.

'Please come join us inside for a glass of eggnog. Annie makes the best there is and it is Christmas after all,' said Mr. Boudreaux.

'I'm afraid I must be getting back, but thank you, Sir,' said Michael.

'Nonsense,' he said with the same dismissiveness as his daughter. 'I insist.'

A moment later they were all seated in the living room, Ashleigh moving quickly to secure the seat beside Michael before Marianne could, a smirk of defiance as she smoothed out her skirts.

'Don't you want to change?' asked Marianne spitefully.

'I will in a moment. Why, I'm still shaking. A glass of eggnog will soothe my nerves.'

Michael looked about the room. It was a shrine of wealthy decadence, with the loveliest Christmas decorations he'd ever seen. They even had a tree on which hung sugared fruits and handmade garlands of popcorn strings and beads, the branch tips sugared like snow. A bushy green garland extended over the mantelpiece with sprigs of holly worked through, their shiny red berries like rubies among the foliage.

The sound of tinkling crystal glasses signalled the arrival of the eggnog, carried on a large silver tray. Michael breathed a sigh of relief, eager to drink it as fast as he could and get away from this family – so spoilt and blindsided by their wealth that they had abandoned the most humane behaviour to their fellow man. He looked at the tray bearer and was struck suddenly by a sight so vibrant as to render the rest of the room to a dull grey. Elegant hands held tightly to the tray, the rolled-up sleeves of her cornflower blue dress, stark against her dark skin. Her white apron layered over it, was pulled tightly around her waist and her hair was concealed beneath a woven red cloth, revealing the stark beauty of her face. As she brought the tray to him he took a glass, thanking her, meeting her brown eyes but for a moment, before they looked away. She was judging him with *them*, he thought and he wanted to stand up immediately and denounce such a practice.

'Hurry up, Salome,' said Ashleigh grabbing a drink from the tray as the girl moved past her to tend to the others. When she was finished, she went and stood beside the walnut sideboard, the empty tray flat in her hands. She did not look at them but every now and then Michael couldn't help glancing at her, as Ashleigh once again recounted their perilous adventure. Secretly he hoped she was listening, him being the hero of the piece but her face remained stoic, her eyes staring in front of her, until Mrs. Boudreaux declared she could clear the empty glasses. They were right, the eggnog was truly delicious, the brandy warming his throat, while the cinnamon and nutmeg played on his tongue, new tastes he had never encountered before. As he finished the last sip, he rose, sure that Mr. Kempner would by now have thought him very late.

'Very well,' said Mr. Boudreaux, half to him and half to his precocious daughter who had leapt to his side and was whispering excitedly in his ear. Michael bade goodbye to Marianne and her mother as they stepped out into the hall.

'Thank you again Michael for coming to the aid of my daughter,' said Mr. Boudreaux.

'Anyone would have, Sir,' he said.

'Well be that as it may, my daughter wants me to give you a job and what my Ashleigh wants, she tends to get,' he said with a note of exasperation.

Michael smiled. 'I appreciate it Sir, I do, but I have a job at Oak Hill that does me just fine.'

'She will be disappointed,' he sighed. 'I can pay you well. Whatever you're getting at Oak Hill, I'll double it.'

Michael was about to refuse again when he caught sight of Salome in the hallway, carrying out the empty glasses. As she moved by Ashleigh, the girl bumped her arm purposely, causing them to shake and fall on the tray. Salome tried her best to balance them before they crashed to the floor.

'You should be more careful, Salome,' she said.

Michael hesitated before extending his hand to Mr. Boudreaux.

'Sir, it sounds like an offer I can't refuse. When do I start?'

34

SINCE THEIR VISIT TO Staten Island, Evelyn had again refused to feed with the others. She would accompany them as they dined on prince and pauper and Gabriel allowed them to hunt in Manhattan once they adhered to the rules.

'You will grow weak again,' Sasha said, the taste of blood fresh on his tongue as they walked through Union Square, the trees shading them from the moon's light.

'You don't need to worry about me,' she said.

'Why won't you talk to me? I can help you.'

'Like you've helped me already? I can take care of myself. If I want to speak to someone, I'll speak to Gabriel.'

'Perhaps he'll take you from me,' he said. 'I only did as he asked and yet you persecute *me* instead of him.'

'Your will is your own,' she said.

'Not always,' he replied. 'I'm sorry if you do not like this afterlife you have been given, and that you befell it by my hand, but you can't hold on to your resentment indefinitely, for it will never end and this life, as it is, will be worth nothing. Like human life, this existence is what you make it. I was a prisoner for many years after my changing, so I know what you're feeling and how you must wish for death, as I did. But things happen and the world changes and one day you find yourself free to roam again, to experience all that this world has to offer, and even to grasp some humanity from it. I had to come back for Vladimir. I had to see his betrayal face to face and when I did I couldn't bear it. I wanted him to see the horror of what I had become, know the fate he left me to endure. As my brother, that's unforgiveable. I honestly didn't know if I would do it but then I saw him, this grey-haired man, who had wasted the life he was given. No wife, no family – a joyless life, shared with no-one, wasted on his pursuit of useless knowledge.'

'Where is he now?' she said.

'He's in the Hudson or probably The Narrows by now, whatever's left of him. You'll soon come to realise that you cannot feel remorse for those undeserving of their lives. The ne'er-do-wells, the thieves, murderers, betrayers – they will never by mourned by us, our family, and while you are right to seek the infirm, who may welcome your kiss, you can also prey on those that prey on the innocent.'

'A protector?' she said.

'Yes, an aide to humanity. That's what Gabriel wants I think. Not many of our kind tread as carefully as we do.'

'Are there many of us?'

'I suspect so, but this country is so vast that it allows us to move about with ease. Who knows how many there are or how many in Europe, even your homeland.'

'I don't think there are any in Ireland,' she said.

'Of course, there are. Where there is human life, we exist. Do you think all your dead are the result of famine?' he asked.

'You're teasing me now.'

'Where there is great loss of life, they gather, a chance to be invisible.' He paused. 'You thought it a condition of this continent alone?'

'I suppose I did,' she said.

'Talk to Gabriel, he has a path for you. One you may be happy to be on. Now will you please feed?'

'Tomorrow,' she said resting her hand on his. 'Tonight, you take me to Gabriel.'

His concern for her was genuine and she felt the guilt begin to gnaw at her conscience for not confessing, that first of all, she was alarmingly immune to the power of the sun and secondly that she had now chosen daylight hours in which to hunt. There was something about the beginning of a new day, bright light across winter skies, when people were just preparing for the possibilities it may bring. It was a time when the city was vibrant and she loved it. Streets flooded with people as they made their way to work; businessmen in fine carriages, news boys for The New York Tribune and the Aurora yelling the headlines, bakers in white aprons delivering hot baked bread, nannies wheeling prams and holding the hands of children as they walked in the park.

She would sit in the window of the Tontine Coffee House, a hotel once devoted to the business of stocks and trade, and watch all these people living their precious lives. Of course, the city was not without its undesirables, preying on its good souls. There were pickpockets on every corner. Even children as young as seven and eight working in pairs. One would fall at a gentleman's feet, while the other delicately and with lightning speed, lifted their leather pocketbooks, as they bent over to help.

So taken was she by their antics, that she had followed two boys that very morning. She watched as they handed over their loot to an old beggar in the lane behind the Park Theatre. His hair was lank and greasy beneath a crumpled hat that sat back on his ears. He wore a pair of fingerless gloves, his dirty fingers protruding, as he wrapped his treasures in a scruffy old cloth, sending the boys on their way. As they turned to go, he grabbed one of them by the shoulder, thrusting his hand into the pocket of his jacket. He withdrew a coin and gave him a hard slap to the head for his impertinence. With that the other boy fished out his own and handed it over, thankful not to receive a thick ear for his trouble. They ran off back into the throng, as the man wandered down the lane, glancing around before removing two bricks from the end wall, securing the stash safely inside.

He was so absorbed in his task, that he never heard her approach, and he jumped when he turned around and saw her standing there. Did he think her a threat? Not likely, but she had seen his hiding place and with a click, he drew out his switchblade. He swiped it at her, hoping to frighten her but she didn't move. When he came at her again, she caught his hand, crushing his fingers as he dropped the knife. She welcomed the surprise on his face, the disbelief that a woman could best him – that she was strong enough and smart enough to do so. She sent him backwards with a shove. His hat sailed away as his body hit the wall and he fell, gasping for breath. Oh, he knew now. He was no match for her. He tried to crawl away, but she pulled him upwards by his ankle and turned him mid-air, sending him crashing down on his back. He didn't move and she suspected he'd broken several bones.

The desire to feed overwhelmed her and she took his hand, biting hard into his wrist. She could enjoy this moment away from Sasha's glare, allow herself the satisfaction the blood brought, without any criticism. She did it her way and she felt no remorse for it. At least she agreed with Sasha on that. If she chose well, there would be no remorse. Only a feeling of rapturous pleasure.

When she was done, she felt an urge within her, a familiar feeling reborn. She cradled his head in her hands, the strength of his blood flowing through her veins, and she felt it grow stronger and stronger, until her fingers tingled at the prospect. Strands of his hair began to singe beneath her fingers, catching fire, the flames spreading quickly down his body. They made light work of him, his clothes disintegrating, the smell of his roasting flesh but for a second before a final surge of heat and then they vanished. All that remained was a charred corpse of black and grey speckled ash.

Evelyn sat back on her knees in wonder. The fire was still part of her, now stronger than before. And she was so glad of its return. For the first time since her transformation, she felt like her old self. Her energy, her passion and she realised that she was now very powerful indeed. As she stood, she shook the soot from her cloak, small fragments of ash lifting into the air, before his remains collapsed, sending black snowflakes cascading around her.

35

JERAMIAH FOSTER HAD TAUGHT Harley Kramer all he knew about rope making and the art of tying knots. His own father had shown him when he was just a boy, and it was a skill he felt his privilege to pass on to those around him. As Michael arrived at the overseer's cottage that night to introduce himself, Foster was on the front porch demonstrating the fine art of noose making to his willing pupil.

'Aw, I almost got it that time,' Harley said, as he pulled tightly on the rope, the noose unravelling.

'You tie a noose like that, you're gonna be chasing that negro for a mile before you catch him again. You make a noose, you gotta make sure it's nice and tight.'

Foster only then looked up at the intrusion and saw Michael standing there.

'You the new boy?' he said, his eyes squinting at him.

'Yes, Sir,' Michael said, looking at the perfect noose dangling from Foster's hand.

'Mr. Boudreaux said you'd be coming down. I hope you got the dedication – them slaves is hard work. Harley, take the boy on over to the cabin and show him the slave quarters too, let him get his bearings. It's a five am start. You miss it, you're out.'

Michael said nothing as Harley, himself only a year or two older than Michael, led him through the cypress trees. He was slight of build, with hair like straw, shoved back behind his ears. As he grinned proudly, rows of brownish yellow teeth urged themselves from his mouth, twisted and buckled at the front, as if in a rush to escape their host. He has stopped walking, pointing to a small grove containing two small but well-built cabins.

'That there's your one, on the right. The small one. Not been occupied for a while, needs cleaning but I'll get a slave on it. You worked with them before?'

'No,' Michael said. 'But I've got the drift of it.'

'You ain't never seen nothing like them. You have to watch yourself. They are wily creatures. You gotta keep them in line.'

'How long have you been here?' Michael asked.

'Since I was fifteen. After my daddy died, Mr. Foster offered me a job and my Mama said it was too good an opportunity to turn down. He's a great man.'

Michael doubted it, going by his rope making class and as he followed him, their path darkened, the trees more closely set, their trunks majestic columns rising from the earth. Set behind them in a clearing were a row of six wooden shacks resting on each other for support with loose planks and gaping holes apparent in each. If these people were such an asset to the running of the plantation, it didn't show in their housing.

Outside one, a campfire smouldered, the last wisps of black smoke curling in the air. Harley stomped his foot through it, spreading the ash and half-burnt sticks with his boot.

'What did I say about fires out here!' he shouted. 'Come on out here, y'all. Come on now.'

Slowly people started to emerge, the young men first, their eyes tired, their expression weary, followed by the older slaves, including Bailey. He was carried under the arms by two others, one of which was Salome, her short hair without its turban. Forty slaves lined the front of the shacks and Harley surveyed them all, counting them. Michael hadn't noticed the whip on Harley's belt until he unleashed it, the leather flying out with a crack.

'Listen up. This is Mr. Michael. He is working for Mr. Foster now and for me,' he said with pride. 'He'll be keeping a close eye, so you watch yourselves now and behave. I'll be getting you a whip tomorrow,' he said to Michael. 'So, who here lit that fire? Come on, own up. I don't want to have to punish all of ya.'

Salome stood out from the rest of them without hesitation.

'I did Mr. Harley,' she said.

Immediately he gravitated towards her, his eyes delighted that the prize was such a pretty one.

'You know the rules Salome, don't you? You'll burn this forest to the ground and the rest of us with it. One stove not enough for ya?' he said sweeping his hand from the start of the line to the end.

'Sir, the stove top is full. I only lit the fire to boil up some mullein leaves for Bailey's wounds,' she said, her eyes never leaving Harley as he moved closer.

'Well Bailey got what he deserved, didn't he now?' he said turning towards Michael. 'Show him Bailey,' he said. 'Show Mr. Michael the punishment that is dealt when you do things wrong.'

Bailey winced as he moved and Salome went to help him.

'You stay where you are,' said Harley. 'Leave him be.'

Bailey removed his shirt with difficulty, the fabric clinging to the sores on his back and turned to show them. The rest of the slaves remained very still, no emotion on their faces. Michael fought to contain himself when he saw the state of the man's back, layers of skin torn away, weeping red furrows criss-crossed all over his skin. Every inch of his back was covered not only in this punishment, but the raised scars of years of abuse, etched like a hellish map down the poor man's spine.

Harley watched Michael's reaction closely. 'What do ya think a' that?'

Michael took his eyes off Bailey. 'Did you do that?'

'I sure did,' he said proudly, 'though Mr. Foster likes to add a few himself too. Just to make sure the message hits home, ya know.'

'It's going take a lot of practice, to be as good as you two,' Michael said.

Harley laughed. 'Well there's a whole line of practice right there in front of you, whenever ya want.'

'What about that one to clean my cabin?' Michael said pointing to Salome who was still out in front of them.

Harley shook his head. 'No, that one deserves a good whooping for the fire.'

'I'll give it to her,' Michael said, 'right after she cleans my cabin.'

Harley wagged a finger at him. 'Don't you go getting no ideas here, Michael. Salome is Mr. Foster's, to do with as he will. So, have her clean only your cabin,' he said guffawing. Michael wanted to punch him right in that bedraggled mouth of his.

'Alright get back inside,' he shouted as they left the clearing, dragging Salome by the hand.

When they reached his cabin, he let go of her, shoving her towards Michael.

'Put your shoulder into each crack of the whip. It'll strike harder,' he said. 'You'll pick it up. Here you can use mine tonight. I'm going back to the boss's house, see if I can't make me the perfect noose.'

He threw the curled-up whip to Michael, who caught it in one hand and walked off through the trees, whistling happily through his buckled teeth. Michael tried the rusted door handle expecting some resistance but it opened easily. He stepped back for her to enter, and she stood still, as if to go inside would somehow give her permission for what might happen within its walls.

'It's okay,' he said softly. 'I won't hurt you.'

She raised her eyes for the first time to look at his face, seeking the sincerity of his words.

'Harley uses this place sometimes,' she said as he stepped inside lighting a lantern. He was about to ask her what she meant but he caught the look of repulsion on her face.

'I see,' said Michael, a knot of disgust tying itself in his stomach. 'Did he take you here?'

'Oh me, no,' she said. 'I'm Mister Foster's. He won't let Harley touch me.' Her words stung him as he imagined the life she and the other women had there.

'You have nothing to fear from me. I promise you that,' he said.

She followed him inside, the room dimly lit by the lantern, the corners still dark. There was only a bed and a small stove but the floor was full of dried mud and leaves as if they had flown in to escape the season and dried there on the floor, now brittle under their feet.

'Harley never closes the door much. No other folks come down here.'

Michael grabbed an old broom and began to sweep them, first into a pile in the middle of the room and then towards the door, expelling them furiously back out into the open, them and the business that brought them in. Salome joined him, filling her apron and shaking them outside where they flew away into the breeze.

'You're not going to whip me, are you?' she said, coming back inside.

'No, no I'm not.'

He expected her to thank him then realised that she didn't owe him that. Instead she continued her work, her step a little lighter than before.

'Can I ask, do you like Miss Ashleigh?' she said.

'What makes you say that?'

'Well she wanted you to stay. I heard her tell her Mama so.'

'Do you think that's why I stayed?'

'I don't know. You're not like Harley or the others and she's pretty,' she said crushing the leaves as she carried them outside. He joined her on the porch, the broom catching the last of them.

'I don't see it,' he said pausing to look at her, awaiting her reaction. If she was pleased she didn't show it.

'You need the money, maybe for your family?' she suggested.

'Nope,' he said. He caught the look of relief this time before she could hide it, and realising her mistake, she smiled at him.

'I stayed because I saw how they treated you and it's not right.'

'So, you're a crusader, here to save us all, is that it?' she said shaking her head.

'Maybe,' he said defiantly, 'maybe all of you, maybe just one of you. I stayed because here, I have something to fight against, and I need a good reason to keep fighting because the world's gone to hell and there are still some good people in it, fighting back.'

'Is this fighting?' she said.

'You're staying alive and you're helping your people,' he said. 'You fight every day.'

'You don't belong here.'

'Neither do you,' he said.

'You're going to get yourself killed. They may hate us but Mister Foster hates your kind even more. Them that don't understand the order of things in the south.'

'Not everyone agrees with him. Mr. Yates at Oak Hill doesn't keep slaves. He's a good man.'

'Oh, you think he'll give me a job if I asked...maybe walk on outa here with a nice reference from Mrs. Boudreaux. Sure.'

Michael realised his naivety.

'I'm sorry,' he said. 'I didn't mean to offend you. I only want to help.'

'You need to help yourself outa this mess,' she said, 'You're gonna get yourself in trouble.'

'I'm already in trouble,' he said. He knew it. He wanted to right any wrong ever done to her. Help her, save her, love her. Everything. Now.

'You're dangerous,' she said. 'Not like the others. Danger in a whole other way.'

She put her hand to his arm. A stray leaf sat on his shirt sleeve and she removed it, letting it flutter to the floor.

'When you live...no survive, as we do, you learn that each day could be your last. Nothing is planned but no good minute is taken for granted.'

She edged closer and he didn't dare move, leaning up to kiss his cheek, her breath warm on his skin. He wanted to put his arms around her but he was afraid of ruining it. It was her choice to make.

'I never kissed a dead man before,' she whispered.

She drew back and he didn't know whether to smile at her or not.

'Will Harley check if I punished you?' he said.

'No, I don't think so but you should pretend to crack that whip just in case.'

As Harley sat on the porch of Foster's house putting the finishing touches to his latest noose, Salome's tortuous cries carried to his ears. The new boy was doing good on his practice, Harley thought, pulling tightly on the noose as it held its knot. Perfection at last.

36

EVELYN FOUND THE DESCENT into Gabriel's underground labyrinth so much easier to navigate this time. Her vision in the darkness was impeccable and she could make out every skull and with it every fracture, chip and concave bone that went into its construction. She wondered at the cause of such damage. Were they made while flesh or simply in the building of this strange haven beneath the city?

Sasha walked in front of her, taking her hand as the path forked. He led her to the right, as it sloped downwards deeper into the earth and the cavern opened before them. This time it was empty – no revellers or curiosity seekers. Only Gabriel lying on his back among the stone slabs, his eyes closed, his hands resting casually on his bare chest, the sides of his long morning coat draping over the edge. As they approached, he sat up, drawing his boots up underneath him to sit cross-legged, like a wicked pixie sitting on a toadstool. He had painted his eyes with kohl from corner to corner, dark smears trailing down to his jawline – a warrior ready for battle.

'Come, come, my friends. Please sit,' he said pointing to a stone opposite him. 'We have so much to discuss, but firstly Evelyn you must tell us of your discovery. There can be no secrets now.'

Evelyn pulled herself up to sit on the tomb opposite him. She prepared herself, straightening her back, readying herself for their reaction.

'I am immune to the sun,' she said. 'I have tested it many mornings and it does not seek to change me in any way. If anything, it strengths me,' she said, smirking at Sasha who looked dumbfounded beside her.

'That's not possible. I have seen the ashes of vampires left in the sun to perish,' he said.

'Go on, Evelyn,' said Gabriel, raising his hand to silence him.

'My fire gift has returned to me.'

Gabriel smiled, beaming from ear to ear.

'That is very good news indeed. Have you tested it?'

'Yes.'

'On a human?'

Evelyn looked confused. 'Yes, of course.'

She told them about the inferno she had brought to the man and they listened intently. The more she spoke, the more hurt Sasha's expression and she felt only the slightest tinge of guilt. Gabriel though, was delighted, a headmaster pleased with his prized pupil.

'Then you are ready my dear for what is to come, and not a moment too soon. You are a vampire Evelyn, but also a weapon against your own kind. You are a walking sun to your night time enemies, capable of destroying them with your power. A secret weapon to assist us and mankind against the foe that is making its way here. Sasha, your maker Woltacht has gathered an army and sends them now to lay waste to this city. It is our task to stop them.'

'Woltacht is dead,' Sasha said.

'I'm afraid not.'

'How else would I have escaped him? He kept me like an animal in a cell, weakened and hungry for blood. The night I left I awoke to find my cell and so many others open and I was the only one left. I walked outside to the courtyard and a rain of ashes from the hundred or so bodies disintegrated from the daylight. He was among them, his cloak resting among his remains. I left that night and thanked the heavens that I had been spared this mass suicide and been given a chance.'

'By him?'

'By…'

'God?' said Gabriel.

'I had my freedom and I took it and I sought out my brother, the only person I could punish for what had happened to me.'

'Woltacht didn't sacrifice himself with his men. He lives. He moved beyond the Kolyma Mountains, taking the chosen few.'

'I don't believe you. Why would he let me go?'

'He took you in the first place because he knew he was about to be infiltrated, I don't know how. Regardless, he turned you. Favoured you for immortality over a blood slave, thinking that he would one day send you back to your brother and ultimately to me. And here you are…the infiltrator.'

'You think me a spy?' Sasha said, his eyes shooting between Gabriel and Evelyn.

'Are you?'

'No! I thought he was dead. I had no knowledge of this.'

Gabriel uncurled his legs and dropped to the floor where he stood beside Evelyn, his hand resting on her knee.

'I could ask Evelyn to burn you, simply on suspicion, but I will hold my mettle for the battle and we will see where your loyalties lie. I do hope it is with us,' he said.

Evelyn saw the fear in Sasha's eyes and a part of her enjoyed the reversal of power, her hand coming to rest on Gabriel's, pledging her allegiance.

'If what you say is true, Gabriel' she said. 'We need Sasha.'

'Indeed,' he said. 'Forgive me Sasha, but your appetite for revenge has been sated. How are we to truly know now your motivations?'

Sasha looked at Evelyn.

'She knows them. They've been clear since I met her.'

'How do you know he advances now?' asked Evelyn.

'Long before you happened upon him Sasha, Woltacht sent out a group of his soldiers west, to the Earthen City. A band of vampires, primitive in their ways, raised by him, the best that Castle Valla had to offer. Woltacht sought to even up the number of vampires to humans, making them the superior race, turning the best while the rest would be enslaved like livestock. A new world order. As a keeper of the grey world in which humans and beast collide, I couldn't allow that to happen and we fought back. The Earth belongs to the humans, it was created for them, not us. We are merely the shadow walkers. Anyway, into Moscow they crept in the dead of night, killing indiscriminately. They slaughtered families in their sleep, swords and hatchets working alongside their teeth and though we lost many, we were able to overcome them and capture their survivors, leaving them exposed to the rising sun, a reminder to Woltacht of our superior powers and the limitations of his. With his best soldiers erased, he had to start again and he did, amassing great numbers and that's when I approached Vladimir to see if he would go to Castle Valla and give himself to Woltacht, with immortality as his prize. Well, you both know how that turned out. Vladimir came back to me unchanged, our mission a failure, until you showed up Sasha and so the stories have begun to be whispered again, that he now has a new stronger army assembled and ready to unleash outside of his homeland, on the very being that defeated him the last time. We don't know when they will reach this island, they may already be here. Woltacht is a master of cloaking his presence but as his charge, you may feel him where I would not, and I am trusting you to share this information with us. Evelyn, you will stay with me now. His forces will look to better the odds by my demise and I would like you by my side, where we can protect each other. We must assume Woltacht knows nothing of your power. A day walking vampire would be of great interest to him, as you can imagine, and there is no end to the lengths he would go to get to you. Even through Michael.'

'Michael is gone,' she said sadly. 'Is he safe where he is, in Ireland?'

Gabriel looked to Sasha to answer her.

'He's not in Ireland. He gave Baker the slip before the ship set sail. It seems he had a change of heart.'

'Why didn't you tell me?' she said.

'Because you drove him away yourself, for his own safety. Did it really matter where he went?'

'It matters now,' she said. 'Where is he?'

'Baker had a dock worker follow him. He left New York on a coach headed to Philadelphia. From there we don't know.'

'So, he's out there somewhere. We have to find him. I want him with me,' she said.

'It will be done,' Gabriel said. 'Michael is never it seems, too far away from trouble. He won't be hard to find.'

37

THE PENDULUM SWUNG IN the grandfather clock, as Michael paced in the hall. He took a deep breath and knocked on Mr. Boudreaux's study, or as he'd heard him call it 'his only sanctuary in this godforsaken henhouse'. Michael feared the worst, that he and Salome had been discovered. They'd been meeting every night since they'd first spoken. Even Thomas knew that when the master summoned you, it wasn't a good thing and so he had passed on the message to Michael with a look of worry and concern. When he entered the room though, Mr. Boudreaux's face was only one kind of flustered – the kind reserved when it came to his youngest daughter. He waved his hand impatiently when he saw Michael at the door.

'Yes, yes, come on boy the quicker we get this done, the quicker you'll be back,' he said. 'Now see here, my Ashleigh is heading into town and wants you to drive her. I need you back here, Mr. Foster has a lot of work for you today so make it quick, see that she gets the things she needs and bring her straight back. She can take to socialising in town, but I've told her to spend whatever in hell she's going to, and get back. She won't go with Bailey and I don't trust any of the rest of them.'

'Yes, Sir.'

'Like a thorn bush she is this morning – gets that from her mother. Tell me why must women be so much trouble? Telling her mother and I, that she won't marry George Cassidy this summer when it's all arranged. Anyway, take her to town and see she buys whatever she wants. It may help the situation.'

Michael thought perhaps he would have preferred his other fate, as the thoughts of spending the afternoon with Ashleigh was unbearable. Nonetheless he had Thomas ready the horses for the carriage and shortly after he pulled up out front, as Ashleigh came down the porch steps.

'Isn't it a glorious day?' she said. She was wearing her prettiest dress, with matching yellow bonnet tied with a huge bow under her chin, her ringlets tucked inside. He helped her up into the carriage. Through the window, Salome was clearing away the mid-morning tea.

'Indeed, it is,' he said quickly, taking his eyes off her and seeing to his passenger.

The skies were a slick of clear blue as they rode along, and Ashleigh babbled on about which items she might get in which store, while Michael threw in the odd comment to appease her. When they had spent the morning in town going through every boutique for dresses, bonnets, and shoes, Michael loaded up her purchases and they made for home. Soon they were out in the country roads again and Ashleigh removed her bonnet, taking the afternoon sun on her face. Her golden hair shone in the sunlight and Michael suspected she had spent all morning refining it. She moved closer to him as he held the reins, slipping her gloved hand around his arm.

'I've told Father I won't marry George Cassidy. No matter what. He's a plantation owner's son, down in New Orleans. Wealthy but my he's insipid and ugly too. My Aunt sent his picture to Mama. He won't do and I've told Father. I won't do it. I'll marry when I am good and ready, to a man of my choosing. Lord knows they form a queue at the State Ball every year. There has to be better than George Cassidy.'

'I don't see you have much to worry about,' said Michael. 'You can have any number of...' (he wanted so badly to say *idiots*...) 'gentlemen. They are yours for the choosing, I imagine.'

'I just think there's so much more to be explored before you settle down to be an old married woman, don't you?' she said.

'I don't think your father would be pleased to hear you say that.'

'Do you think I'm pretty, Michael?' she asked, inching closer to him before pulling the reins in his hands. The horses came to a stop.

'I don't think, Miss Ashleigh, I should answer that,' he said, trying to pry the leather straps from her.

'Michael, there's only you and me here,' she said, the carriage standing among the shaded line of trees.

'We should go,' he said.

'Kiss me,' she said leaning into him, her full rosy lips parted.

'Now, wait that's not a good idea. Come on,' he said.

She smiled at his flapping, delighted to have taken him by surprise.

'Just one kiss.'

'Your father wouldn't approve and I like my job just fine,' he said. He started to pull the reins free from her fingers but she yanked them back, angry.

'You will kiss me, or I will tell my Father that you forced yourself on me. He is ever so protective of my virtue.'

'That's ridiculous,' he said. Before he could react, she planted her lips on his, their soft flesh pushing against him. She held them there a moment before she gasped, swooning, a little girl thrilled with her conquest.

'I knew I would kiss you today,' she said bringing her fingers to his lips to wipe off some wayward rouge.

'That's enough,' he said, pushing her hand away angrily, rubbing his mouth with the back of his hand. He grabbed the straps and pulled hard on the reins.

'Michael, you're such a baby,' she giggled.

The horses trotted onto the road again and he didn't speak a word for the remainder of the journey, pushing out to the other side of the bench, much to her amusement. He cursed himself for playing into her hands and knew he'd set a world of trouble in motion, the moment his lips met hers. She, on the other hand, comfortably basked in the kiss all the way home, and as he helped her out she whispered, 'It will be our little secret', before skipping up the porch steps.

Later that night as he walked with Salome in the woods, her hand in his, he told her what happened.

'You shouldn't have kissed her.'

'I didn't. Before I knew it, she was on me.'

'Your lips have a power – a magical effect on a woman,' she said, nudging her shoulder into him.

'That depends on who they kiss,' he said as he put his arm around her.

Something slithered on the ground beside her bare foot and she reached down, carefully picking up a tiny snake, it's forked tongue sliding back and forth in its mouth.

'Don't be fooled by Miss Ashleigh,' she said, bringing the snake to her face, as it curled itself around her wrist. 'She's dangerous. Always has been. As a child she would have nightmares, terrors that would wake her in the night screaming and sometimes, she would sleepwalk right out of her bed and across the lawn to the woods. Imagine it, a ten-year-old girl, waking from a nightmare, frightened and lost, with no idea of how she had come to be there. One night, she must have walked deep into the trees, because we heard her cries. Joshua, Thomas' daddy, ran to her and she, still trapped in that nightmare, cried out against the demons that sought to drag her down, banging her head against the ground, her hair mussed up with mud and leaves. He thought if he held on to her tightly, he could calm her, waking her and the episode would end, but she swung out at him, scratching him and even biting his arm so hard she drew blood.

We all stood in the trees watching, young Thomas holding my hand. His daddy eventually soothed her, singing to her as she wept into his shoulder, glad that the demons weren't real and she was safe. Bailey ran to fetch her Mr. Boudreaux to come and take her but he didn't understand what Bailey was saying. He ran into the trees and all he saw was his daughter in the arms of a black man, his face dragged by her nails, blood running over his arm. And I saw her. She drew her head up and the shame and embarrassment hit her that we or anyone else would see her like that. Barefaced she told her daddy, that she could remember being lifted from her bed by a man, and she had woken to find Joshua laying her down in the woods and that's when she started screaming for help and fighting him off. Well, Mr. Boudreaux went from deathly pale to purple in a heartbeat. Rage will do that to a man and he had Joshua immediately taken by Mr. Foster for hanging. Bailey and the other grown-ups protested but they were beat down, and that night they hung Joshua from that tree that hangs just over the edge of the lawn, and made us watch, even us kids, and I saw her standing at her bedroom window with her Mama and she was smiling. No-one ever gave her cause for that again and word is she's slept like a baby ever since.'

'Jesus.' Michael said.

'So, now you see,' she said, freeing the snake back into the undergrowth. 'We take a great risk, especially if she's taken an interest in you herself.'

'Then we'll leave, run away from here. Somewhere they won't find us.'

'They always find us when we run,' she said.

Michael considered her words, an image of his sister flashing into his mind, and with it the thoughts of her and Sasha eventually finding him, their teeth bared in attack.

'We just need to make sure no-one finds out,' she said.

'Sorry, yes, you're right.'

'What is it? Sometimes you look so lost in there,' she said as he leaned away from her. 'There it is again, a look in your eyes, something that you try to keep hidden from me.'

'It's safer if I keep some things to myself, that's all.'

'You've lost someone. Someone you loved.'

'It's not what you think, really. You'll think I've taken leave of my senses.'

'You're the most sensible white person I've ever met,' she said smiling. 'I doubt it.'

Michael looked around as the wind hissed in the trees. It swayed the branches, the leaves crackling and he realised he was about to tell her a secret, the wood already knew. Saying it out loud would be a catharsis of sorts, for these creatures were as real as they were.

'My sister...' he started, trying to find the words. 'We ran into trouble after we arrived in New York. Got ourselves mixed up with some people, well…creatures I suppose, that took my sister and changed her into one of them. A thing that lives on blood. I know how ridiculous that might sound but…'

'Vampires,' said Salome. 'When you live a life surrounded by evil, you learn of all threats that lie in wait for you. It's a duty among our people to educate each other about such things. Stories have passed down through generations about them. Are you afraid she will come for you?' she asked.

'She drove me away, in fear I suppose that her maker would kill me or she herself. I don't think they know where I am, but I know the day will come, when I will see them again. You have to tell me what you know. Is there any way for her to be saved or at least freed from them?'

'They care only about the blood. That hunger drives them to commit murder without mercy. They must have it at any cost, but you should talk to Meega. She has lived in these woods as long as I can remember, hidden from the slave masters. They tried to find her once, when she spread word that we could chew the cotton root to kill the babies inside us. All the unwelcome babies – for who would bring a child into this. The next generation of slaves. They went deep into the woods, but they never found her. She shows you the way, only if she allows it.'

'Do you think she'll talk to me?' he said desperately, but the wood already gave him his answer, as a flurry of dead leaves fell from the branches above them.

38

DESPITE THE CHILLY NIGHT, Michael could feel the sweat dampen his shirt. They had travelled beyond the plantation, moving through the thickest part of the woods. The air here was warmer, the canopy of leaves and branches overhead keeping its climate temperate below, a little world untouched by the seasons. The ground itself was thick with branches, some from fallen trees, some just twisted and briary, growing along the path, making it difficult to navigate – if that is indeed what they were doing.

'It feels like we're going in circles,' Michael said.

'Be patient. We will know soon enough,' said Salome, working her way through the thicket, her feet sinking in the swampy earth.

'There,' she said, 'look.'

Through the trees to their right, peeping through the foliage, came the soft glow of light from a wooden hut. Once a hunter's cabin, it looked like a hurricane had run through it, for it leaned to one side, cradled in the trees. The roof was on the verge of collapse, branches lifting it from the inside. The only thing that kept it on was the tapestry of vines, binding it together. Salome caught Michael's hand and led him towards it, knowing that if they were lucky enough to find their way through the trees and watery perils, it was because Meega let them. She knocked and gently pushed open the door.

'Hello Salome,' came a voice from within. 'You brought me a guest.'

'Yes, Meega,' she said. 'He needs your help.'

Meega was seated with her back to them by the fire, her small frame hunched over, her bony hand poking it with a stick before throwing it onto the flames. Her grey hair showed no signs of thinning. It framed her face like a lion's mane, her dark skin loose and wrinkled, her brown eyes, shining brightly as she extended her hand to usher them in.

'You sit here,' she said to Michael, 'beside me.' She pointed to an upturned crate.

'I wondered when I would see you,' she said. 'I felt you bring the darkness with you when you arrived in these parts.'

'Do you know why I'm here?' he asked.

'You got vampire trouble,' she said, nodding her head. 'Messy business. And they are after you? Are you hunted?' she asked with a glint in her eye.

'No,' he said, 'at least, not for now. It's my sister. She was turned and I need your help to free her from them.'

She reached out her frail fingers and put her hand on his chest, feeling his heart thump inside.

'You are strong. Your sister is also very strong. You are very alike but there is no cure for this disease of the blood. Free or not, your sister will always remain one of them. I see fear in your eyes. Do you fear her?'

'Yes,' he whispered.

'A wise answer,' she said. 'How they do crave that blood. Makes them do crazy things.'

'How can I free her from her captors?' he asked.

'You kill them,' she said matter-of-factly.

'I didn't think that was possible.'

'There are ways,' she said moving close to him. 'Now, listen to me very carefully for you walk a very danger-ous path. These creatures will kill you before you've even realised they are there. They are quick and strong, but they walk only in darkness for the sun burns their skin. At dawn, they must recede to the shadows until the sun falls again. If you can capture one, which is a feat in itself, the sun's light will burn and destroy it. The second way is a blade through the heart. Wooden stakes work equally well but require close range and more force, a blade will kill more efficiently.'

Meega put her hand on his suddenly, gripping it tightly, her eyes losing their brightness for a moment.

'You need to be careful,' she said releasing him. 'I can feel other forces watching. Maybe it's a crow high in the trees or a snake writhing through the earth outside, but I feel their eyes on me, and you in turn. They are trying to find you.'

She stood up, straightening her back as far as it would allow, as she shuffled off into the corner, among the boxes and crates piled high.

'Think I still have it…' she muttered. 'Ah yes, here it is.' She took out a small tin and opened it carefully as she sat back down, emptying its contents in Michael's palm. At first sight, it looked like a pebble you might find washed ashore. It was small, fitting neatly in Michael's hand as he closed his fingers over it, it's exterior cool and smooth. It was grey but for a thin streak of flesh-coloured pink that ran through it.

'It's a sun stone,' she said. 'Keep it with you and you will feel its heat when a vampire is near. It may give you just enough time to act if you're lucky.'

'Thank you, Meega,' he said, putting it in his pocket.

'Good luck. You have a fire within you. You're a strong one. I just hope the thing still works.' She let out a chuckle then, before tapping him lightly on the chest and nodding her head in affirmation.

When they reached the edge of the woods, dawn was almost upon them. Michael held Salome close for a moment, his head resting on her shoulder. He took a deep breath, inhaling the essence of her, that it may last him until he would hold her again.

'You're going to go back for her, aren't you?' she said. 'You're going to fight.'

'I want you to come with me to New York. Can you do that? Can you run?'

'Yes,' she said. 'I'll go with you. I'll go anywhere with you.'

'We'll leave tonight,' he said unable to contain his excitement. He kissed her, not wanting to let go and she pulled away, her hand eventually dropping his, as they parted. Michael watched her as she disappeared among the trees. One more day. That's all it would take. He would keep her somewhere safe in New York as he tried to free Evelyn, and both of them at last would have the freedom that belonged to them. He turned back for his cabin, taking care to make as little noise as possible but from the trees behind him, someone watched. They moved slowly as they followed him, taking great care not to be seen or heard. As Michael crept back to his cabin, carefully turning the handle and slipping inside, the figure stopped behind the bark of a nearby tree, consumed with only one thought.

New York? I don't think so.

39

As DAWN BROKE IN Manhattan, a glaze of white frost covered the city. Snow had yet to fall but the clouds lay overhead, in wait. All along the banks of the Hudson, the edges of the water froze to the sides, ice breaking off to float downstream into the harbour, swallowed by the flowing current. Gabriel and Evelyn sat on horseback, each of their steeds snorting steam into the cold air as they made their way north through the city. Gabriel looked uncomfortable in his clothes, like he was suffocating beneath their many layers, but their task was to blend into their surroundings – to act and travel as humans did, avoiding unwanted attention. Over his black suit, he wore a heavy grey coat and a gentleman's top hat, tilted ever so slightly on his head. Evelyn too was dressed for the weather, a long woollen coat fitted to her body, a ladies riding hat on her head, three tall feathers complimenting its design.

Gabriel had explained the reason for their journey, but as they reached Kings Cross Bridge, she could see the doubt in his eyes. The decision to leave the island, even for a few hours had not been taken lightly. He would be exposed. It was imperative that they reach Olivia by noon, for he wanted the security of his Manhattan lair come nightfall. The small hamlet lay east of Sleepy Hollow, a tiny, self-sufficient community nestled between mountain and lake that rarely bothered the world around it. For almost a hundred years, Olivia had thrived, free of the maladies that gripped many parts of Westchester County. Founded by Reverend Marshall Hooksbury, he had led his small group of sixty parishioners on a mission to find the place 'chosen by God himself' in which to take shelter from the growing world. A widower, he had lost his wife to tuberculosis and with her their unborn daughter, who never took a breath outside her mother's womb. He had named her Olivia and when he saw the beauty of the setting, he knew God had led him to this place, and that he must name it for her, as surely as she was at the Lord's side.

It was snowing as they reached the outskirts, the first of the houses dotted on the mountain side among the trees. They followed the road as it led them into town. A few inches of snow formed a blanket on the deserted main street, untouched by footprint, hoof or cartwheel.

'Do you hear that?' Gabriel said, slowing his horse.

Evelyn listened carefully, not picking up any sign of life and shrugged her shoulders.

'Exactly,' he said.

Two rows of wooden store fronts faced each other, and at the end of the street as the road narrowed, stood a large church, its cross pitched high above the rooftops. Its wooden lattes were painted white as if made from snow and ice, the crystals glistening as Gabriel and Evelyn rode towards it. At the top of the steps, stood a tall figure dressed in black. Evelyn could not pick up his scent and she looked at Gabriel, who was smiling. The man wore a black cassock that kicked out at his heels, a small crucifix sitting smartly around his neck, his blond hair trimmed close to his head. He gave a welcoming bow to Gabriel as they dismounted their horses.

'I didn't think you would ever grace this town with your presence,' the man said.

'I needed to talk to you.'

'Come inside. Aren't you going to introduce your companion?' he asked.

'No,' Gabriel said curtly, 'I'm not.'

Evelyn slid her hand back into her glove.

'She is not here to meet you. I am. Stay here a moment,' he said to her, removing his hat. 'This could be over quicker than I thought.'

Evelyn nodded, turning her back to them, taking in the deserted street. She could hear their voices inside.

'I didn't think you were fond of vampires,' the preacher said.

'I've learned to be fond of many things I once disliked,' he said, walking up the aisle. He turned at the altar and sat on the step facing the empty wooden pews. The man looked wounded for a moment.

'You know I feel you sometimes, watching me, even after all this time. I find it somewhat comforting that you still take an interest. But now you come to see me in the flesh. Why?'

'Woltacht.'

The man looked surprised. 'I heard he was dead.'

'Not so. He brings new followers now on New York.'

The preacher sat in the front pew, silent, lost in thought.

'We fought hard for Moscow,' he said after a time. 'I don't have any fight left in me. That's why I came here to disappear, to be among them and preach His word.'

'Redemption is a foolhardy pastime, Jude,' he said.

'And yet you find yourself also playing the game. Why not just let Woltacht have his way? Isn't the Earth damned anyway?'

'Perhaps, but I like my part in it. There is a balance. Woltacht will destroy that and then we will find nothing here but misery,' Gabriel said.

'Who's the girl?'

'A friend.'

'And there was me thinking you never wanted any,' he said.

'Perhaps I'm too choosy,' said Gabriel. 'Have you seen anything or heard of any vampires in these parts?'

Jude shook his head. 'Maybe you're wrong and they're not coming.'

'That may be, but he's had years to plot his retribution on us. Also, one of his breed is with us now.'

'A defector. How interesting. Do you trust him?'

'Yes,' Gabriel said without hesitation. 'Do you remember when we came here first, sent to this purgatory to redeem ourselves? You asked me if He would ever need us again, ever reach out to us or whether we would be doomed to endure the mortal world, trying to find an existence in it for ourselves?'

'He will never need us again,' Jude said wistfully. 'There are just some things you can't undo.'

'He needs us now,' said Gabriel. "Whether He realises it or not.'

'You don't need me,' said Jude letting out a sigh. 'You are the stronger and more powerful one.'

'And you have always been the wiser one, Jude. Together we're stronger. I don't know if you feel it but something pulls at my powers. My visions now are poorly drawn at best and without them my knowledge shrinks, putting us all in danger.'

'He said he would never take our gifts.'

'Exactly, so if it's not Him, then the other options may be too dangerous to comprehend.'

'Close your eyes. Let me see inside your mind,' said Jude.

Gabriel shut his eyes, welcoming the darkness. Jude closed his too but he opened them almost immediately, shaking his head. He rose from the pew and came to sit beside Gabriel on the altar, turning into him, placing his hands carefully either side of his head. It was the closest thing to an embrace for both men and Gabriel looked at Jude, his eyes closed in concentration and felt a sting of regret. After a moment, Jude took his hands away.

'I can't do it,' he said. 'Something clouds my mind, blocking our sight and strength. It means to disorient us.'

'You must come back to Manhattan with me,' said Gabriel.

'My place is here among my people.'

'These are not your people Jude. I am.'

Jude stood putting his hands into the folds of his cassock.

'I am trying to atone for the things I did, the things *we* did Gabriel. I have carved out this life in the hopes of finding some sort of peace. I won't ruin it by jumping into a conflict with you. It's no longer my fight.'

Gabriel pushed himself up from the step. 'Then God help us all,' he said standing eye to eye with him. He put on his hat, straightening the rim and turned briskly towards the door. As he reached it, Evelyn flung it open.

'I think we've company,' she said.

40

'THERE,' EVELYN SAID POINTING to the hillside. 'Look.'

A cloudy trail of snow kicked up into the air as something moved rapidly through the trees towards them, shaking the firs as it descended – three white streaks of danger, gaining ground by the second.

'Secure the horses round the back,' Gabriel said, running to his, the ground crunching beneath his boots. Grabbing the reins, he handed them to Evelyn. Jude came to the doorway, his eyes following the trail down the mountain. Quickly he slammed the door, shutting them out. They heard a key turn in the lock.

'Seems you picked a side after all,' Gabriel shouted.

Evelyn ran to him. He was standing in the middle of the road, facing down the row of storefronts. The trail could no longer be seen in the trees and the snowfall had stopped, bringing with it an eerie stillness.

'They're watching us,' he said. 'How are you with dogs?'

Up ahead, some thirty yards away, a large hound crept across the snow, it's head hung low, it's eyes fixed on them. It was a beast of an animal, muscular and strong, its black coat long and shiny. It stopped in the middle of the road and raised its head, to let out a long howl, summoning its companions to join him. Two others emerged, one as white as the snow, the other grey, each as menacing as their leader. All three looked to Gabriel and Evelyn, their long noses bowed, eyes bright for the kill.

'Go!' shouted Gabriel, pushing Evelyn in the opposite direction. She moved at speed, the white beast breaking into a run after her, while Gabriel darted to the right, the grey one taking after him. It was fast and it slid on the snow as it tried to catch him in its jaws, but he made good ground, disappearing behind the first building.

Evelyn made it into the store on the left. The white hound had stopped and was now pacing in front of the large glass window, watching her inside. It was a general store with all sorts of goods and she looked around for anything she might use. At the back were the apothecary shelves, stacked with medicines and potions. She threw them to the floor, the glass smashing, the contents spilling out onto the floorboards. Through the window she saw the dog move back to the street, before turning and running towards her, straight for the glass. It flung itself into the window as the glass shattered and Evelyn went down on one knee, pressing her palms to the floor as the alcohol in the liquid ignited.

The dog landed on a sea of fiery waves. If it was in pain it didn't show it, its eyes narrowing as it looked for her in the flames. She ran towards him, her coat on fire, consumed by her own defence. The dog bared his teeth as it leapt up to meet her. She swung a punch to the side of its head, the force sending him to the floor, his body splintering the wood. Evelyn came at the beast again but this time it was ready and it rolled over on top of her, the flames high around them. Its jaws pressed close to her face. Drool dripped from its sharp teeth onto her cheek and she thrust her hand upwards with all her might into the flesh of its belly, holding it there as she spread the fire to its insides. The dog didn't even have time to yelp in pain. It was dead within seconds and as Evelyn pushed it off her, a long mournful howl came from the black hound on the road outside.

Gabriel had rounded the corner. At the back of the property was a door and he threw himself inside. He slammed it shut as the body of the grey dog pounded against it, its sharp nails screeching as they tore at the wood. Even in daylight, the store was dimly lit but there was no mistaking the industry inside. Coffins lined the walls, a variety of wooden resting places, their lids leaning against them, waiting for their passengers to the next world. Gabriel plucked a claw hammer from the nail where it hung, letting go of the door. The grey dog burst inside. He twirled back to bring the hammer down on the dog's head. It missed its skull but severed its ear, as it moved sideways. He swung it again but he wasn't quick enough and the beast went for him, knocking him back into a pile of curled wood shavings, the hammer flying out of his hand.

Something in his coat pressed hard into his side. He reached into his pocket and found a small silver pistol. Jude – it had to be. As the dog came at him, with snarling jaws, he aimed and pulled the trigger. With a loud crack, the bullet hit the dog in the face, shattering it into a bloody mess. Skin, hair and matter spattered the walls. Through the window, he saw the general store erupt in a ball of fire as the black dog howled outside, watching the flames.

Stepping over the fallen beast, he walked out the front door, wiping the blood from his eyes, his pistol aimed at the remaining dog. Evelyn walked through the flames, facing him on the other side. The trigger clicked but no bullet discharged from the chamber. He squeezed it again and again but nothing happened.

'Damn it,' he said, tossing the gun as the animal ran at him, Evelyn giving chase. Gabriel sprinted up the wooden boardwalk until he reached the end. Only forest lay beyond it. He threw himself into the last doorway, the beast not far behind. At first glance, it looked like a sheriff's office, but it had abandoned the rule of law for that of religion. Instead of gun racks, the walls were a library of religious tomes and scriptures, overlooked by a crucifix hanging on the wall. Reverend Hooksbury's legacy it seemed, had held fast. There was a holding cell at the back complete with iron bars and shackles. Fresh blood ran down the wall. Someone had atoned for their sins quite recently. Gabriel backed himself in to the cell, waiting on his attacker. The beast charged in, its jaws salivating at the sight of him trapped there. It leapt into the air, extending its nails, ready to tear him apart. But it did not meet its prey. Instead, it met the brute force of the back wall. Gabriel appeared from the shadows outside and flung the iron bars shut, capturing him.

The dog whimpered. Blood ran from its mouth and broken nose. Evelyn marvelled at Gabriel's trick. Of course, he had appeared on an ocean of ice for her. He could project his image anywhere.

'Evelyn, will you do the honours?' he said, pointing to the animal.

As she approached the cell, a familiar scent rose to her. She stopped, looking at the floor. Something wasn't right. She knelt, pressing her ear against the boards.

'What is it?' Gabriel said.

'There are vampires here,' she said, her fingers spreading across the floor. 'Lots of them.'

The black dog leapt to his feet, barking wildly.

'There must be hundreds down there,' she said.

'No wonder the town is empty. We must find the opening.'

They looked about the floor. There was no sign of a hatch but Evelyn spotted four grooves worn into the wood. The table on the far side of the room had been moved.

'There,' she said. 'It must be underneath.'

They shifted it easily to one side. A small iron ring lay set into the wood.

'Can you do this?' Gabriel asked.

'I'm certainly going to try,' she said, and she pulled the ring, the trapdoor opening with a cool rush of air. She quickly lowered herself into the pitch blackness, dropping down to a tunnel crudely dug into the earth. As she moved through it, she hoped the earthen ceiling would hold, the thoughts of being buried alive not one she wished to encounter with so many of her own kind. Gabriel followed behind her and together they made their way slowly along, following the scent of the undead.

Evelyn's vision in the darkness was tinged in green and blue and when they reached the end of the short tunnel, the colours seemed to ignite with the picture before her. In a wide cavern, lay hundreds of sleeping vampires. She felt Gabriel's hand on her arm and she turned as he pointed to a family lying asleep together. Two parents, each with a protective arm around their sleeping children, their little faces frozen in their immortal dream world. Evelyn had never thought that a child would be made endure such a fate, and she looked on horrified as they surveyed the others, spotting more children among them.

She didn't know if she could destroy a child, vampire or not but the alternatives, that this army would reach New York was too horrific to contemplate. She reached a hand back to Gabriel, telling him she would go on alone. Carefully she made her way through them, stepping between the gaps, until she stood in the centre, the vampires spread out around her like fallen petals. Closing her eyes, she summoned the fire. She would need more power than ever before. She envisioned the flame growing inside her, taking it to molten red, then white hot, urging the heat stronger and stronger. Instead of releasing it, she contained it, intensifying it until it exploded outwards – a bright light as harsh as the midday sun. It blasted the vampires where they lay, it's light and heat so intense that it turned them instantly to ash.

When she was satisfied that every one of them was destroyed, she dropped to her knees, the light vanishing, plunging them back into darkness. Gabriel crouched at the entrance, shielding his eyes until it was over, awestruck by her power. She moved back to him, stepping between their bodies as before, her ankle touching the arm of a male vampire. His body disintegrated like grains of sand until there was nothing but the scorch marks of where he'd lain.

Gabriel looked at the vampire family, still holding each other in death, taking care not to disturb their resting place. When they reached the surface again, the black hound wept in its cell, howling for its lost compatriots.

'Burn it all,' Gabriel said.

Evelyn nodded. 'And Jude?'

'He's gone,' he said. 'He travels at great speed, perhaps to tell of our exploits or to run as far away as he can from the retribution that will be coming. We have disabled an army here but the top tier is still out there and they'll be coming for us – not tonight perhaps, they will come here to see the damage themselves – but certainly thereafter.'

'Let them come,' she said.

41

ASHLEIGH ALLOWED THE SEEDS of jealousy bloom into revenge. The power of its secrecy, allowed it to flourish in her mind as she considered her best course of action. That morning, she rose with a spring in her step and as she watched Michael speaking with Bailey and Thomas at the stables, she felt her heart swell with expectation. She had considered perhaps blackmailing him in return for the kisses that Salome had stolen from her, but then Michael had kissed a slave and that tainted him beyond repair. She had laid awake the night after their kiss, dreaming of his lips again on hers, when her desire could no longer contain itself and she'd thrown on her housecoat before sneaking down to his cabin. It was Salome she had seen first through the trees, and from there she had stumbled upon the pair, brazen in the dawn.

Her mouth watered at the thoughts of their punishment and the importance of her discovery. She imagined the reactions of Foster and that idiot Harley, not to mention her father who would erupt at such a flagrant breach of his moral code or her mother who would weep for humanity. Ah yes, the shock would be shattering, the punishment almost surely death, for it could not be condoned. Much as she wanted to, she knew better than to gloat to Michael that she had unmasked them, as passionate men were unpredictable and he might take to silencing her. No. She knew what she had to do and the part she would play.

42

THAT EVENING, FOSTER AND Harley emerged through the trees, a length of rope swinging idly in each of their hands. They were afforded a certain level of autonomy when it came to dealing with the slaves, and Foster was grateful to Ashleigh that he was the first to hear about his new employee's deception. He knew all too well that Salome was a temptation for any man, but how dare that upstart take what was his, and how dare she give herself willingly to him. They would take Michael first and restrain him while they waited for Salome to finish her service in the house. Ashleigh would alert her father at the right moment, when justice was in hand, and Foster could be seen to have a handle on things. If Mr. Boudreaux had to bring the news to him, it would surely come with his swift dismissal, his own overseer having no knowledge of what was going on right under his nose. This he could control.

Harley had subdued Michael with a swift punch to the gut as he'd opened the door of his cabin to them. Then they'd tied him to a chair and for an hour Harley beat him. He refuted their claims, over and over until at last he relented, knowing that their intel was too close to the truth to have been anything other than an eye witness. They even teased his plans to flee with her to New York and finally he had to admit it, though he insisted that it was not Salome but another girl from a different plantation. For this, Harley beat him some more until he stopped talking again. It was only when he took him to the edge of the trees, where the lawn stretched up to the house that he began to scream her name. Foster was dragging her across the manicured grass, one hand embedded in her short hair, the other gripped tightly to his shotgun.

Harley knocked him forward on his knees, tying a piece of cloth around his mouth to subdue him as Salome struggled with Foster, one shoe falling behind her as she scrambled to get her feet under her. He shoved her down on the grass beside Michael, both of them kneeling before him.

'I'm gonna miss you, Salome,' he said, bending down to stroke her face. 'Your position's gonna be a hard one to fill, but you know little Agatha's coming to that age now, isn't she? Starting to grow into a fine young woman.'

Salome leapt to her feet and sprang for him, landing a blow to his face. He hesitated as he considered hitting her with the butt of his gun, then turned to Harley.

'Hang her,' he said.

His words were music to Harley's ears as he brought out his noose, slinging one end of the rope over the thick branch of a nearby tree, before slipping the loop around her delicate neck.

'What in God's almighty earth is going on here?'

Mr. Boudreaux stormed across the lawn, loading his own shotgun, his fingers fumbling with the shells. He was followed close behind by Ashleigh, shrinking timidly behind him, but following pace for pace, her ringlets bouncing like a riot each side of her head.

'Sir, we have a serious situation. This here negro has been fornicating with the new boy. It's against all goodness and they're gonna get God's swift punishment,' declared Foster.

Harley worked the rope slowly through his hands as Salome was pulled towards the tree.

'You should have come to me immediately. Only for my Ashleigh hearing the commotion, I'd be oblivious. Pick that boy up,' he gestured to Foster.

When Michael was stood facing him, he pulled the gag down over his chin.

'What have you to say for yourself?'

'You're wrong,' Michael blurted out in a panic. 'It wasn't her.'

Ashleigh stepped forward. 'I saw them Daddy, in the woods. It's her all right,' she said with a smirk.

'No, no you're wrong,' Michael said.

'Shut him up, Foster. I don't want to hear anymore. If Ashleigh says it, then it is so.'

Michael fought it in a frenzy of desperation.

'You jealous, stupid little…' he shouted before Foster gagged him again, pulling it tightly into the corners of his mouth. Mr.

Boudreaux cocked his shotgun at him but Ashleigh put her hand gently on her father's elbow.

'No, Daddy,' she said. 'I want to see them hang together.'

He lowered the gun, shaking his head.

'A sorry state of affairs indeed. Alright sweet pea, but come back to the house. You can watch from the porch steps,' he said.

He was aware suddenly of a line of slaves gathered among the trees.

'You get back to your quarters, now. Justice is being served here tonight,' he shouted, putting a protective arm around his daughter as they walked back across the lawn. Ashleigh strained her neck to see what was going on.

'Go back,' said Foster to the slaves. 'Or there'll be punishment for all of you.'

In the leafy darkness, the men didn't move, Bailey and Thomas among them. Harley let go of the slack on Salome's rope and took another noose, looping it around Michael's neck. He and Foster took one each as they pulled hard, hoisting them until Michael and Salome's feet left the ground. They kicked the air as the men tied the ropes and stood back to watch their handiwork.

43

MICHAEL FELT AS THOUGH his throat had been cut. Every fibre of the rope seared his skin, made worse by the slightest movement of his body. His throat had squeezed shut and he gasped, the air unable to get to his lungs. He didn't notice the sun stone until it had landed on the grass in front of him. It had burned a hole through his trouser pocket, its orange and pink fissure glowing brightly in the darkness. He twisted his body to look at Salome, feeling a jolt as the rope snapped and he was falling backwards, carried on the air back into the trees. His body met the ground with a thump and he pulled the noose over his head, flinging it to the ground where it landed beside a pair of familiar cowboy boots. He looked up to see Wade towering over him and screamed a hoarse cry as he scrambled back into the undergrowth.

'Don't kill me,' he said. 'At least not yet.'

'Kill you? I just saved your sorry ass,' said Wade. 'It's good to see you, pal. Now get yourself together, we gotta make like lightning if we're to get back tonight.'

Michael listened to his words, trying to decipher them.

'You're not going to kill me?' he said.

'Nope, now come on, let's go.'

'No,' Michael said, 'I have to save Salome.' He struggled to get to his feet.

'Stay here,' Wade said sternly. 'I'll get her,' and he disappeared into the darkness.

44

HARLEY AND FOSTER WERE still trying to grasp what had happened. One minute they were hanging their captives, the next Michael was gone in a whoosh of furious wind, a straggle of rope left dangling from the branches. Salome had stopped moving, her struggle finally over, until she too was falling, caught by the arms of a strong black man who laid her carefully down on the ground.

Foster didn't recognise this slave. He wore a suit more expensive that any item of clothing he owned, but a negro was a negro no matter what way he looked at it. He drew up his shotgun moving closer to him, when the man disappeared into thin air. Then someone grabbed him from behind, their strong arm across his collarbone. Hot pain burned in his neck, as the man latched his mouth to his skin, drawing every drop of blood from his trembling body. Harley couldn't believe his eyes. He drew his hunting blade from the sheath in his belt. He faced foes on all sides – Foster's negro killer, the slaves advancing from the trees, Salome panting on the grass and then a cowboy, who smiled at the odds so favourably stacked against him.

As Foster's body slid to the ground, he thought better of his grandstanding and dropped the knife. He made a dash along the treeline as the slaves emerged. Some charged after him, while others made headway across the lawn. The other strangers didn't follow. He may have a chance yet. But they were smiling, looking past him and when he turned around again, a red-haired woman was coming towards him, walking at a leisurely pace.

'Well, your mama must be so proud of you,' she said. He kept charging, sure he could push her out of his way, but she braced herself for his assault. Every bone in his hands splintered on impact and he let out a high-pitched wail. The slaves had stopped their pursuit and they watched as Velle grabbed one of his hands, squeezing each broken finger into the next. She twisted his arm, forcing him face down onto the grass, where she sat on his back, his legs kicking out under the back of her dress.

'This'll only hurt a bit,' she said as she sank her teeth into the crook of his neck. Quickly she drank and when she was done, she reached her hands around his jawline and pulled swiftly to the left, until she heard it crack.

'There,' she said. 'Naughty boy.'

**

ASHLEIGH HAD WATCHED IN awe at the ease at which both men were dispatched. She scanned the treeline for Michael. He had completely disappeared. Half of the slaves had already made their escape but the others favoured revenge and they came upon the house brandishing torches. Things were about to get very bad indeed. She ran up the porch steps but a stranger stood there, leaning on the door, one foot crossed over the other, his hand resting on the jamb.

'Please,' she said. 'You must help me.'

By the time the words came out, she realised her mistake. The man's appearance was disarming. He was beautiful in an odd way, his skin smooth and pale but in his eyes, she saw a monster. She backed slowly down the steps lifting her skirts as the man followed her.

'You can see pretty good from here' he said pointing to the hanging tree. 'You had the best seat in the house.'

Sasha moved to his left as a shotgun pellet came whizzing through the wooden door, narrowly missing his shoulder. Ashleigh saw her chance and disappeared into the porch shadow, running as fast as she could along the edge of the house. Sasha looked back to see Mr. Boudreaux framed through the hole he'd put in the front door, his shotgun in his arms, newly reloaded.

'You're going to need that,' Sasha said walking down the steps away from him.

45

HARLEY'S KNIFE LAY ABANDONED in the grass and while the others watched him run away, Salome slid her hand across to grab it. She clutched the handle now to her breast, as she watched Sasha approach. He must be the leader. She had heard the red-haired woman speak and knew that she was not Michael's sister but the others certainly fit his description perfectly. They had taken him. Somewhere among the trees, he lay dying. They would kill them all until their thirst was quenched.

The leader glanced at her as he spoke with the cowboy. What would they do with her? Kill her too? Michael was gone and with him, hope of ever leaving Raven Wood alive. He was coming towards her. She closed her eyes, as his hands reached under her and then she thrust the knife into his chest, the blade finding the soft flesh of his heart.

46

A CRY RANG OUT that silenced the whole night. The sound of agony and fear bound together. Sasha clasped the handle of the knife. Had she done it? Finished him? Perhaps he could reverse it, remove it so quickly from his heart as to render it futile. He went to pull it out but her hand came upon it again, ready to finish the job. She must have known the chance she took. To kill just one vampire, when three others were waiting – ready to avenge him. Lincoln swept in, his hand pulling the blade out and with a flick of his wrist, he slashed it across her neck, silencing her forever.

Sasha was still. In truth, he was afraid to move. He hadn't seen any vampires killed in such a way so he didn't really know what to expect. Was his heart on fire, or was he imagining it? The dark blood ran like hellfire through his veins. But instead of burning him, it was hard at work restoring the tissue, rebuilding torn arteries. The blade had missed the chamber by millimetres. He closed his eyes, knowing all too well, how close he'd come. Michael's voice called through the woods. The girl was dead. His love. Sasha let out a sigh.

'Go, get him Wade,' he said. 'It's time we left.'

Wade looked at the fallen girl and shook his head.

'Man, he's not going to be happy.'

The calmness of the cold still night disappeared. A rush of wind powered through the trees, whipping the branches into a sudden frenzy, the low hanging cypress trees swishing their manes. There were screams from the house and the sound of gunfire as the slaves advanced, invading the ground floor. Wade had done his best to prepare him, but Michael was railing against his grip as they returned. He flung himself to the ground where she lay. It was wet with blood, the blades of grass black in the moonlight.

'She attacked me Michael. Lincoln was only protecting me.'

He touched her face. 'Go back to where you came from,' he said, his voice a monotone. 'I'm not going anywhere with you.'

Behind them, a large fire blazed in the ground floor of the house and the Boudreaux's who ran out were set upon by the mob as they took their revenge.

'Evelyn needs you.'

'Really? Then, where is she?' he said. 'You have taken everything from me. Why don't you just kill me already?'

'Honestly? Because she wouldn't want me to. Your sister is very important. She needs you with her. You're in danger out here.'

Michael laughed.

'Danger follows me, wherever I go. And I'm not going with you. Not now. Not with any of you.' He glanced at Wade.

'Then you leave us no choice but you know that fighting us is futile?'

'Fighting is all I've ever done,' Michael said.

He swung for Sasha, a punch landing squarely on the vampire's jaw. He didn't react and when Michael went to hit him again, Lincoln was ready.

'No,' said Sasha putting up his hand.

Michael rubbed his aching fist.

'You should have left us alone. Why couldn't you just leave us out of it?' he said.

'I won't fight you Michael,' Sasha said.

'You're fucking animals – that's all you are.'

'Does that include *me*?'

Michael spun around. Evelyn's feet touched the ground as she made her descent, her cloak catching the wind. She took a step towards him and he backed away. The glass panes of the first-floor windows exploded behind them, flames screaming out of every window.

'We have to leave,' she said. 'Please Michael. I'll explain everything when we're home.'

'Home? This is not our home. It's dead and gone in the grave with our father. We should have crawled in there with him and never come to this place,' he said, the tears coming at last to break him. 'Now I will bury *her* and I will crawl in with her where I belong.'

'No you won't, because we didn't come this far, fight the fight we've had to get here, to give up,' Evelyn said. 'We can be part of something Michael, something that matters. Something we never could have understood before but now it has found me, found us and we can do something with our lives.'

She looked at Salome.

'I'm sorry for your loss, I am and we have suffered too much of it but like it or not, I need you now and I need you to come back with me. I can't do it if you're not safe, and I don't want to.'

'What about them? You're staying with them?' he said, flinching as something hit his hand, his fingers catching it. It was warm, nestling against his skin and he ran his thumb down the glowing fissure of the stone as it rested happily back in its owner's palm.

'We're a family now,' said Sasha.

'You're not my family,' Michael said. He lunged at him, and Lincoln's arm caught him, pulling him backwards. Michael swerved and punched him in the jaw. Pain sung in his fingers but he brought his other hand up, ramming the sun stone into his mouth. Lincoln fell to his knees, his human reaction one of panic as the stone slipped to the back of his throat. More than that he realised it was no ordinary object but one of magic, burying itself deep, revelling the darkness, the heat, the moisture. When it ignited, it was sudden – a white flame that burst through him, throwing his head back before it consumed him totally, his body falling asunder as it hit the ground. They all watched, horrified.

'What did you do?' Evelyn cried.

Michael didn't answer, awestruck by the stone's power. It had proven useful after all. He doubted he could kill them all but Lincoln's life for Salome's was a start, and the loss for Sasha was a handsome reward for the taking of his sister. He saw Sasha move almost at the same time he felt his teeth tear the flesh on his neck. Now they burrowed deep, severing the artery before he was pulled back. Evelyn had flung him into the trees, with a warning to stay where he was. Sasha just licked the blood from his lips. Michael knew himself it was over. He held his hand to the wound but he couldn't stem the flow. He stumbled back to Salome.

'We can't leave him here to die,' Wade said.

'Absolutely not. Don't you even consider it,' Sasha said. 'Not after what he's done.'

'Lincoln killed his girl. He was never gonna take it well.'

'She put a knife in me.'

'Shame it missed,' Michael said. He slumped down next to her body. 'Just go…all of you.'

He took his hand from his neck and let the blood flow. He would be with her soon. But Evelyn wouldn't go. Instead she fell to her knees, lifting his head onto the folds of her gown.

'You should leave,' she said to the others. 'Gabriel needs you.'

She wouldn't look at Sasha. He looked eager to go anyway as he paced back and forth. What would his sister make of him now?

'Come,' he said.

He disappeared first. Velle took Wade's arm and soon they were gone too. Evelyn brushed her hand through his hair.

'Oh, Michael, I'm so sorry.'

'I was coming back to save you,' he said. 'We'd decided. This is probably how it would have gone, but I would have kept her safe. And she would have lived. I would have got her out of here.'

'There is so much to tell you and now there's no time. But I don't want you to go. I can't do this on my own. Please stay with me. Ask me and I'll make it so.'

'To be one of… them?'

'One like me. The strongest you have ever been. Never sick. Never hungry again. There is so much at stake, battles we have yet to fight, ones we can win. And we can help this world, be the good in it, despite the bad. Please, Michael don't leave me.'

He watched the ash as it swirled in the air, the last remnants of Salome's killer drifting away.

'Fire,' he said, '…destroys them?'

'A powerful one, yes' she said, 'but they are our friends, despite what's happened here tonight. We need them and Wade is your friend, Michael. There are others far more dangerous to us. You have no idea.'

He was close to death, and suddenly scared to face it. What if there was nothing beyond it? What if she wasn't waiting for him? That they couldn't be together. That these precious weeks were all they had. His sister had found a way to cheat not only death but also time.

'Do it,' he whispered.

He felt her skin on his lips and then her blood. It dripped into his mouth but he felt nothing. Was she too late? Death had dug its nails in, dragging him onto a long, dark and lonely road. But it couldn't have him. He would fight it, with everything he had. He gripped his sister's arm and the flow increased. He was drinking now, the blood flowing inside him. Changing him. When it was enough, Evelyn pulled herself away. His head fell back across her arm, and he smiled as the sun stone flew back into his palm.

47

ASHLEIGH RAN THROUGH THE azalea bushes, keeping her head low. She heard glass breaking and a scream from the upstairs balcony and she stopped, peering out through the leaves at the mob laying waste to her home. They were severely outnumbered, lambs to the slaughter, and with Foster and Harley killed by those creatures, escape was her only option.

She looked to her left down the side of the house and made a run for the stables. She was pretty good on a horse. She knew how to get the best out of them, just like the slaves and she knew if she rode hard she could reach Oak Hill and sound the alarm. Maybe catch some of them. Imagine if she was the only Boudreaux left? She let that thought propel her as she ran, the wind catching her skirts, pushing her legs to move as fast as she could.

When she reached the stable door, she stopped to catch her breath. She was not alone. Inside Bailey stood fixing saddles to the horses. He jumped as he heard her voice.

'Bailey, fix that horse for me,' she said.

He almost agreed, used to her commands.

'No, Miss Ashleigh. I won't. Now you get yourself outta here 'cos I don't want to have to hurt you. I'm leaving.'

She laughed, mocking him.

'Give me that saddle. I'll do it myself. You always were worthless,' she said.

She leaned in to pull the leather straps tight, when something sharp hit the back of her head. An inky blackness invaded, tiny silver stars spiking through it, as she tried to grasp what had happened. Pain rang in her ears. Her hand went to her head, meeting a slick of blood oozing from her scalp. Her palm was covered in it and she felt a sharp sting in her brain as she fell amongst the hay, the stars swimming now back and forth. Through them, she saw the spade in Thomas' hands. She felt nothing after that. By the third strike she was dead and Bailey and Thomas made their escape into the night.

48

A BRIGHT MOON HUNG low in the Manhattan sky, it's reflection rippling on the surface of the water as Sasha, Wade and Velle shot across it. No-one had said a word since they left, each feeling the loss of Lincoln. When he had joined them, they knew that their family was complete. Sasha knew even then, that he had a friend for life. He may not have 'needed a pack' but Lincoln found a peace with them and they felt it even then, that having him with them made sense, that they could navigate this world better together. Now their family was broken, a hole left in all of them that would never be filled.

Their feet touched down in the alleyway and Sasha felt a sudden swoon of nausea. He steadied himself against the narrow walls, the memory of human bile rising in his throat as surely as if it were there. A rush of horrific memories flooded back to him. The rise and fall of the hammer as they drove the nails into his palms. The pounding feet. Woltact's torn mouth. The feel of him on his skin. He could smell the innards of his cloak. Feel the fabric touch his face.

'You okay?' Wade said.

'We need to get to Gabriel now,' he said.

Woltacht was close. He had to be. When they approached the entrance, the door was slightly ajar, with no sign of the green eyed old man who kept its watch.

'I don't like this,' said Wade as they made their way inside.

The tunnels felt all the deeper under the surface such was the silence, maddening without the usual music and revelry to keep the claustrophobia at bay. The walls seemed to loom closer, the ceilings lower, smothering the sound of their footsteps as they made their way along. The large cavern was lit by torch and candle light but empty, a theatre without its nightly audience. Behind it, lay Gabriel's private retreat and they knocked on the thick wood as they entered, but he was nowhere to be seen. Piles of old books and papers lay scattered over every surface, the floor a sea of them, and there in the corner behind a large tomb he sat, frantically flicking through page after page.

'Come in, come in,' he said, waving his hand.

'What are you doing?' Sasha asked.

'I'm looking for an old manuscript. One that will help me summon the assistance we may need should things get critical.' Mafdet padded over to him, nuzzling into his shoulder and he stopped his search for a moment, rubbing her under her ears.

'Evelyn's not with you?' he said. 'I haven't been able to see any of you. I was worried.'

'Things didn't exactly go to plan down in Georgia,' Sasha said. 'But she'll be here soon.'

'And Michael?'

Wade shook his head as Gabriel realized that Lincoln was not among them.

'There were losses?' he asked, softly.

'On both sides,' said Sasha.

'Well there may be more yet my friends.'

He recounted to them his visit to the town of Olivia with Evelyn, of the dogs sent to purge them and the astounding power of Evelyn's gift in destroying the sleeping horde.

'They will come for us. Perhaps this very night. By now they will know what she did. Sasha, find Evelyn and take her to your brother's house. We will find the manuscript and meet you there. We are like flies trapped in a bottle here. It's not safe.'

Sasha left them, hurrying through the tunnels. When he reached the surface, the feeling hit him again, crowding his senses. He retched, as he was overpowered by the scent of his maker.

49

FAR BELOW, WADE AND Velle began sifting through the yellowing scrolls.

'Where is everyone?' Wade said.

'I have been deserted it seems and with my abilities compromised, I am blinded. When I couldn't see you in Georgia, Evelyn insisted on going herself and well I couldn't very well stop her. Perhaps my disciples got wind of what was happening and deserted me. It wouldn't be the first time.'

A deep rumble sounded overhead and the three of them looked to the ceiling. 'Maybe that's Sasha with Evelyn?' Velle said rising.

'No, not them,' Gabriel said, listening as many footsteps could be heard echoing through the passageways. Moving quickly to the edge of the tomb, he freed a jewel encrusted scabbard hidden underneath.

'Ready yourselves….'

'Got any more of those?' Wade said.

'There's a trunk over there.'

Velle looked on enviously as Wade took up a silver dagger. He threw it to her at whizzing speed and she caught it in one hand. Wade reached back into the box and pulled out the only pistol, its handle beautifully engraved with flames.

'That's Desdemona, the Wolf Killer,' Gabriel said as Wade checked it for ammunition. Six silver bullets gleamed in the half light. Mafdet stretched her bones on the rug and snarled.

'Be careful, pretty one,' he said, readying his sabre. 'We need to flank them. Wade, you go right, Velle left. Mafdet you come with me and get out the far side if you can.'

Velle nodded and blew Wade a kiss. He winked at her and opened the door to the chamber just as an arrow whizzed by his ear. He slammed it shut as two more pierced the door with such force, they almost broke through the wood.

'Jesus,' Wade cried. 'Get behind me.' He opened the door enough to get his fingers through and grasped the wood, pulling the door off its hinges.

'Go for the archer,' he said to Velle, her dagger poised.

'You bet.'

Wade pushed out. Two more arrows hit the wood from the right and Velle leant sideways, throwing her dagger into the air. It whistled across the room and struck the archer, a woman, in the shoulder. She gave a grunt as she removed the blade, blood running down her bare arm. She was dressed for battle, her breastplate polished brightly, her green eyes ablaze with fury. She hurled the dagger back into the door and waited for Velle to take for it. When she did, she shot an arrow into her hand, pinning her, as she readied another. She didn't see Mafdet until she was upon her. The lynx leapt from the shadows, knocking the bow from her hands.

Velle pulled the arrow from her broken flesh, and kissed it, before hurling it with all her might back to its host. Not even the archer had time to register it before it struck. It tore through the metal of her breastplate, into her leather vest, her skin and her heart. She collapsed to the ground, her eyes turning a milky sea green, their power diminished.

Without the cover of her arrows, the other vampires moved to attack. Velle counted nine of them, their eyes brimming with the same hate as the woman. They closed in, forming a semi-circle around them.

Wade flung the door outwards, as Gabriel swung out his sword. He was an accomplished swordsman. He'd had to learn. He would not survive Earth on his wits alone. Because of his position, he was rarely questioned but if it led to a fight, he had to be ready. He couldn't always rely on his disciples to do it for him. He tore his sabre across the body of one of the vampires, tearing him in two. As he fell, he finished him, the tip of the sword sinking into the vampire's heart. Another came at him and he took it down with his mighty blade.

Wade aimed Desdemona and fired. The assassin's heart exploded on impact into a cloud of dust and the others scarpered for cover. Velle ran out to grab one, and landed a ferocious blow to the creature's face. His jaw moved to the left, swinging from his skull but he managed to smack her with the back of his hand, sending her flying over a row of tombs. She leapt up as Wade shot at him, the bullet hitting the wall behind him as the vampire moved towards her.

'He's mine, Wade,' she screamed. She flew at him and delivered a punch to his gut, the two of them falling back to the floor beside the dead woman. She drew up her dagger and plunged it into his heart. A shot echoed off the walls as Wade took down another.

'You killed my dogs,' a voice boomed from the back. His Russian accent chopped through each word. Gabriel eyed their master, walking slowly towards him. The man looked like a wolf. He snarled, his lips drawing back to reveal his long sharp teeth.

'Hound killer. I will feed you piece by piece to their mother,' he said.

Gabriel readjusted his grasp and swiped his sword through the air. But the wolfman came at him, his movements a dark distortion, quick and swift to avoid every blow. He was in Gabriel's face before he knew it. A bullet flew by him from Wade's gun and he avoided that too, moving to allow it to pass him. Wade turned as one of the vampires sprang at him and he fired Desdemona with precision, every bullet counting as it hit its target mid-air, the vampire disintegrating.

Gabriel struggled as the wolf man held him. He was no match for his physical strength as he drew his jaws closer. But he did not attack, instead bringing his fingernails into his back, just behind his shoulder blades. There he ground them into two old but deep scars that resided there. Gabriel let out a cry, the wolf grinning as he tore into the flesh. For a moment, the image of the bare-chested man disappeared, replaced by something else. For his truest form was not that of a soft-skinned human but a blackened thing, its limbs like branches of a dead tree, deprived of light and water, hard ridges running all over his body. His face was a mass of knots and lumps as if badly beaten and never healed and his long hair was a bunch of featherless quills, only their spikey stems remaining. Gabriel tried to beat his wings but remembered they were gone, ripped from him, the wolf's hands now set deep in their place.

He stared into his eyes, electrified by the fight and beyond them, using his gift to explore his mind, to find his master's location. His powers strengthened and the wolf twitched his fingers, easing his grip a little.

'Stop it,' he said, trying to pull a veil over his thoughts, but he couldn't and he released his hold on Gabriel, backing away as Velle crushed the skull of another under her boot.

'Fall back,' he shouted to his two remaining assassins and with that they disappeared at speed back up the tunnels.

Gabriel fell to the ground, his back on fire with pain as he thought about what he'd seen, the image floating in his mind as his visions slowly restored.

'Oh no…no, no,' he said. 'We need to get to Sasha and Evelyn now.'

50

'Do you always feel this amazing?' Michael said. He stood up, stretching his arms above his head, every muscle taught. 'Indestructible.'

'You're only indestructible, until you're not. You know only too well with Lincoln, that we have our vulnerabilities,' she said.

'Yes, but I will never be sick another day in my life and I'll never grow older than I am now. That is an amazing gift.'

'You've taken to it well,' she said.

'I would be a fool not to. The alternative was…well, not an option. So, I welcome it just as you have.'

'It took me a little longer.'

'That's 'cos you're a better person than I am,' he said.

She smiled. 'I doubt it.'

Evelyn had seen something in his eyes as the transformation had taken place, something she hadn't possessed. He had shed his grief and was welcoming every stage, re-born and revelling in the pain, knowing he was one step closer to his new powers.

'You and Sasha would do best to give each other a little space, until things settle down,' she said. 'You've both lost someone.'

'Aren't you angry with him?' he asked.

'Aren't you? I'm not ashamed to admit that I'm glad that we're together again. I missed you. It will be Sasha who will not be pleased with me about your turning. So best to keep out of his way for now.'

'He'll have to get used to it,' Michael said. 'I won't be leaving your side again.'

She took his hand as they rose into the air and for most of the journey north, Michael whooped and hollered, the wind running its cool embrace over him, as they disappeared into the thick clouds, finally coming into New York. He marvelled at its scope from the air and as they swooped down over the waves, he dipped his fingers into his bright reflection, his sister's nothing but a silvery shadow.

'Who would have thought when we came here on the Eleanora, that we would see those very ships from the air,' he said.

'We have to keep this city out of Woltact's hands,' she said as they landed in Washington Square. She had explained the situation to Michael as they flew, but she wasn't sure how much attention he'd been paying.

'You still have the stone?' she asked.

'It has *me*,' he said. 'It seems intent on staying in my possession.'

'Good, it gives you an advantage. Use it if you need to.'

He took it out of his pocket, its surface a constant low glow in honour of its host, when it started to grow brighter, the colours throbbing.

Sasha landed at Evelyn's feet, his eyes immediately diverted to her companion.

'You turned him!'

'You left me no choice.'

'You should have let him die,' he said, walking around him, inspecting him like an inferior insect.

'We're not all capable of killing our brothers,' Michael said, confident that he could match Sasha blow for blow this time.

'That's not helping,' Evelyn said to him. 'Where are the others?'

'With Gabriel. They'll join us at home. We must go quickly…'

He didn't seem himself and she could tell he was worried. He lurched forward, holding his stomach. Was he ill? How was that possible? He fell to the ground.

'What is it?' she said.

'He's here. He must be,' he said panting. 'I can feel him.' For the first time since they'd met, Sasha looked afraid. Evelyn had no wish to meet his maker on the street.

'Let's get him home,' she said putting her arm around him. Michael reluctantly took his other one, lifting him to his feet.

51

THE MANSION ON FIFTH Avenue was eerily quiet. There was but one hour left before daybreak and the rooms lay in darkness, their thick velvet curtains cloaking them from the outside world. Sasha felt a little better, the crushing pain in his stomach subsided.

'Gather any weapons you can, anything of use.'

'The study,' Michael said, delighted at last to have free reign on its treasure. He disappeared and called out to them straight away. When they came to the door, he was standing in the centre of the room. The glass in every one of the cabinets was smashed, shields and old paintings knocked from the walls and the floor was strewn with books pulled from the shelves.

'A break-in?' Michael ventured.

'Do you sense anyone Sasha, your maker?' Evelyn asked him.

'No,' he said quietly, his eyes roaming the damage. 'I sense another but it's not possible.'

The door slammed behind them suddenly, making them jump. The sound of footsteps came on the spiral staircase, the familiar clunking of silver on iron as the walking stick hit the metal. Instead this time its owner did not limp but strode confidently down each step, swinging the cane out until it landed on the required stair.

'Alexander, how I've missed you.'

Vladimir reached the bottom step and stood there, smiling at their shocked faces.

'I killed you,' said Sasha, his eyes clouded in confusion.

'On the contrary, you brought me to the attention of the master and I thank you for it. It took him a while but he came to realise that I was of more use to him, than you could ever be. You were weak and ungrateful of his gift.'

'The master is dead.'

'Come now, you don't believe that. You might have once but not now. And look at our friends,' he said. 'Why, we're all vampires now. I knew there was something about you Evelyn.'

Michael instinctively stepped in front of her and she gripped his arm in warning, ready to fight.

'So, we are quite the party. Though your friends are sadly not here. My new comrades paid them a visit. I expect they are dead by now. Grom was out for blood. Not happy that you and Gabriel slayed his beloved dogs and I expect he made them pay dearly. Bethezba too. And the master, he is angry with you Evelyn, for destroying his growing family. Such promise, gone now. How did you do it? That's what he wants to know. So, you will explain yourself to him, maybe even join him and in doing so, I will spare your brother.'

'I killed you once, I can do it again,' Sasha said.

'I was hoping you'd say that,' he said, sliding the blade from his walking stick. 'I think you'll find the odds more balanced this time round.'

He let out a snarl as his teeth shot down, sharp and deadly. Sasha snatched the samurai sword from the mantle. As they came together, their blades met in a fizz of blue sparks, each pushing forward.

'Can you feel him close?' Vladimir said. 'He's almost here.'

Sasha pulled back and swung his blade around to catch his side. It swiped cleanly through his flesh, as Vladimir pulled back.

'Perhaps he will let you live,' he said. 'Forgive you for your insubordination.'

Sasha brought the blade up again, aiming for his heart as a pain twisted inside him. He backed away from his brother, his sword falling as he felt the imaginary cloak of his maker draped over him, the smell of the old cloth filling his senses. Michael and Evelyn could smell it too. Vladimir gave a long low bow in the direction of the window.

It had opened, a sea of moving cloth drawing back the curtain as it streamed inside. It flew out over them, the hood at first appearing monstrous. Its tip grazed the ceiling before it settled into Woltact's form, the fabric resting in folds at his feet. He raised his arm and from under the cloth his jaundiced fingers moved towards Sasha.

'My son,' he said. 'You have done well.'

Sasha looked at him in disbelief, his maker's face hidden deep in his hood. He curled his fingers, beckoning him closer.

'It is time for you to return to me.'

'I don't serve you any more,' Sasha said.

'You serve me even as you speak. You brought *her* to me.'

Evelyn readied herself, flexing her palms, allowing the energies to move about her body, to bring the fire when she commanded it. She couldn't repeat her performance from Olivia without also killing Sasha and Michael and she eyed the folds of the cloak, calculating how quickly she might reach to touch it and how prepared he might be.

'Bring the girl to me, Sasha,' he said.

'You can't have her.'

'Sasha, we can take her with us. If you care for her, bring her to me. Imagine what we could do here. It is limitless. From here we can spread our kind all over America. This is just the beginning.' Sasha didn't move.

'Bring her to me,' he bellowed.

Michael ran at him, his teeth bursting through, tearing his gums as the blood streamed from his lips. He met the full force of Woltacht's hand as he swatted him away, but it was enough to give Evelyn the chance she needed to slide across the floor. She touched his cloak and it ignited immediately, a yellow flame spreading up the wall of fabric. The fire consumed him and Vladimir drew back into the corner, the flames reflecting brightly in his eyes as he looked on in horror.

The hooded figure bent double, curling his arms in before throwing them open and backwards, the cloak slipping from his body. Woltacht laughed hoarsely as the flames died around him, buried beneath the heavy folds on the floor. He stepped forward, his dirty feet bare, dressed in a simple druid's robe, centuries old. Sliding his hands into the opposing sleeves, he rested them there as he perused the girl.

'That's a nice trick,' he said. 'I could use you.'

The echo of the human he once was hung loose on his hairless body, his face decimated by his slashed mouth, his eyes rheumy as he squinted at her, destroyed by the evil he pursued and the darkness in his heart.

'No, thank you,' said Evelyn circling him.

'As you wish.'

'Come to me,' she said. 'Let me touch you. That's all it will take.'

Woltacht gave her an impatient look. 'Vladimir, destroy her.'

52

Vladimir hesitated, sure that she would burn him if he got close. He hadn't come this far for it to be cut so short. Instead he grabbed his brother by the neck, squeezing him tightly as Sasha still fought the pain inside him.

'You care for Alexander, don't you?' he said to her. 'You move on me and I will kill him and then I'll kill *him*,' he said pointing at Michael.

Woltacht ran his crimson tongue over his broad lips, smiling.

'Now offer yourself to our wonderful guest, just like you offered yourself to my brother. Let him drink from you and give him the immunity he seeks from your wrath.'

Michael gripped her hand as she considered Vladimir's threat. Slowly she released her fingers, taking a step towards Woltacht, his arms outstretched.

'No, Evelyn,' Michael screamed. 'You can't.'

'Close your eyes,' she said. 'Now.'

She released her contained heat, blasting it around the room, the light bouncing off the surface of the precious metals that adorned the walls and mantle. Vladimir pushed Sasha forward, taking shelter behind an iron shield – the heat ferocious, unlike anything it had ever endured in the crusades. Woltacht tried to fight it, his will pushing it back, the blood of thousands coursing through his veins, but to no avail. He could not withstand it and her might won out as he began to burn. Years of living in darkness could not have prepared him for this, as if the sun itself had journeyed from the sky. His body burst into ash and when it had settled, Evelyn looked to Michael and Sasha. Both of them cowered, their heads in their hands, awaiting their own annihilation. When it didn't come, they opened their eyes.

'We're still alive,' Michael said scrambling to her. 'How?'

'Because of him,' she said, looking to the shield and the vampire concealed behind it.

***

As Woltacht burned, Vladimir had closed his eyes, muttering the words he had memorized over and over, not missing a single one. Even when Sasha finally pulled the shield from him, he was still saying them.

'It's a little late for prayer, brother,' Sasha said as the door burst open. Gabriel was first through it, Mafdet at his heels, followed by Wade and Velle.

'We saw the light and thought it best to wait outside,' said Wade relieved to see that they were unharmed.

Gabriel stood in awe at Woltacht's demise.

'You did it. Oh, my Evelyn, you did it,' he said with delight, picking her up and twirling her around. Vladimir eyed him from the corner where he remained curled up, his brother standing over him.

'And you, you cretin,' Gabriel said. 'You will pay dearly for your treason.'

'Wait,' said Evelyn. 'Without him I wouldn't have risked the others with my power. Only he knew they would be safe. Bring him to me.'

Sasha threw him down before her.

'How did you know that would work?' she asked.

'I am a learned man,' he said. 'I read. You know that. If you know how to decipher these books, then all the answers lie within them.'

'Why did you help me?'

'Because I prayed you might spare me. I witnessed your great power and I knew that Woltacht would succumb. That I was on the wrong side. You were searching for answers yourself in this room, weren't you? I can help you find them. Please Evelyn I beg you. Let me join you. Please, Sasha.'

Sasha's fist pounded into the side of his face.

'I say we kill him,' Sasha said. 'He's dangerous.'

'I agree,' said Gabriel. 'Evelyn?'

Evelyn looked at him, his shoulders slumped forward in defeat.

'Give me the stone, Michael,' she said as he dug deep into his pocket. She took it running her thumb over its smooth surface before handing it to Sasha.

'No,' said Vladimir. 'You can't. I saved you. I saved all of you.'

Sasha examined the weapon, the very one that had killed his dear friend.

'Hold him,' he said.

'What will it do to me? No, no please,' he cried.

There were no more words after that, only the stone being forced into his mouth. Vladimir clutched his throat as it lodged there, panic-stricken. His face began to blister, the first wisps of smoke starting to curl around him. They let go of him and he stumbled backwards, turning to the window in terror, as flames engulfed him. With flailing arms, he escaped through the opening, leaving a fury of smoke behind him.

'We have to go after him,' Sasha said.

'He has nowhere to go. The stone will finish him or the rising sun,' said Evelyn, the first light beginning to break in the sky. 'Either one will see to his end. You need to take shelter.'

'Perhaps not any more,' Sasha said. 'Has your blood made me immune to the natural sun, like you?'

Michael looked at her expectantly.

'There is but one way to find out but perhaps this is not the morning for it.'

'Well,' said Wade, taking Velle's hand and kissing it, 'I need my beauty sleep. You folk can debate the matter all you like. I need a rest. You comin' beautiful?'

'Yes Sir,' said Velle, biting her lip. They disappeared upstairs as first Michael and then Sasha, stepped slowly out into the dawn. The street was deserted, the city not yet awoken and Sasha felt the first beam of natural light on his face in decades. He looked back to Evelyn and Gabriel as they stood on the doorstep with Mafdet at their feet. His smile was as broad and hopeful as any she had ever seen. There was no sign of Vladimir and she imagined him ash, carried by the wind, spread across this city she had come to call home.

'You have done miraculous things here,' Gabriel said. 'I'm so glad you came.'

'So am I,' she said.

'I hate to admit it but I don't think we've seen the last of Vladimir,' he said, letting out a sigh. 'I can still feel a glimmer of him. But no matter. Let him go and lick his wounds for a few centuries. He is not equipped to be any sort of threat. Will you stay for a while in New York?'

'That depends I suppose on the two of them,' she said looking at Michael and Sasha. They revelled in the morning sun and though Michael had never lost its magic, it renewed him in a way it had never done before. Sasha stood like a child just allowing it to bathe him, its heat beautiful to him, warming his bones.

'I think a trip to Ireland might be in order. See how it's been doing without us,' she said.

'A sound plan indeed. You have the world at your feet Evelyn. Can I call on you should I need you?'

'I wouldn't have it any other way,' she said. She left him, running down the steps to join the others as Sasha caught one hand, Michael the other and they danced in the birth of a new day.

53

'I THOUGHT YOU MIGHT come here,' the man said, pulling up another chair to the fire. He didn't turn around. He just stared into the flames as the hooded figure walked slowly towards him.

'I'd say it's good to see you, Rako, but it's not. I never thought I'd come back.'

'And yet here you are. Is he really gone, the master?'

'Yes. The girl destroyed him.'

He sighed. 'Grom came back, his tail between his legs, defeated in battle.'

'They were strong. He underestimated them.'

'You got your wish. He turned you after all.'

'And you? I never took you for wanting this life, Rako.'

'Well, the master gets what he wants regardless. Were you followed?'

'No. I am in no fit shape to threaten anyone. It will take time to heal.'

'That we have in spades,' Rako said. 'How is your dear brother?'

'I should rip your head from your spine for asking.'

'Don't do that. At least not on an empty stomach. Not when I have just the thing for you. The master gifted him to me. Gave me one of his own blood slaves, one he's kept alive a long time. I can remember the day I gave him to Woltacht, so perhaps it's only right he returned him to me. Do you remember Caleb Tamersk?'

'I came to see you not long after he was sacrificed.'

'That's right. One taste and you will feel like a new man.'

Vladimir lowered his hood.

'Will I look like one too?'

He turned his face to the light. Half of it was burnt black, the skin disfigured, twisted around his features. His eyelid was closed, sealed by fire. The fingers on his hand had melted, each one glued to the next, a hardened crust around them. He had used them to tear open his own throat and pull the sun stone from his body. It had done enough damage to end the life of any fledging but he had something else on his side and he rested his hand to his chest feeling Woltact's power inside him. He would need time to harness it, to heal, the words of the spell coming again to his mind. He thought nostalgically of his study and his books. *To read*, he thought, *is to learn the secrets of the world.*

Clare Daly lives in Kildare, Ireland with her husband and two children. A former film publicist, Clare worked in the Irish film industry for twenty years before deciding to follow her dream. *Our Destiny Is Blood* is her first novel.

www.claredalyauthor.com

You can follow her on Twitter @cdalyireland or on Facebook at claredalyauthor

Our Destiny...is to return Spring 2018

ACKNOWLEDGEMENTS

FIRSTLY MY THANKS GOES to you, the reader, for taking the time to read my book. When I started it in 2012, it was but a tiny seed and to have you read it now is beyond my wildest dreams. I hope you liked it.

Getting it into your hands was a long fought battle of self belief and I couldn't have done it without the people who supported me and encouraged me to keep going, particularly in tough times. Nicola Costello - you pledged your support from day one and never faltered - thank you and to my friends and willing readers along the way, Stephanie Dickenson, Caroline Lynch, Jane Rooney, Gilly Clarke, Maud Halferty, Lisa Peyton, Jennifer Finegan, Ruth Ivory and Trish Long. Your feedback and support has been invaluable. You have no idea.

On the editing front, my sincere thanks to Esther McCarthy for your keen eye and also to Robert Doran, for your generosity and sound advice that helped me see the wood for the trees. Thanks also to David O'Callaghan and David Stevens for letting me bug you for your always essential advice. To the rejections I've received over the last two years, I thank you.

You taught me a valuable lesson in perseverance and gave me the grit I needed to actually make this thing happen, by hook or by crook.

And lastly to my family, my dad Peter, my sister Carol and my brother Colin for your never-ending support, not only on this adventure but the whole shebang. To my children, Adam and Grace, who can at last hold Mammy's book in their hands (you see there was a book!) and lastly to my husband Vincent, who told me to chase my dream no matter what and is still telling me.